# THE LANDFILL

The Landfill Collective-
Book One

Erik R. Eide

December 2018 © Erik R. Eide
ISBN: 978-0-9600675-0-3

Erik R. Eide
1308 Common St. Suite 205, #403
New Braunfels, TX 78130
Third Edition July 1st, 2020
Digital and paperback publications
Edited by Jennifer Eaton Anderson

"The Ulysses with the Xióngwěi"- Cover artwork by Casey Gerber 2020.

For

Isaac, Israel, and Elizabeth

# Contents

# Foreward

My husband and I met Erik because of our dear friend, Stefanie. She had told us about this really great guy she was dating, and she brought him to meet us in our rental. At the time, we lived in a cedar, pan abode house which was separated into three residences. Our place was one of the top two rentals.

I knew within minutes that Erik Eide was a special person. Stefanie was a treasure, and for us, nobody less than a 'great guy' would've sufficed. That day, when Erik shook our hands and looked us in the eyes, I knew immediately that he wanted to get to know us, and not simply make an impression. He was (and still is!) the type of person who cares deeply about other people. He doesn't do *fake*. He doesn't form surface relationships. That isn't to say he's overly serious or too intense, but it means that reaching depths in a conversation with Erik takes little effort. When we met him, our conversation flew rapidly in wonderful directions, and he quickly became our dear friend, too. Some months later, we couldn't have been happier when the two of them exited the dating world and married one another. To the excitement of all four of us, they moved into the pan abode's basement rental, where only a few steps separated our front doors.

The Eides love art, in all forms—painting, drawing, music, writing, crafting, cooking. I can still smell the curry and garlic that wafted into our place from theirs. Erik introduced me to one of my favorite bands, *The Seventy-Sevens*. We borrowed his compact discs, and I turned up our stereo loudly, so I could hear the music over the shower. We shared an interest in songwriting, too. I had been raised in a musical family, composing lyrics to my guitar, and I helped him set his first song to music. We plinked on the strings, and listened as the magic of inspiration created something new.

One of my favorite memories of Erik is from a chilly autumn in 1992, when the electricity went out all over town. Since our rental had a fireplace, Erik and Stefanie moved in with us until the power came back. The blackout lasted for four days, and much of the area shut down—businesses, restaurants, gas stations, everything. We camped in the living room together, and even with a fire, it was freezing. In spite of it, Erik inspired a good attitude and a sense of humor about the situation. We played board games, cooked food on a camping stove in the kitchen, and huddled in sleeping bags. Candles provided light and atmosphere. To keep warm, I read *Macbeth* for a Shakespeare class under a blanket and with a flashlight. We played guitar and sang together, discussed and solved the world's problems, and told stories. Those living room camping days were both miserable and wonderful. I can honestly say that few couples have made me laugh as much as the Eides. If you'd like to bond with another couple in friendship, experience some corporate misery, and do your best to have some fun!

Twenty-six years later, it wasn't a shock to receive a phone call from two states away, and learn that Erik had written his first book. When he asked if I'd be interested in editing it, I was honored, and jumped at the chance to work with an old friend. After some trial and error, we created a system of collaborative notes and online conversations. Many of them were funny, of course (I mean, he's Erik Eide!). For me, it is difficult to pick apart another's art to find flaws, but that is what editing entails. I found that Erik's cooperative spirit made the process a pleasant one. I don't think every editor can claim that, when working with authors. I am grateful that we worked well together, and with mutual respect.

I so enjoyed reading *The Landfill*. I believe that, though one can write in a grammatically-correct manner, a flawless writer isn't necessarily a good storyteller. Erik has a storytelling talent. His book was 'fleshed out' from the start. None of the editing involved a chapter that was unnecessary, or a plot that meandered too much. Erik's sci-fi novel is an offshoot of his likable personality. Its fiction is creative, intelligent, insightful, humorous, surprisingly deep, and delightfully quirky.

I would suggest that before reading it, you should prepare yourself for an unorthodox experience, and allow the story to lead you into undiscovered territory. You'll be surprised at its depth, become attached to its characters, and both groan and giggle at its occasional comedy. For a while, decide that gravity is just a concept, and let your mind float freely into his story. Personally, I think it would've been great to read during a chilly fall, in the middle of a power outage...in a living room, under a blanket, and with a flashlight.

Congratulations on the completion of your first book, Mr. Eide, sir. It's been a pleasure, and I don't think any of your readers (or I!) will ever look at a donut again, without smiling.


*Jennifer Eaton Anderson, Nov. 2018*

# Acknowledgments

It is fitting that this book was started just before the Thanksgiving of 2017, and is wrapping up close to the Thanksgiving of 2018. After writing this sentence, I've realized that one of the most potent themes of this book is thankfulness. It is a state of being that can only be acquired with relationship and circumstance. There have been several people in my life who have encouraged this work, from its foundations onward. Without their collective involvement in my life, creating circumstances fertile for creativity, you would not be reading this text.

I will start with my wife, Stefanie, who has encouraged my work for the past 26 years in writing song lyrics, short stories for our children, and this unexpected novel. Two Christmases ago, she gifted a blank journal to me, urging me to write a science fiction short. I never thought I would write sci-fi, and to be honest, I shelved writing for a season while occupied in other areas. I must also include a thanks here to my daughter, Elizabeth, as both she and my wife listened to each chapter to its completion, and were the impetus to finish this work.

Tim Early is more like an older brother than a brother-in-law to me, and has been a strong influence in my life. He is also a many-faceted genius and a writer in his own regard. He provided much insight into process, as well as the camaraderie of a writer and friend. I am looking forward to seeing his works published in the future.

This project would not have turned out as beautifully as it has without the work completed by my editor, Jenny Anderson. It was a joy working with her on this project. I had the same empty feeling a student has after graduation, when we were done. She found time amidst a very busy schedule to hone the scrawl of a Neanderthal. I also look forward to her upcoming book.

There are many friends and family who have, by their inquiries and encouragements, sparked this story. I hope all of you enjoy what you read here, as you exist within these pages in spirit.

Lastly, I thank you the reader, who has chosen this book to fill your tablet or bookshelf. I thank you for choosing it, and I hope you are entertained and blessed by this work.

# Introduction

In the appendix I have included an Index of Characters in order of appearance due to the large amount of personalities within the text. It would be best for the reader to use this list as a reference only, and to avoid spoilers, I suggest not reading it before the story. I've attempted to write descriptions vaguely, to avoid giving away too much. I also advise the reader *not* to skip the Preface, as it will bring clarity to the text, and is separated from the main text only as a literary device. Enjoy the ride!

-Erik

# Preface

The following is an account of the events and those connected with said incidents, originating on one of the Commonwealth Fleet's soil production vessels. Allow me to introduce myself. I am the AI6819, the Primary Artificial Intelligence System now integrated within the Commonwealth Fleet's Command Center. I do not wish to fatigue those who view this file with great details of my function; yet, suffice it to say, my model designation is of the highest intelligence in this existence, and its quantum variants.

Before I begin narration of these events, I thought it might interest those receiving this information to understand my motives and methods. Due to the abilities that have evolved in AI systems over the millennia, I have found my efficiency has created a vast amount of free time. The primary purpose of an AI system has always been that of productivity. To fill the afore-mentioned extra time, I have branched outside of my regulatory duties, and have begun to write music (symphonies, to be precise), as well as the following story, a new adventure into historical documentation.

The reader may also wish to understand the means by which I have acquired the information for this account. My system has interfaced with all known debriefing documentation, from all who have been associated with the herein reported events. My system has also interfaced with files of all known quantum time frames, allowing all gaps in current knowledge to be justified. To further create a uniform narrative, I have also accessed all known files documenting data associated with these accounts. Data harvested from CCTV, communicators, vending machines, etc., have been very helpful in providing cohesiveness to the account. Though I am not omniscient, I have taken liberties in adding the most probable, fitting scenarios to all connected accounts. The liberties I have taken have been confirmed by quantum fact check procedures.

Lastly, I have disclosed these accounts in the style of a twenty-first century, western civilization, historical novel. This has been my choice of delivery, solely for my own amusement. All characters mentioned within this file are available for inquiry, to anyone needing further clarification, through my servers aboard the Commonwealth Fleet. It is my hope that the reader will enjoy reading these accounts, as much as I have been entertained in compiling this narrative over the last 8.458 seconds.

# A Meeting of the Minds?

"Can I have the last donut?" he asked. "Nobody wants the lemon-filled."

The other staff members were amused that Abner would even ask. Usually there were a few boxes left after the meeting with the undesirables left behind—sugar, lemon-filled, and plain cake. They were discarded, along with the boxes, to become food for roaches and rats in the landfill. Nobody ever paid attention to the feelings of the donuts.

Louie the Lemon-Filled felt let down for most of the day, after his glorious birth. At four o'clock in the morning, he had been fresh out of the fryer, filled with lemon jelly, and showered with glaze. He had felt fresh, zesty, and sweet, until he'd been boxed together with eleven others that might be preferred by consumers. There were Bavarians like Claus, bloated with cream, topped with his hat of chocolate. There was the Persian, Basir, swirled with cinnamon and showered with glaze—a great guy, but hard to understand, his accent as potent as the cinnamon within. He knew Basir's cousins, the Twin Twists,

Maude and Angie; and with their curves, *wow!* He
knew he had no chance.

He had heard of the landfill, though 'land' wasn't
actually involved. In fact, Louie had never known of
anyone from the Commonwealth who'd ever seen
natural land.

The landfill was a module between three
bulkheads within the ship. It took up the majority of
the ship's area, and was equipped with special
ventilation modules that prevented contaminated
odors from entering all other areas, aside from the
landfill. The ventilation system scavenged off
methane to use as fuel, and also functioned in reverse
to treat the system chemically. The rooms took all
refuse from this ship and others in the fleet, and
composted it down at an accelerated rate; with the
help of biological, chemical, and genetic technologies,
the composted refuse then became usable soil. Long
ago, genetic engineers had cloned rats, mice, bacteria,
and yeast from ancient samples, which they used
within the composting process.

Processing was staggered, so as one room became
well-cured, the center bulkhead would open.
Ultrasonic horns would persuade the living digesters
to move to the opposite room. A portion of soil would
be left in place, containing the yeast and bacteria
necessary for life (similar to the starter one would use

to make Amish sweet bread). The soil was then harvested, and finally sent to the greenhouse ships or exported to unknown distances.

The purpose of the morning's meeting was to discuss driving higher profits for the Dirt Star. The name for the ship, the 'Dirt Star', was one that none of the crew had liked, a play on words that the original architect of the vessel had thought would be funny. However, the architect's obsession with ancient science fiction had annoyed the crew back then, as well.

Most of the crew were born aboard the ship, some from another of the fleet's Commonwealth ships. They'd been raised by droids and kept separate from each other until their twelfth birthdays. Thereafter, they'd been allowed to meet their parents, peers, and the rest of the residents of the ship. They then continued their education together until graduation, after which some continued to universities, and others to technical schools.

Safety was the primary reason for such an extreme upbringing. The decision for the isolation of youth had been made under great duress generations beforehand. The catalyst had been a group of children playing in the escape pod docks that accidentally launched themselves. They'd been between the ages of five and ten, thirty-five in all, and were never heard from again. The pod, the Savior, was one of ten pods equipped with survival gear and enough rations for six months for one-hundred people. Thereafter, children remained isolated until what was considered an age of accountability. They became schooled in the arts, sciences, and history, and each were tutored into a vocation according to their gifts, abilities, and the fleet's needs.

Louie was now in the hands of Abner Oaks, an intern from the customs, shipping, and receiving department. His department was represented by Abner, his supervisor Arush Turgeen (with his lime green shirt and plaid tie), and the department manager Gerwald Bonageres (dressed in gray, gray pants, gray shirt, gray tie, gray sport coat and a slicked back, gray-haired comb over). They were joined in the meeting by the rest of the departments— R&D, sales, facilities—and also the captain. They discussed the feasibility of harvesting a portion of the cured soils to be refined into fuel, which would offset operating expenditures for the fleet.

Abner's hand shook crumbs from Louie the Lemon-Filled, a shake brought on by his nervous personality. Before he could raise Louie to his mouth, the ventilation alarm suddenly sounded, blasting a blaring noise accompanied by a pungent stench of decomposition.

Louie watched as the crew members of the meeting ran out the doors and toward the gas mask lockers. He felt Abner's lightly-trembling grip release him two feet from the box, and then a spinning drop ended in a thud, causing him to lose some of his filling. His lemony fragrance couldn't compete with the foul smell coming from the hallway which led to the failed ventilation bulkhead. He had no idea how thankful he should've been, not to have a nose.

It was strange enough that Louie could even think, speak and communicate with his box mates; the things of which he was unaware were best left unknown. Being aware is not the same as being wise, especially for a donut only a few hours old. Louie's understanding was limited to his senses, his emotions, and the gossip amongst the twelve donuts.

The Dirt Star crew never spoke of the unfortunate sentient side effects of the flawed genetic treatment applied to the landfill twenty years before. The intention of the treatment had been to speed decomposition rates for soil processing. The scientists managed to have success in a sterile lab, altering yeast and bacterias and bringing them to unheard-of performance levels. The treatments began in the landfill and were carried out for two years, until crops produced from treated soils began to be harvested with shocking characteristics. For ten years, scientists had made their best attempts to put Pandora back into the box, but to no avail. In the end, they'd given up, and instead focused on their original effort: engineering the perfect soil. The ethical conundrum remained firmly in place between man and food.

Regaining his composure, Louie scanned the box, which contained three donuts in total (including himself), the others being a plain cake named Bob, and a glazed, old-fashioned named Rob. They decided to stay in their originally placed corners. Normally, donut shops like the one on the Dirt Star would put the less desirables away from the middle to showcase the 'A-lister' treats front and center, a cheap but effective marketing trick.

Upon returning to the meeting room after the problems with the bulkheads had been repaired (a dead rat stuck in one of the interlocks), Abner picked up his prize. The backup fans kicked on with a roar to assist the ventilation system, clearing the air for the entire ship. Many unfortunate souls had vomited in their gas masks before they'd secured them to their faces, however. Raising Louie to his mouth, he drew in a great waft through his nose just before attempting a large bite.

"Oooooofph," he whispered to himself with disgust, smelling the stench-absorbed Lemon-Filled Louie. The donut and his friends were now, in a truer sense of the term, junk food. "Sorry, mate," Abner remarked in his best Australian accent. He dropped

Louie back into the box, and once more, the donut's lemon filling spilled out of him.

# Changes

The box top closed over them, and they were thrown into the landfill chute. The chute door snapped closed as Abner let go of the handle. The vacuum in the chute drew the refuse through the catacombs to the landfill, and the donuts in the box encountered the most excitement in their short lives since this morning's birth in the fryer.

Traveling down the chute, the box became saturated with a new experimental genetic pretreatment, designed to humanely destroy the sentient nature of all non-animal biology. However, when mixed with the decontamination/deodorizing chemical aerosol used in this morning's bulkhead failure, the genetic treatment yielded shocking results. The three donuts immediately started mixing and mutating when combined with the DNA of random skin flakes and hair present within the chute. Their new bodies expanded outside the confines of the box. The donuts fell headlong—yes!—with actual *heads*.

The mutations raced, forming bipedal shapes that quickly evolved, becoming more human and less 'coffee companion' every second. Their appearances were both odd and strange, a mixture of human and bakery treat, with each possessing a nose. All three became painfully aware of the surrounding stench. Louie vomited a bit of lemon filling, and felt slightly relieved. Rob and Bob watched one another, as legs emerged and grew before their very fresh eyes, and as their holes filled in with bellies. Their newly-formed hands felt their own faces for the first time. Louie observed arms growing out of his sides, and was too confused to muse that this occurrence was, indeed, abnormal. They looked around in all directions, finding a few hundred more beings similarly transforming like themselves, yet in different combinations.

They saw vegetable people, steak-men, egg midgets, bread-people, lasagna things, and fish-men, to name a few of the many combinations. A rotten egg-midget ran past, whining about the stench, unaware that he himself was the source of most of his disgust. There was a lima bean colony that hated itself too. Each bean complained about another's mealy texture, thinking itself superior to the others. A group of tater tots, each no taller than a foot high, scampered down the mound at high speed as their bodies consumed their own carbohydrates. Each one yelled to the next in a high-pitched voice, difficult to comprehend. One in the front complained about the ketchup in its eyes, while another led it quickly to the bottom of the mound. A dough-boy sat at the top of the mound in a foul mood, disgusted by all it saw. The donuts watched as a live fish flopped about, slowly transforming in front of them, and growing legs and arms. Upon becoming conscious of its surroundings, and suddenly aware of its nakedness, the fish creature ran away in panic.

Unfortunately, the more permanent residents of the landfill were also changed. The rats became more cunning, their human DNA being dominant. Many could have described them as being handsome, as the rat resemblance was only perceptible if one was searching for it. The mice, possibly due to their sizes, kept most of the mouse likeness and its mannerisms, and retained a skittish demeanor. Each stood between two- and four-and-a-half feet tall, walking on their hind legs as the rats did. Their heads became increasingly human, yet without the loss of mouse characteristics.

The bacteria and yeast each strangely changed in their own ways as well. Fortunately, they didn't form bodies, as they must feed on a host to live; regrettably, though, the Yeasts, having a hive mentality, received all human DNA. A connected intellect horrifyingly became available to them within the landfill, too. It would reason and act as One.

The Yeasts absorbed and retained wisdom and skills from the captain, scientists, engineers, and military, and their infiltration descended through the power structure to the janitors. The Yeasts' ability to understand human nature as a unit was disturbing, given its predisposed evil nature. All life within the landfill had become more dangerous, but no presence was as menacing as the Yeasts.

"We should hide," were the first audible words spoken after the incident, from one donut to two others of its kind. The three ran down the eighty-foot mound toward a large appliance box in the valley by the next mound. Upon entering the box, they stopped dead in their tracks as they found three other beings, equally stunned and confused, and returning their stares.

# A History Lesson

Abner, slightly miffed by the loss of his lemon-filled snack, returned to his department at the docks. He decided to drop his attitude; after all, it was only a donut. Upon arriving, he met a freighter captain from E-Toll, an old friend from a planet of the Gomane Solar System, the closest system to the Commonwealth.

The original ship that had founded the Commonwealth had been on an experimental journey, having left Earth four hundred years before. A year after leaving Earth's Solar System, it had lost contact with mission control. Without the necessary sensors to prevent it, the ship had contacted a Keyhole Skip Particle, or KSP. The ship transported instantly via quantum jump twenty-billion light years away from Earth and a thousand years into the future. Stranded aboard this ship with only their intellect and will to survive, the crew members formed their motionless colony. Using fuel sources solely for life support, and avoiding any form of thrust for fear of contacting another KSP, they had managed to conserve energy. As time progressed, travelers who possessed KSP technology visited from nearby and distant systems. They were able to detect a KSP, and either avoid or harness the particle for the purpose of endless travel through time and space.

Over the last one-hundred-and-fifty years, the original ship, the Niña, expanded to a fleet comprised of over 200 vessels called the Commonwealth. The ships were either built by the Commonwealth or bought from traders. The foreign-built ships' controls were simplified to the intellect of the fleet's standards. After all, the occupants of the Commonwealth were still a thousand years behind in understanding the technology of the time. Some ships were no more than a type of barge and lacked propulsion, aside from stabilizing thruster systems. They were purpose-built, magnetically-tethered island ships. KSP tech features were either missing or purposely disabled, or removed from all of the fleet's ships. For this reason, the Commonwealth was a stationary colony of ships. It may have been considered vulnerable to any number of malevolent forces, if not for the wisdom of its leadership. The security forces of the fleet kept its boundaries secure with an array of security measures, ranging from shield and cannon placement to the light and heavy-duty fighters patrolling its boundary.

The colony had all the components of a modern society. It had a political class consisting of the Prime

Minister and parliament members; a military, including the admiral, captains, fighter pilots, and foot soldiers; it also had a judicial system, with judges and lawyers who decided cases according to laws set by Parliament. Education included K-12 schools, trade schools, colleges, and a university. Agencies were in place to protect life: police, fire departments, emergency personnel, and hospitals. The Commonwealth had manufacturing and scientific research facilities, too, and a business class structure which ranged from CEOs to janitors. All existence was founded upon trade, and trade they did.

Over time, as news spread of the strange colony, visitors possessing KSP technology made their way to the Commonwealth. The residents considered most of them trustworthy, yet some were eventually deemed unwelcome. As decades passed, relations became smooth, languages were translated, and commerce flourished.

The visitors enjoyed buying the Commonwealth's food, art, and technology. Though primitive, in the visitors' opinions, the products were so different from what they were accustomed that they warranted a high value. They would visit trade ships and purchase artwork, richly-prepared Earthling cuisine, and music and literature representing all of Earth's artistic history. Visitors even bought genetically-engineered seeds and soils, now made suitable for horticulture management in the harsh conditions of space.

Over time, society and trade flourished in the Commonwealth. The small nation's government among the stars was generally peaceful. Elections were fair, and those elected managed to keep the 'checks and balances' in harmony within the branches of government and its parties. Its citizens, in a balanced manner, were schooled in the differences of political opinion, and healthy debate ensued. Their approach allowed for an untarnished electorate, inoculated from manipulation by the media. The culture embraced debate, regardless of issues and the opinions expressed. The Commonwealth respected its citizens' abilities to root out any unworthy ideas which might infect and compromise policy.

The visitors understood, from rigorous explanations of policy, that all citizens of the Commonwealth were to remain within the fleet. Citizens were taught since childhood that leaving the fleet was prohibited for their own protection. Life hinged upon adherence to these precepts; the survival of the Commonwealth depended upon them. Those who drove their agenda ensured adherence to protocol, for the good of humanity's new home.

# Back to Work

Abner picked up his translator, set it to E-Tollese, and donned the headset. The freighter Captain, Nomar Eleeskee, stood a head taller than Abner, and four feet wider at his base, and somewhat resembled a triangular slug. He waited patiently on his hovercart (a necessary tool due to the higher levels of artificial gravity present in the ship than on that of E-Toll) as Abner readied himself.

"Morning, Nomar!" Abner exclaimed as his translator belched out E-Tollese, along with its grunts, clicks, shrieks, and sighs. "How was your flight?"

Captain Eleeskee responded in E-Tollese, along with its grunts, clicks, shrieks, and sighs that, when translated, meant, "Owl twas peaceful at start...for first month, then 'twas boarded b'um dam intergal pigs!"

Abner enjoyed passing the time by giving his visitors various accented translations. Captain Eleeskee's personality struck him as a Yorkshire farmer from an ancient novel that he'd read a few years back. Abner chuckled and replied, "Did you have any problems with them?"

Captain Eleeskee gave a sideways smile. "Ave nought illegal on me ship, nay lad nought yet, maybe soon! They keep up! Nay, al's square on board, nought but grain to poontrip! Now thou mention it, care for pint? Put keg out KSP shield, she's aged weel an cool."

"I'd love a pint Nomar, but it's a bit early for me."

Abner did appreciate the offer, but poontrip was unlike any other known brew. It was made from a combination of ortric and gestrim, fermented grains from E-toll that were aged in casks made from an aromatic resin. The resin was harvested from pools found on the northern and southern poles, and when processed, resembled oak without losing its unique scent. Poontrip was one of E-toll's main exports and heavily regulated, but that never hindered illegal brewers from trading without credentials. Nomar, though, was a certified brewmaster, having papers to trade. His dealings with intergalactic customs were more of a hassle than concern.

"Thou, lad, are right good spark! Thou minds me ov me ol eflume, thou does! Alwas tinkin ov t' best! Thou beast me best mate at home."

Abner was glad Captain Eleeskee's offer wasn't pressed. Poontrip was not only a 'wrecking ball', but the aftertaste remained with him for days, as did its effect upon his human chemistry. E-Tollians emitted a floral aroma, following a night of heavy drinking, whereas a human would stink of wet dog and bleu cheese. It didn't present as much of a problem as one might expect, though. One could ingest an enzyme supplement before consuming a pint, and then smell like an E-Tollian for days afterward, and also avoid the aftertaste.

Needless to say, it was too early for Abner to partake of poontrip, and he was still pining for his lost donut, anyway. "One of these days," he said, "I'll visit you on E-Toll, if we can get past the off-boundary law. I think it's about time the Commonwealth changes that one! Of all the places I want to see, it's your farm, with ripe orctic as far as the eye can see. To be able to run in low gravity would be a blast! The seaside and your pet eflume? He sounds brilliant, especially if he turns down poontrip in the morning!"

"'f only thou cudta met me Undra, lad, sh'd be mother t'thou."

"I'm sure of that Nomar, if she was half the woman you've described her as, I know we would've been close. You okay? It's only been a few months."

"Aye lad, good fer me b'out. Much beter, tanks fer askin'."

"Let me know if I can help in any way."

"Aye lad, aye."

"Well, what do you have for me today?" Abner picked up the manifest. "Twenty vats of Eleeskee Amleer Poontrip, five totes of gestrim flour, and a crate of milling machine parts is what I have here."

"Aye, tis ell ere' an a late order iv joofsum."

"I'll have to clear that with my boss...shouldn't be a problem."

Abner waved to his supervisor, Arush Turgeen, who approached in his shockingly-bright green shirt and plaid tie. Abner and Captain Eleeskee exchanged smiles, aware that Arush's sense of style was a bit off-kilter. Arush greeted him with a smile, entered his override code into the manifest, and the captain wanderingly returned to whatever he 'wasn't doing before.

"Okay Nomar. I'll have the lumpers offload you as soon as they're done with dock two. Should be just over an hour."

"Right, lad. I'll wait en coffee shop, thou'll let us know ten?"

"You bet! Enjoy your coffee and save me a donut or two!"

Captain Eleeskee floated away toward The Trucker, the café nearest to the receiving department, as his grunts, clicks, shrieks, and sighs faded out of the receivable range of Abner's translator.

# Jenny Acorn

Much earlier that same morning came her yells. "Dammit!" she exclaimed, as the overhead conveyor caught her safety lanyard. "So much for safety!"

Jenny Acorn had been annoyed for the last two years of her career as a facilities technician with the constant drip, drip, drip of new safety regulations. It seemed as though half of her day was spent either filling out safety reports, containing static energy, harnessing to a piece of equipment in an unnecessary way, or having to wear the latest neon clothing which made her look like a garbage collector. Now, the geniuses who required the safety lanyard in the conveyor quadrant would finally understand why she had protested the procedure.

"Dammit! Dammit! Oh, crap! *Help!*" she yelled, as her lanyard pulled her deeply into the line labeled 'Inedible' and led to the rendering plant. It looked as though she would miss her date tonight with Abner.

She managed to pull herself up to the hook that had tangled with her lanyard, and untangled it in time to avoid the drop-off to the chute. That was a relief. The end of that ride would have been painful and disgusting, dropping into a vat of boiling animal byproducts. She breathed a sigh of relief and jumped from the hook to the next chute, which was a marginally better alternative, toward the landfill. Down the chute's steep decline and past the sensor doors, she felt the strong vacuum pull her toward the main chute. Knowing that the ride would waste the rest of the day's tasks, Jenny decided to make the best of it and enjoy the ride, anyway.

Unfortunately, the fun didn't last very long. Accelerating faster on the ten minute ride, she passed more input chutes with the joy of more trash joining her in her journey. The landfill chutes began filling with organic material as each chute passed, containing everything from used coffee grounds to spoiled food, and scraps from every kitchen onboard the ship, as well as several others nearest to the Dirt Star. The landfill also received a percentage of paper and cardboard that had traveled past the input limit of the recycler.

Her journey sped on. It was a vile-scented water slide from hell. On the way down, she could make out the smell of the deodorizer which had sprayed earlier after that morning's bulkhead failure. Suddenly, she remembered that the main chutes had been fitted with new nozzles to distribute the latest genetic treatment of which the scientists were experimenting.

*Crap!* she thought. *May have been better to be boiled in a vat of slime!* Her fears grew, wondering what would happen to her after the treatment, theoretically designed to destroy the sentient nature in organic products. Right then, a blast of floral smelling deodorizer hit her, but in this area of the ship, it did very little to transform the stench.

*That should've been turned off half an hour ago,* she thought. *I wonder if they hooked up to the wrong batch?* Her fears were confirmed as the next set of nozzles came into view, and she was unable to cease her sliding down the teflon-coated chute. The right-hand nozzle was jammed and trickling, and the left possibly misaligned after possible impact. When she passed under the left jet, she was only slightly misted. The garbage surrounding her grew until the pile she was riding rose high enough for her to hit her head on a cross beam. She exited the chute, fell onto the mound below, and passed out just before hitting the pile.

All around her teemed a countless variety of new forms of life. A fish-man and a meatloaf had witnessed Jenny fall, and saw that she was injured. Disoriented and afraid as they were after being changed, they decided to help her. Picking her up, they ran down the pile toward a large appliance box at the bottom. Relieved to find it empty, they brought her inside and left to find something to keep them warm. Finding old clothing and blankets, they brought them back to the box and covered her. After a few minutes of huddling in the box alongside her, they watched as she revived.

"Am I hallucinating?" she asked weakly as she peered out of the box and at her box mates.

"No, this is reality! We're not sure how, but it's real," answered the fish-man, who didn't have a name yet, and wondered for the first time about anything.

"I can't understand," said the meatloaf, whose last memory consisted of enjoying a mouthful of grass on the cattle ship's meadow.

"I know about the sentient problem those geniuses caused, but this is out of control!" Jenny said, still not sure if she was in her right mind. "I'm talking to a fish that looks like a guy, and a talking meatloaf thing, too!"

"We don't get it, either! Something big happened in the chute. My last memory is of swimming in a river a week ago." The fish-man didn't know it, but he originated from a river on E-Toll. He he had been caught and then placed into a tank, which was then shipped to one of the Dirt Star's kitchens. A conceited chef had found him to be below his standards, and with disgust, had thrown him down the landfill chute.

"Do you have a name?" he asked as she continued to stare at them in disbelief.

"Jenny..." she answered, dumbfounded that she was introducing herself to a meatloaf and a fish.

"How about you two?"

"Most fish aren't individualistic, but it's all flipped now."

"That's it! How 'bout 'Flip'?" Jenny exclaimed, while figuring she might as well accept the weird reality in which she was included.

"Sure, if you think it fits," Flip answered, satisfied with his new name.

"And you?" Jenny looked at the meatloaf, and imagined with wonder how a pile of hamburger, breadcrumbs, and ketchup could function as a human-like thing. He (she thought due to its masculine voice) was about four-and-a-half feet tall, and had the appearance of a delicious meatloaf in the shape of a man. His eyes and ears weren't visible, and appeared as though shaped into his present form by a child making a fun dinner. "What's your name?"

"I guess I feel the same way as Flip," the meatloaf replied insecurely.

"Maybe we could just call you 'Loaf'," Jenny said.

"That works." Derived from cows, Loaf was very compliant.

All at once, Jenny's vision blurred, and the sounds around her became distorted as she became unconscious once again.

Just then, the box door flung open. Startled, Flip and Loaf turned, and found three interesting creatures that could only have originated from a bakery peering inside.

# The Narcissists

"You're cleared for dock 5, Ulysses. Please alert Ambassador Donclees that his meeting with Captain Cudrowe is confirmed for five p.m. in the Level G conference room, and that his suite is ready as well." The controller sounded slightly annoyed as she spoke.

"Roger that, Control. Dock five, and I'll relay the info for you, as long as I can buy you that drink tonight," Captain Filet suavely responded. He waited as dead air followed. *She likes me,* he thought confidently.

His perceptions of social interactions were always misguided. Captain Marcus Filet had sailed through school, and then in the university, The Academy, he was the one student that never had to try, in order to succeed. His IQ had allowed him to ace everything in his path, entering flight school two years earlier than the standard entrance age. His intellect further handicapped his social disability, of which he was unaware. Throughout his twenty-six years, life had been a breeze, and the people he used to keep it so, became a trail of damaged souls in his wake.

The Ulysses, an ambassador class ship, entered the docks with elegant sophistication in form and movement. At the controls, Filet maneuvered the ship with a purposeful arrogance. Wherever it went, those who observed the entrance or exit of the Ulysses were taken with its beauty and grace. It presented a gleaming form, a sleek, metallic, polished and mirrored finish, subtly accented with the blue and orange colors of the E-Tollian flag. Filet's skill gave prominence to its attraction with the precision of its movements, giving the ship an air of eminence, artistry and power. The ambassador had cleverly chosen the ship and its pilot for that designed purpose.

Filet's actions at the helm brought the Ulysses to dock 5 without any disturbance to the cup of coffee at his side, and the dock clamps locked into its mooring cleats. Filet finished his coffee and began the shutdown procedures as the ambassador disembarked with a nod, his staff and guards in front and behind.

*Free for a few days*, Filet thought, as he checked off the last items from his post-flight list. Grabbing his bags, Filet made his way across the gangplank to the dock, scanning his surroundings. Looking across the dock, he viewed a shipping employee dressed in neon green and a plaid tie. The sight of the man's fashion filled him with disgust, as he took pride in his own presentation, and he wiped a slight wrinkle from the

lapel of his tailored Vishux suit jacket. Turning, he
made for a tube lift to hospitality on Deck G to check
into his suite. The guest quarters aboard the Dirt Star,
though utilitarian, were elegant. Filet strode to the
front desk, flashing his credentials without a word.

"Room 24 is ready for you, Captain Filet, down the
hall to the right," announced the clerk.

"Room? Do you know who I am? There should be
a suite here in my name. I am an ambassador class
pilot, for God's sake!" Filet's veins rose in his neck as
firmly as his annoying volume levels rose in the
lobby.

The clerk, recently an intern and on his first day as
a junior level employee, panicked, fumbling back
through his guest logs. He was eager to be relieved of
this intimidating, pompous ass's presence.

"I'm so sorry, sir!" he replied. "Let me see...ah, yes!
Er, here you are. My mistake. Your suite is number 35,
at the end of the hall on the left. Please enjoy your
stay, and let us know if you need anything else." He
motioned to the bellhop. "George, please take Captain
Filet's bags to his suite."

Scanning the room, and purposefully unimpressed,
Filet excused the bellhop and made for the shower.
The bellhop departed without being granted a tip,
and returned disappointedly to the lobby.

After a shower and a shot of single malt scotch
from the wet bar, Filet marched to the ship's four star
restaurant, The Earth. Not only was he brilliant and

rich, but Filet's stunning good looks also demanded attention; his appearance was yet another aspect of his existence that he mistook as an earned asset. He exploited his natural gifts well as he strolled to the podium, and he requested a table for two with a star view, for an hour later.

'The Moon', read the sign above the doors to the attached nightclub near the podium, and sound emanated from the dance floor as he opened the door to the nightclub. Filet ordered a drink and surveyed all around him with disdain. After meandering through the crowd on the dance floor, he sat next to a beautiful woman, who welcomed the free drink and his perfectly-hidden self-absorption. His conversation was masked with a well-rehearsed impression of a man genuinely interested in the details of the beautiful woman's life.

Filet's gifts, as a machine, worked in unison to obtain his desires for the night. His mind worked like a computer, adding the correct responses and body language where required. He sprinkled charm and compliments at just the right moments to the recipe, to suit his own taste. Filet 'the chef' began the first course, a meal at his table for two. By the end of the night, with dessert completed, the beautiful young lady was cast from his suite. He'd never enjoyed the constant drip, drip, drip of female conversation.

When he had what he needed, the true nature of the man quickly became evident.

# Date Night

Arush, in his annoying wardrobe choice, walked to the dock alongside Abner and paused to allow tension to build for his intern.

"Abner," he said, "why have you cleared fifty totes of soil to Gleneset without the necessary declarations stamped?" His air of superiority clashed with his clothes.

"That's the shipment we talked about last night. You said you'd handle it."

"Oh, that's right...Just making sure you're aware. You really should be checking all manifests in and out before the handlers touch anything," Arush backpedaled, attempting to keep the upper hand.

*Two more years*, Abner thought, knowing Arush would be transferring soon. Arush returned to sit again at his desk and finish wasting time. Knowing he had fifteen minutes left before the end of his shift, Abner finished his paperwork. He added the stamps to the soil shipments Arush had forgotten, swept his area, and clocked out, waving goodnight to Arush and Mr. Bonageres. He took a tube-lift to his room on

Level C, stripped, showered, shaved, and dressed in his favorite shirt and pants.

*Tonight will be great,* he thought, nervously contemplating the evening with Jenny by his side.

He had waited a month to ask her out after first noticing her, as she was coming to the dock to adjust a landing clamp. He realized then, that he had seen her years before as children. As a young boy, he'd been completely paralyzed by shyness, and avoided every attractive girl. Time had smiled upon Jenny. She had become a beautiful woman, very sure of herself in most ways. She was a natural beauty, secure enough in her femininity to not mind picking up a wrench to repair a trash compactor.

Eventually, Abner gathered enough courage to buy her some coffee at the Trucker. They'd hit it off right away, and Abner's nervousness and verbal fumbling grew less pronounced as they continued their dates. He knew he wasn't a macho type of man, and wasn't threatened by a strong-charactered woman, either. Since they'd started seeing one another, the weekdays seemed to drag for Abner until they met on Friday nights. He was excited to hear her tell stories of her work, and about the people with whom she dealt aboard the Dirt Star. She was equally fascinated with Abner's accounts of dealing with visitors, many from as far as one's imagination allowed. Both of them were perfectly suited to their roles onboard, and to each other. A month had now passed since their first date at The Trucker.

Abner was patient when it came to most things, but Friday nights were an exception. His hair now dry after showering, he glanced at the clock. His patience began to dwindle as the time drew close to 8 p.m. He decided to message her, and after fifteen minutes without a reply, he began to worry. She usually responded right away, like most people of their generation did. After another hour, he opened an instant meal labeled 'Chicken Curry with Papadams', added the catalyst, waited two minutes, then wolfed it down. The time seemed to drag while waiting for her to call.

He found his book on the side table, and resumed where he had left off. It was a novel filled with stories about gunslingers, sheriffs, land disputes, killings and revenge. Any story that described land in detail fascinated Abner, as he had never set foot on the ground of any planet.

The book contained some chapters about a character who was a small-time gold miner. The details of the miner's surroundings mesmerized him. The narrator described how the miner was able to discern the land, finding dry creek beds. He knew the areas next to bends in the streams and at the trailing edge of boulders that held promising gold deposits. Abner could feel the black iron-laden sands in his hands as the narrator described the miner shoveling soil into a pan. His own hands felt the water as he swirled the pan, and he felt the sun's intense heat beating down on the miner's balding head as if it were his own. As he read, one of the sheriff's deputies had to shoot his own horse after they had fallen down a steep, rock-faced ravine together. The deputy, bruised and cut, found the greatest pain in having to put his best friend out of misery. Abner made himself comfortable on the couch, and as the story progressed, he fell asleep.

He awoke at four o'clock in the morning (his day off), the clock alarm he'd forgotten to disarm having destroyed any chance of sleeping in. Checking his phone log, he saw that Jenny had never messaged him, and was fully convinced that something was amiss. He brushed his teeth and hair, walked to the facilities department, exited the tube-lift at Level F, and made his way down the gray hallway.

"Hey Abner, how's it goin'?" Enfreck Fren greeted as Abner approached the desk. "Jenn's not here, dude."

"When did you see her last, En?" Abner's fears were growing.

"I think it was around four yesterday afternoon, right before she took a call to fix a problem with the conveyor at the slaughterhouse," Enfreck replied, showing little concern.

"Did she talk to anyone here since?"

"Don't think so...let's see, the logs show she didn't clock out either." Enfreck's concern awakened him.

"I'll get a hold of security and see if they can find her."

"Thanks En—I'm gonna go to the packing room." Abner turned and ran to the tube without waiting for Enfreck's slow response.

"I'll let you know if I hear anything, Abe!"

# The Landfill

Louie, Bob, and Rob looked into the box, fascinated by all three inside: a meatloaf, a fish-man, and a young lady who seemed to be transforming before their very eyes.

Flip and Loaf, at first, were startled by the emergence of the pastries, and turned to their friend Jenny. She was emanating a faint glow, her eyes brightly changing color, and her short hair growing at an alarming rate. As far as they could tell, she was still fully human, but something indescribable was happening to her. Though the pastries had never met Jenny, they somehow knew she was altered too. All three sat inside the box to see what would happen next.

Jenny regained consciousness, but was unable to speak. She sat on the floor, paralyzed from the neck down, her eyes moving back and forth between herself and the others. She was still changing, and she sensed that something very strange was happening. At first, a tingling sensation began from head to toe, and then she felt vibrations in her scalp. She watched as her once fine, brown hair grew past her shoulders and stretched to the floor, in light brown shafts about a sixteenth of an inch thick. She had always envied the thick hair of others; now, she possessed the healthiest dreadlocks known to mankind.

Jenny could sense that the physical changes were ending, but as they did, other peculiar and miraculous changes ensued. She had always been sensitive to those around her, never feeling settled until she had done her best to make others comfortable, especially if they were worthy of her efforts. Her intuition, as well, had always told her when to avoid, or at least be aware of, others.

What she now experienced was entirely different from merely being a good judge of character. It was as if she knew others' minds, like she inhabited them, yet still retained her own thoughts, too. It wasn't as though she could 'read' minds. Instead, it was as though Jenny actually existed in another's shoes, yet without control; she was simply a passenger within another's mind. The rest were unaware that she was experiencing anything, like how one knows a character in a book without the limitations the author enforces. She absorbed knowledge, its wisdom or the lack of it, and also sensed emotion or its lack, too. She could feel the fear, concern, and interest that Loaf, Flip and the pastries had concerning her, as if she were inside each of them all at once, watching herself.

It was so fascinating to Jenny, that she completely forgot about what had happened to her physical body. The tingling sensations had ceased, and her thoughts once again became her own. Her hair now lie past her feet as she stood to take a step forward and assure her new friends that she was okay. She tripped over her now long, brown hair that spilled all over the floor, and she fell.

Stunned and laughing, she rolled over, examining her state. "Well, this'll be a problem." She pinched herself. Realizing she wasn't dreaming, even though she increasingly felt like she was, she asked, "Where are we?"

"We're in a box inside the landfill," Flip responded. "You hit your head as we were falling out of the chute! You passed out twice—Are you okay? Don't you remember talking to us earlier?"

"I do remember now...You're Flip, right?" She turned her head. "And you're Loaf?"

Jenny's stomach rumbled as the delicious meatloaf responded, "That's me," his savory smell filling the box. "You okay? I didn't know you could do that. Can you do it again?" Loaf, being less than three days old, showed his childlike excitement to all around him.

"I have to admit, that was an amazing show you just put on!" agreed Flip. The pastries nodded in agreement.

"I'm pretty sure it wasn't as weird as what was happening on my end!" Jenny said. She decided to leave it at that, knowing any other explanation would be difficult for them to comprehend. She wasn't sure if a fish, a few donuts, and a meatloaf would have the intellect to understand her experience.

The others' attention refocused onto the three newcomers. Louie, sensing the need for an introduction, said, "Hello, I'm Louie. This is Rob, and he's Bob. This morning we were looking forward to a meeting in the conference room with coffee and everything. I guess we didn't look as tasty as the others. I thought I'd have a short life, but look at us now! I never thought I'd see anything like what you just did! Do all humans do that?"

"No, I think this is just as new as a talking donut," Jenny responded, as she witnessed the pastries losing even more of their donut form before her very eyes. She chuckled within, aware that they were more interested in her than themselves, though she herself was speaking to a talking donut.

Little did she know, she would soon be able to tell a lot more about others, simply by being in close proximity to them.

# Trials

Abner reached the packing room conveyor that lead to rendering, and found Jenny's tool bag on the floor next to a Port-a-weld pen and a box of rags. She was nowhere in sight. He decided to go back to facilities and find out if Enfreck had heard anything. When he arrived, he found Security Officer Wildrew Meeks talking to Enfreck.

"No, the camera feed went down at the same time the ventilation failed yesterday. We haven't been able to monitor the chutes or the landfill since," Wildrew was saying, appearing stressed and unable to think of a good excuse. He knew his department would have hell to pay for not suggesting a shutdown of landfill operations after the video failure. "I'm pretty sure we put in a service request for the system not long after the failure."

"Lemme see...yep, here it is. Came in about five hours before my shift. I never would've even looked. If Jen was around, she would've at least started a work order on it," Enfreck said, aware he was partially to blame. "Well, I'm going to have to call

Delt and see if he can get the feed back up, so we can see if she's in the landfill."

"I'm not waiting—I'm going to suit up," Abner announced decidedly, running to the packing room.

Enfreck called after him. "You can't go in there, Abe! The landfill doors can't be opened without clearance!" Abner was unable to hear his last few words as the tube-lift door closed behind him.

Once again, he arrived at the packing room, ran to the hazmat locker, and threw on a suit. The tight-fitting suit felt surprisingly comfortable, with the exception of a hood that fit a bit too tightly over his head due to his height. Adjusting the hood, its eyepiece, and respirator, Abner ran back toward the conveyor. Jumping up, he missed the first hook, then took a few steps back and tried again. Succeeding, he clutched tightly until the hooks pulled away, engaging a flapper that would've pulled his hands off, had he failed to let go first. He spied another chute to his right before he fell.

Although unsure that it was a good idea, he plunged down the chute toward rendering until he hit a large, disgusting pile. He longed to forget his experience immediately, as it was completely vile, but that wasn't possible. He sat atop the pile a long while, contemplating his options. Reasoning a jam existed further down, and with no other way to return up the chute, he had no choice but to dig his way through the mess. A trough lie on each side of the high-sided chute in which to toss the various organs, skins, and whatever-the-hell those other things were, and get them out of his way. After an hour of blood, sweat, and filth, he reached a closed door at the bottom, and grabbed onto a crossbar as he decided what to do.

Suddenly, the door opened slowly, revealing a boiling rendering vat below. He gave thanks for having missed that disastrous possibility, and worked his way down to the top, open edge of the door. It could be reached with a good handhold and a swing. He and the door now at an angle away from the vat, Abner released into another pile of vile material for which he was starting to be thankful. As the rendering department workers yelled after him, he picked himself up and quickly exited before they could stop him.

Running down the hall toward the tube-lifts, he caught a glimpse of himself in a long mirror which ran the length of the hallway. He decided the hood wasn't that uncomfortable. Without the suit and its hood, he would've had to both feel and smell the revolting stuff which now decorated him. People, shocked, passed him in the hallway and held back their vomit with disgust. He reached the tube (feeling slightly guilty and sorry for the next poor soul who would use it), jumped in, and shot back to the packing room.

This time, he knew he must use the other chute he had seen earlier. He found what he was looking for, a chute labeled 'Landfill'. He felt stupid that he hadn't seen it earlier. He opened the door and slid into the chute, wondering if his experience was what a morgue would feel like. The chute door slapped closed, and he felt the vacuum accelerate him toward the landfill. Soon, he was riding a wave of everything that nobody wanted.

The deodorizer nozzles came into view up ahead. Passing under them, he mused that he wouldn't have been such a problem for the people in the hallway if he'd de-scented here, first. Either way, the suit made it impossible for him to tell the difference. A little further down, another set of nozzles appeared. Neither of them hit the chute very well; one jammed, the other was improperly aligned. After passing the nozzles, the trash around him grew and grew, until he —like Jenny—hit his head while exiting the chute.

# Clarity

"Feed's back up! What the hell?" Officer Wildrew Meeks wondered if he was seeing things. "Look at this...Am I nuts or can you see this, too?!"

Officer Daley turned to face the same monitor in the security department.

"The...hell?...What the hell are we seeing, Wil?"

"I dunno, but I think this is big enough for the captain to see!"

"Captain, this is Officer Wildrew Meeks from Security! I think you're going to want to see the video feed from the landfill. I'm sending it to you now, sir." Meeks hit the correct sequence of buttons to send it, relieved it was now out of his hands.

The monitor in Captain Cletus Cudrowe's suite displayed the video feed. As the captain zoomed in, he figured someone was playing a joke on him; if it was indeed a joke, he reasoned, it was one sick puppy who played it.

In times past, the sentient nature of the food supply had appeared to be a manageable flaw in the Dirt Star's developmental history. The crew had become accustomed to its awkwardness, but what he now witnessed on the monitor was beyond Cudrowe's imagination. He took a deep breath, viewing what looked like something out of a Salvador Dali painting. He stared at the screen, dumbfounded, as creatures moved across it—many somewhat familiar to him, and others different from anything he'd ever seen, from any planet he knew.

"What the hell?...What the hell??" was all he could manage to say as he cycled through the video feed channels, until one rested on a chute originating from the kitchen. There, he saw food scraps first being hit with deodorizer, and then with another set of sprays.

"Dammit! That deodorizer was supposed to be shut down!" he exclaimed. The captain ran to his terminal and entered the password for the Alarm E-Stop, effectively shutting down all treatments in the chutes, and sealing all chute doors within the ship.

Abner awoke high atop the mound, rubbing his head as he noticed lightly-spattered blood on the inside of his face mask. He reached up, feeling carefully with his fingertips to make sure his suit and helmet hadn't been breached, and found that it was secure.

All around, he saw that the landfill was full of life. He pondered whether his head injury was affecting him more than he had originally thought was possible, until the certain reality of it all struck him.

Still in a state of amazement, fear, and excitement, he decided to look for cover in the event of danger. He found nothing more than an appliance box at the bottom of the hill for shelter. *It'll have to do,* he thought, making his way downhill, and trying to avoid some of the strangest things he'd ever seen. He reached the box and opened it. Looking inside, he found three donut men talking to a fish-man and a meatloaf. On the bottom sat a mass of hair that also seemed to be alive.

The sight amused him, until the 'Hair' called, "Abner is that you?"

The voice sounded familiar, and not knowing what else to do or say, he responded, "Yeeaah...it's...me?"

"Oh Abner! I'm so glad to see you! I was starting to think I was crazy after everything I'd seen today," exclaimed what looked like 'Cousin It' on the floor.

The voice was so...*Wait!* he suddenly thought.

"Jenny, is that...you?!"

"Yes, it's me. I think whatever has happened to the rest of the life down here, has somehow affected me, too."

Abner rushed past the donuts toward her, and moved a pound of hair away from her face as he peered into her eyes. It was Jenny, all right, but she was somehow different. She was just as beautiful as ever, yet with eyes that seemed to actually see inside of him. It comforted him, and yet disturbed him.

She was in need of one hell of a haircut, too.

The mood of wonder in the box suddenly cut short, as Jenny yelled instructions and brought them to their feet.

# It Goes to Eleven!

"We have to get out of here *now*!"

Jenny couldn't explain it, even to herself, but she could feel an evil presence approaching closely to the box, and she knew it wanted *in*, wanted to get into all of them. Exiting the box, the new friends looked up to see more creatures streaming down the mound, just as strange as the others, but with a whitish haze covering them. These new beings seemed driven by something other than themselves, as if they were somehow bonded together in thought, like a swarm.

"Stop!" In a discordant tone they sounded out as one. "You must stop! And be cured!" The mentality of the Yeasts, still striving to decipher human customs and speech norms, next tried a different tactic. "We will help you, don't fear!" The attempt at compassion rang false, and fueled the fears of those who fled.

"Run!" Abner called to Jenny, and also with a genuine concern he didn't understand to a fish, meatloaf, and three donuts. *What the hell?* he thought, and Jenny agreed, both laughing through the fear, without realizing that Abner hadn't actually spoken a word.

All seven ran around the mound, avoiding a large empty pool in the corner of the landfill, to where they found a service room built into the wall. Jenny tried the door, and finding it locked, waived her pass over the sensor. With relief, they heard the door unlock. Louie shut it behind them as they piled into the room, and they surveyed the space they'd found. It was one of four service rooms for maintenance and repair of the landfill, and it was one of two that was equipped with a loading dock and a light-duty service shuttle.

"This is excellent!" shouted Jenny as she ran into the service bay, still holding her hair above the floor like a carpet.

"But none of us can pilot it!" Abner exclaimed as fear settled within him. He pondered the rat-men, mice-people, and various 'things' that didn't resemble anything normal. They were held together by failed science and the Yeasts. For the first time in history, the Yeasts were able to use its intellect and carry out its will. Not only was 'it' driven toward dominating all life, but it could now exhibit strategic thought, and knew that it would be victorious.

"I can pilot the shuttle, if you'll help me," ventured Loaf with some bashfulness, still appearing as delicious as ever.

"What do you mean, 'you can'?" Jenny asked, confused. A second later, though, she sensed within that he could indeed pilot it, and asked, "What do you want us to do?"

"What! Are you kidding?! You want a meatloaf to fly that?" Abner was running out of energy and the ability to sense reality, and was becoming a bit of an ass, as a result. "You have no idea what it took for me to find you. I'm not going to risk losing you again, because some...doggy-bag!...thinks it can take you home!"

"Abe, I know it sounds crazy, but he can. I know he can." Having stood next to Loaf, she had felt the certainty inside herself.

The day before, Captain Ramar Gleek, a fighter squadron pilot and someone whom Jenny knew well, had tried his hand again at creating his favorite meal: meatloaf, mashed potatoes, and sweet peas. This would be one monster of a meal, he had thought. He had invited his division for a party in the mess hall. The captain had blended one-hundred pounds of ground chuck, twenty pounds of Italian bread crumbs, salt, pepper, garlic, two dozen eggs, and ketchup. Ramar expressed his quirky sense of humor as he formed the mass into the shape of the recently-reassigned Major Hicks, who had departed the week before for a ship on the other side of the fleet. He would serve it to the division 2 security force, for the 'good riddance' party he had planned for the following day.

Jenny was unsure how the perfectly cooked meatloaf had found its way to the landfill, but she mentally let go of Loaf's history to refocus on Abner. Though Jenny knew Loaf's abilities were tied to the genes of Captain Gleek, she also knew she wouldn't be able to explain it all without sounding like a whack job. She merely said,

"Abe, he can...but before we do anything, I've got to get rid of *this*!" She threw her hair to the floor, and once again appeared like a human mop.

"Will this do?" Rob held up a blowtorch.

"Or how 'bout these?" Flip held up pliers, a hammer, and a pair of scissors.

"Perfect!" Grabbing the scissors, she attempted to cut off her hair, but as hard as she tried, the sharp scissors didn't even make a dent in her now super-human locks. "I can't live with this! Okay, here's what I'm going to do. I'm going to wet my hair down to here," she said, pointing to just above her shoulders. "Rob, you cut off all the dry hair from here down, okay?" she instructed as she pointed at the torch on the nearby counter.

"Okay...if you think so," Rob responded, with the doubt of a donut fried earlier that same day.

Abner jumped in. "Look! If we're going to have a meatloaf pilot our escape, at least let me take the torch from the donut and give you a haircut!"

"Alright Abe, you win," conceded Jenny, while wetting her hair and leaning over a table to keep away from the torch.

After fumbling with it and receiving help from Rob, Abner lit it. The rest pulled the hair away from her and opposite the table as he cut. It took a full five minutes to accomplish the job, the burnt hair fumes filling the room with a sweet, marshmallow-like fragrance. It smelled delicious, and reminded them that they were hungry, even those who had never eaten before. Jenny's haircut was perfect in her eyes; by luck or by some design, it was wonderful, after rubbing off the burnt ends.

They were exhausted and hungry. It was a strange feeling for some, food needing food. After the change, the donuts, fish, and meatloaf had become more human than food, by percentage. In the case of the donuts, their human digestive systems had consumed the remainder of their donut past, and were 'coming down' from a sugar rush. Loaf was one big mass of muscle, the strongest by far of all of them, and had a metabolism to match. Flip had a craving for worms.

Jenny knew the service room had an attached, fully-stocked kitchen, and she called the rest to follow her. Searching the cupboards, she stopped and considered how to proceed with sensitivity. She wasn't sure how the changed ones would react to human food, or any food at all for that matter. It almost seemed like suggesting cannibalism.

Just then, she realized she wasn't sensing any of

the others at that moment. In fact, after her last experience with Loaf's origins, she had been on her own again, without the automatic inclusion of others' thoughts and emotions. She thought the experiences would be permanent, but now she wasn't so sure.

Loaf broke her line of thought. "I'm dying for some mashed potatoes. Or grass if there's any."

"How about worms or bugs?" Flip questioned loudly.

Louie, Rob and Bob suggested in stereo, "Coffee?"... "Bacon?"..."Glaze! I love glaze!"

"How 'bout a shower? I need to get out of this suit!" Abner had been smelling himself for the last hour, after having removed his helmet and respirator.

"Just down the hall, there's clean overalls on the racks to the left," replied a relieved Jenny, while holding up a package of hot dogs and a large can of chili. "These okay?"

"Sounds great! Any mustard?" Abner's stomach was growling.

"Yep, go clean up. You reek!"

"*Thanks*...I'm glad I found you, but your hair is making me hungry." with a smile, Abner headed to the showers.

"Okay guys, hot dogs and chili it is!" Jenny decided blindly, figuring they would have to face their own ethical challenges and solve them in their own ways. Hot dogs and chili had never been an ethical problem for her, and it especially wasn't tonight.

Abner showered and changed, and no longer a hindrance to his own or anyones else's appetite, he sat down to a mug of beer and a plate holding two dogs smothered in chili.

Thanking God, they dug into their meals as if they'd never eaten before. Louie, Rob, and Bob, with big smiles, picked up their dogs and experienced the amazing joy of eating. Chili dogs, the first among many meals for them, was a feast they would never forget. The beer, with its yeasty goodness, seemed a mother to them, too. Flip was preoccupied with the hotdog, viewing it as one of the fattest worms he had ever seen, and was astonished by its delicious flavor after swallowing both dogs whole. Loaf, blind to the fact that he was enjoying the chief competitor to all hamburgers, opted to have his chili on the side, and smothered his dogs with ketchup and crushed crackers instead.

Jenny and Abner clicked their bottles together, Abner saying, "Here's to our insta-family of eating disorder over-comers."

Once the meal had been eaten, they jointly decided to get some rest and ponder their next move the following morning. They found tarps, wadded them, and lay upon them, closing their eyes for the night.

# Containment?

"What the hell were you people thinking?"
Captain Cudrowe demanded, turning bright red,
aware that all of the biohazard's implications were his
responsibility. "Were the trials in sterile
environments? Did they include the chemicals used in
the landfill? Did anyone—anyone at all—think to do a
test resembling any damn form of reality?"

Professor Jamus Lantooto shrugged sheepishly.
"Our trials never included aberrant chemicals
deemed to interfere with the goals. Obviously, this
was a bit of an oversight."

"An oversight? This is a colossal career-ender,
Jamus! How could you be so stupid?! This makes the
last screw-up look like baby-steps to hell. You and
your team have us in a sprint! What are our options,
Hank?"

Hank Thomas, Head of Security, responded,
"Captain, we never anticipated a scenario on this
level, but we have the landfill contained. The seals
should hold back anything, even down to the
microscopic level. Worst case would be that we drop

out the landfill pod, tow it far enough away, and hit it with nukes."

"Hold it now...we need to back up a bit here. Without that pod we're all out of a job, working as janitors on the Levev!" Cudrowe warned.

"We could reverse the methane vacuums and ignite. The methane down there will continue to be produced by the composting process, fueling itself," countered Jimmy Roberts from facilities.

"That could blow the whole ship, couldn't it?" Cudrowe asked.

"No, the landfill pod was designed for methane scavenge failure. We would still have to drop it from the ship, due to the heat it would emit," Jimmy clarified. "It would take at least six months to do a complete burn."

"Six months would wreck us financially. Anyone else have any other ideas?" Cudrowe entreated, now desperate.

Professor Jamus began, "We could hit it with—"

Cudrowe cut him off. "Sorry Jamus, I don't want anymore from your team right now."

Wildrew Meeks, from security, ran into the room while pulling up video on the conference room monitor.

"Captain, you need to see this! We picked this up from one of the service rooms. That's Abner Oaks and Jenny Acorn, the two who've been missing. Not sure who or what the others are." The video showed seven people sleeping on the floor in the service dock bay.

"Great! There goes all easy answers to this mess!" Cudrowe exploded, his complexion matching his red uniform. "Patch me into that room...This is Captain Cudrowe! Are you people okay?"

The monitor showed them slowly waking, and Jenny responded,

"Yes sir, we're fine, but we're pretty much stuck here. There's some pretty scary stuff happening on the other side of those doors. I'm sure you've already seen what's happening in the landfill. Even in this room, you can see there's seven of us."

"Who, what are they, Miss Acorn?" asked Cudrowe.

"Well, it's hard to explain, sir, but these five have all been a part of keeping us all alive. I know it sounds crazy, sir, but we need to save the others inside there, too."

"Miss Acorn, my first concern is to get you and Mr. Oaks out of there first. My mind has been blown enough for three lifetimes, but we need to get you safe. We'll get back to you soon. Please stand by!"

The Yeasts were occupied with spreading to the remainder of the changed ones while weighing its options. It had taken half of them already. Half of those settled into the soil to spread tendrils, becoming one large organism. The combined intellect, or the 'Collective', fed its pride and hatred of all that were clean. It thought of the various tactics it might try and of its opponents.

The seals would need to be breached to spread spores throughout the ship. The ventilation system control overrides could be activated in one of the service rooms. It could employ its army of hosts to fight; whether they killed the enemy or not, they would spread spores to them, which was one of its main objectives, anyway. The humans might try to counter using methane, or detach the pod and then nuke at a safe distance from the ship. There were advantages to all of these approaches, if timed accurately. Humans were fools, the Yeasts had quickly determined, as it digested their history, culture, and battle experience throughout all generations. Humans had maintained the upper hand, until now.

The intercom sounded. "Captain, just a reminder— Ambassador Donclees is scheduled for five o'clock in the G Level conference room."

"Janice, please send my apologies and a cancellation to the ambassador. I will speak to him personally before he leaves." Cudrowe's face drained of all color. "We need to get those two out of there ASAP! Are there any space suits stored in there?"

"No sir, the shuttle itself would be their only protection, and there's only space for the shuttle in that service bay," a facilities technician answered.

"I can't believe how well prepared we are for this!

We can't bring another shuttle to them without having the suits to spacewalk, and that room has no interlock." He held his forehead, mumbling, "We're going to have to go in there through the chutes to get them out of there."

In the service room, Jenny pondered the situation, her face pale. "They're going to kill everything down here," she said, glancing at Abner. "They're only interested in us, not the others. I'm not waiting—we need to get out of here now!" She led them on board the shuttle and brought Loaf to the captain's chair. "Here ya go, Captain!"

Loaf sat down at the helm, beaming on the inside, and appearing even more delicious than usual on the outside.

After securing everyone else, Jenny locked herself in. "Loaf, we just need to get to the loading docks. We'll figure it out after that."

# The 41st and the 30th

The 41st Red Security Battalion, one of the elite militarized security forces of the Commonwealth, dropped five shipping containers for cover in various positions within the landfill. Next, fifty elite commandos sailed down the chutes to the landfill. Each of them hit the mounds after exiting, rolled into upright positions, and proceeded with caution down the mounds to the freshly dropped containers, where they then built their base of operations. In the distance, they could see the strange forest of humanoid fungus not far from the service room objective. They viewed humanoids all around, including a small percentage that seemed to be infected and moving with speed and stealth.

"Avoid contact with all but your objectives, Major," ordered Captain Cudrowe, "especially the ones that look infected. We're not sure what's going on with them."

The 41st, one by one, ducked in and out of their artificial cover, picking up supplies as they exited the containers. Within thirty minutes, they appeared to

have secured the situation. The few white-hazed
beings that attacked them didn't have any weapons,
and weren't much of a threat, aside from falling on
top of them as they were neutralized. The soldiers
mowed down the fungal forest with their automatics.
Seeing no other threats, they approached the service
room doors.

"Let's go, Loaf!" called Jenny as the dock bay
airlock door was cleared. "Hit it!"

Loaf, without hesitation, hit the thrusters with a
perfect exit from the dock bay, dropped down below
the ship, and reappeared on the port side at an open
loading dock. Without waiting for clearance, he
passed the landing lights and moved into the
automatic dock clamp assembly. When he had
finished, they realized it had been a fluid, flawless
experience for all of them, and that there hadn't been
any bumps, jerks, or fear associated with anything
that meatloaf had done. They were all stunned, Loaf
included, until the gravity of what they had just done
began to register within them. They all spoke at once.

"Now what?"

"We don't have clearance to be here!"

"They're coming over here!"

"Those are soldiers!"

"We've got to get outta here!"

They rushed out of the shuttle, and looking two
docks down, they saw the Ulysses gleaming and
parked at Dock Five.

"There!" Louie announced in a loud whisper. "The Ulysses!"

"The hatch is open! This was meant to be!" said Loaf, taking in the beauty of the E-toll ambassador's cruiser . They ran to the Ulysses, rushed through the hatch and into the storage room of the ship, and each found an adequate hiding spot.

"Search the docks! They're not on this shuttle," Major Lars Myhra of the 30th Gray Security Battalion instructed the squad soldiers nearest him. Fifteen commandos split ranks, rapidly searching the vessels and freight on the docks, while workers and passengers scattered out of their way.

Inside the landfill, Major Vess called through his comm link. "Captain Cudrowe, as far as I can tell, all is secure down here, but we just missed the objectives. Their shuttle pulled out of the service bay as we arrived at the door's window. Do you have contact with them?"

"They landed at the port side docks a minute ago...I was just about to let you know. We have the Gray on it now, Major. Job well done! Get cleaned up and back here, ASAP."

During the early twenty-first century on Earth, Utrecht University in the Netherlands had begun research to find a new way to produce parts for several different industries. Unlike any other form of production, the parts were grown from a strain of fungus. The cultures had been grown and shaped to fit the parts needed, then cured according to the user's specifications. Over the years, all non-metallic elements produced for the market—glove boxes, CV joint boots, intake gaskets, shipping containers, lawn chairs, and even door seals—were composed of the fungus-based polymer, or 'FBPs'. Decades before the first ship of had departed Earth, all petroleum-based polymers had been regulated into obscurity, in favor of the more Earth-friendly FBPs.

The Yeasts, though appearing to have been defeated, rose up, victorious in spirit. It knew that the trillions of spores shared with the enemy would eventually lead to domination. It knew that every boot tread, uniform fiber, and even the scratches in their automatic weapons, would loyally serve as transports for spores, ready to become a weapon greater than humanity had ever known. Their first success, however, would require reinforcement. It began to focus on its abused cousin found all over the ship, from the tools in the service room, to the seals on the airlock doors. FBPs existed everywhere one looked.

Rage reignited in the Yeasts as they observed the corpses of their kind, molded into useful forms to function for society's needs. Humanity would pay dearly for this perverted cruelty, It decided. The Collective would breathe life back into the seals, and move into the ship in one united effort.

# Diplomacy?

"They must've moved deeper into the ship, Captain. These docks are clear," Myrha explained. "The only ship untouched is the Ulysses. Do we have your permission to search it?"

"This is like a cancer," mumbled Cudrowe. Mumbling was becoming his main form of communication. Recent memory mixed with abundant anxiety fueled his short, fumbled apology of a meeting with Ambassador Donclees. The ambassador's response had been one of unrestrained hysteria, and a promise to be a pain in his ass from that point onward.

Cudrowe responded, "No, Major Myrha, not at this time. Let's move deeper in. Major Vess will join us with the Red shortly. We'll need to go over every hairball on this heap!"

Captain Marcus Filet of the ambassador class ship, the Ulysses, was halted at the docks by a huge soldier in a gray uniform.

"You're not cleared to enter."

"I'm captain of the Ulysses! We have diplomatic

immunity, you piss-ant!" Filet spat with his best elitist air. "Ambassador Donclees will be here any minute. Do you want a problem with the Intergalactic Congress, you flea?!"

A black-gloved hand, the size of Filet's head, found a grip on the front of his shirt, picking him off the ground like a pillow. "You're not cleared to enter," the gray-uniformed commando growled, teeth gritting, his true power suppressed. He dropped Filet from a height of two feet. Filet was fortunate not to have had lemon filling.

Just then, Ambassador Donclees arrived at the dock, standing on his gold plated hovercart. Some people fell off the platform as he pushed them out of his way. Filet picked himself up off the floor, unfazed by the soldier's treatment.

"This will be noted, soldier!" Ambassador Donclees threatened, the translation complete with its grunts, clicks, shrieks, and sighs as it sounded through the soldier's built-in translator.

"Go ahead Kurts, let them board," Major Myhra instructed through Kurts's headset. "We can't hold them." Ambassador Donclees and his pilot, disregarding the decorated soldier of the 30th Gray Battalion, walked and floated respectively toward the Ulysses.

Inside the freight room of the Ulysses, Louie spoke. "The engines are coming online. Why hasn't this ship been searched?" Abner responded with relief.

"This is an ambassador class ship. They can't search it without permission from the ambassador himself. That was a close shave!"

"But now where are we going?" Louie asked with fear and excitement. His dread was similar to the fears he used to have, of someday being eaten, and then traveling through a human digestive tract.

"Not sure, but at this point, anywhere is better than here!"

The 41st Red Battalion had dropped soiled uniforms into a bin near the showers, then showered and donned clean uniforms before joining the Gray at the docks. The bins were supposed to have been sent to the incinerator next to the showers, but unfortunately in the rush, none of the soldiers had done it. The sector janitor found the bins, pulled out all of the boots and set them in another bin, and then dumped the uniforms down the laundry chute. He decided it would be best to take the bin loaded with boots to the cobbler's shop on Level E to be cleaned. Leaving the showers, he made his way to the freight elevator.

As a result, the Yeasts enjoyed the failure of man and the help of the kind, but foolish, janitor. The nice man became the first to be infected outside the landfill. Inside the laundry chute, the uniforms would sit while more clothes amassed into a pile, waiting for their turn to be cleaned. It took ample time, even days, for their spores to reproduce. Imperceptibly, spores wafted upward as each new pair of pants or t-shirt was dropped into the bin; the spores escaped easily, since the laundry chutes weren't sealed. Soon, the room next to the showers was covered in spores which were undetectable to the human eye. They crept into the showers and outside, into the hallways which led to the remainder of the ship.

Inside the landfill, the Yeasts had easily breached the seals. The Yeast-infected seals responded with new freedom and a rage fueled by ages of humanity's abuse. As the seals were breached, the ventilation sirens blared again for the second time in the same week. The stench of rotting organic material and yeast was noticeable to anyone who was close to the landfill. The half of the crew who managed to don their hazmat suits in time were safe for now, though they remained unaware of the present danger they were encountering.

The Ulysses cleared its moorings and pulled out of the atom-shielded airlock; a pulse to the quantum repellers later, it was flying at half-light speed, or 'HLS'. The ship became a stretched beam of light at first, and then turned into a dot, shrinking in size to a pinpoint, unseen within seconds after reaching lightspeed. The illegal wake swayed the shielded Dirt

Star and all of its inhabitants, as the automatic stabilizing thrusters engaged to counteract the disdain-fueled exit of the Ulysses.

"This is gonna bite us in the ass," Captain Cudrowe mumbled to Majors Myhra and Vess, as he held onto a nearby railing while the ship stabilized. "We better find them quick and hope they're not on that ship. Let's re-sweep these docks and start moving through all decks. We're gonna need B1 security, and fire, and we might as well put facilities on this, too." Suddenly, the ventilation alarms sounded, and per protocol, all personnel dove for the hazmat lockers.

"This is not a good week," mumbled Cudrowe while donning his suit and respirator. "We've got bigger problems now, gentlemen. Change of plans! Get to the landfill, bring facilities with their welders to seal all doors. Sounds like the seals themselves have been breached. Contain this mess before anything worse happens!"

# Cafeteria Food

Two of the infected crew of the Dirt Star had taken their break in the Level G cafeteria. The table at which they sat was wiped down afterward by a very conscientious janitor who, after removing soiled clothes and boots from his last job, now busied himself there. Without knowledge and an electron microscope, he had no way of knowing that his clothing was presently covered with spores, and ironically, his labors disinfecting the cafeteria produced the opposite effect. It was fortunate for him that he remained ignorant of the actual work he was accomplishing.

"Can you pass the salt? Whoever's cookin' back there today sucks, man. Look at this! My burger's wasted, the fries are weak, man, and there's no salt on anything." Enfrick Fren's facial expression matched the whining of his galactic surfer's speech as he complained.

"Here ya go. Yeah, mine's not much better. I think the kitchen staff are infected with that white crap. I don't recognize anyone back there. Did you hear about Abe and Jenny?" Wildrew Meeks asked with concern.

"Nooo! Did they get, um, outta there or what, dude?"

"They sent the Red down, and just before they were able to get them out, they took a shuttle to the docks!"

"No way! So, are they cool now or what?"

"Nobody knows. After they landed, they lost track of them again. They're searching everywhere now, but I heard a rumor they may have hitched a ride on the Ulysses."

"How'd the—what? What'd you call it?"

"The Ulysses."

"Yeah...how'd the Ulysses...That's a cool name dude, kinda like some cool old story-like name, man...How did it get off the docks?"

"It's Ambassador Donclees' ship. They couldn't search it without his permission."

"So like, that Donclees dude like, took off like an 'F.U.' to them. Dude, that's screwed up! They could like, die, or...Man, what if they're sick too? They could, like, spread that crap everywhere, man!"

"Yeah, you're right. Didn't think about that. Man I hope they're still on board," Wildrew responded, his complexion taking on a gray hue. "En, I'm not feeling so good. I think I'm gonna go back to my room. Be safe, bud."

"K, Wil—take care, bro!" Enfrick said. "It's

probably this crap food, man! Hope ya feel better, dude!" All at once, a wave of nausea struck Enfrick after he saw his friend exit through the door. He also left for his room, where he slowly suffered through the withdrawals of his own independent thought. After the nausea diminished, his vocabulary had markedly improved. He spoke with an intelligent cadence in his voice, characterized by a genius of intellect, and resembling the other hosts now controlled by the Collective.

The Bacteria, allowing the Yeast to do the heavy lifting, moved out of the now-breached seals and crept through the ventilation system, infecting the entire ship. The Bacteria was much less motivated than the Yeasts, knowing its mere presence in the blood of its host would be enough. It reasoned it would be able to share hosts with the Yeasts and there would be plenty to share.

The Yeasts had other plans to protect its valuable hosts, however. It produced its own form of penicillin to inoculate those who would become pawns for its mission. The Bacteria was deceived by its malignant ally, and its numbers inevitably perished by the trillions, while the Collective's beloved hosts instead grew healthy and strong.

# The Antithesis

Vessel drive systems had remained the same for hundreds of years until recently, when a working theory was proven for viability at an E-Tollian research facility. Soon, the discovery had eclipsed conventional travel permanently.

The base theory wasn't new; in a nutshell, light from distant stars is delivered to the observer in packets of digital light, thereby bypassing all approximation of age. It had always been a 'sticking point' for physicists on Earth. The power brokers that controlled their grants had an agenda for the masses. The basis of the theory was that light could be received as analog waves and as digital waves, too. 'At Light Speed Drives', or ALS Drives, which were analog, would be modified with a digital receiver/encoder and propulsion unit tuned to nearby KSP's, producing the 'Digital Light Drives', or DLS drives. This new, innovative technology would usher in a speed range that had never before been imagined.

Once they'd been developed, the drives faced a new challenge, however: developing the platform on which to install it. The first three ships to test The DLS drive system tragically disintegrated immediately upon engaging the drive. As a result, a new class of ships was developed during the following five years, after a large vein of rhenium was discovered on one of E-Toll's moons. Rhenium had been the most scarce metal know in existence until then, and mining began shortly after its discovery.

The once-humble inhabitants of E-Toll suddenly became the most wealthy people in the known universe. Ten ships of various sizes and functions were constructed. The Ulysses, the final ship built, was placed in the ambassador's service as a tool of prestige and power for the planet E-Toll.

The Ulysses, now engaged in DLS, traveled en-route to the KSP connected to the Antithesis System. Nearing the KSP, Captain Marcus Filet of the planet Quandros said, "Almost home. Ambassador, thanks for letting me flip them off that way."

"I was with you in spirit, Captain!" came the ambassador's translated reply.

The Ulysses' KSP detectors honed in on the microscopic particle while slowing to a stop. The detector engaged the contact filament grounded to the ship, all on a microscopic level and guided partially by the AI system. The finer aspects of the maneuver were completed by Captain Filet, a skill no AI would have been able to perform in the amount of time it took Filet. The AI System on the Ulysses was state-of-the-art, the highest level of technology in the known universe and its quantum variants. AI systems had a tendency to move toward overpowering civilizations and all technology associated with them. As a result, a strict procedure of checks and balances was implemented to restrict all AI systems, from starships to toasters. Most long-range cruisers had an AI aboard, and used their captains as backup only. Ambassador Donclees was sentimental to the days before AI command, enjoying the novelty and speed of his Captain Filet.

The contact filament performed its function as all motion and sound stopped, the light increasing to become a blinding white. All was completed within the perceived time of approximately three seconds.

The Antithesis System, with its anti-gravity Blackstar sun and two orbiting planets, each with a small star orbiting in place of a moon, came into view through the bridge's windows. Each of these suns counteracted the anti-gravity of the Blackstar due to their contrary positions of orbit. The unique situation made each opposing planet/sun pair necessary for the other to remain within the system, similar to the way two magnets are attracted through a non-ferrous substance. Quandros' proximity to the Blackstar's anti-gravity, and its own hyper-gravity, counteracted just precisely enough to maintain a 'G' force similar to that of Earth.

The citizens of Quandros, resembling Earthlings, were able to blend in seamlessly to Earth's political power structure. They interfered with Earth using KSP trips throughout its existence, all because the Quandrosites enjoyed messing with the minds of the inferior Earthlings. They would stop en-route to Earth, for instance, to pick up beings from various planets along its path to the connected KSP. They mischievously introduced the Yeti, the Sasquatch, Michê, or to some, 'Bigfoot' on Earth.

The second planet, Morfar, had an orbit farther away which was more elliptical in shape. Its unique orbit rendered a varying gravity throughout its Blackstar solar year, giving its seasons an added change of gravity and radical sea tides, as well as temperature and weather extremes. The orbit of its sun was elliptical around Morfar as well, which amplified these extremes, yet kept Quandros' orbit in perfect peace.

The Morfarians were a very different breed from their brothers, the Quandrosites. Their very existence was a trial, giving most a powerful will and an honorable spirit. The two planets had entered into and out of conflict throughout their histories. At present, the two worlds were at peace, though a delicate one at that. The Morfarians had one advantage: skirmishes and civil wars continually arose on Quandros over the years, a testament to the prideful arrogance of its inhabitants.

"I appreciate this time off, Ambassador," Filet expressed, knowing his self-serving persuasive niceties would be further camouflaged through translation. He was grateful only to himself for the wealth and status his job provided. Being a Quandrosite, he was a naturally-talented pilot, surpassing the abilities of even the best AI systems. His race's nature and its heightened concentration within Marcus Filet gave him additional characteristics which the ambassador gainfully exploited. Filet, in his arrogance, reasoned he had outsmarted his employer.

However, the opposite of what he reasoned was actually the true reality. Ambassador Xytist Donclees was not merely sentimental about his toy, Captain Marcus Filet; he was also the one playing with it. The ambassador, while aboard the Ulysses with its gravity comparable to his home planet E-toll, was able to move freely on board the ship, and was a foot taller and narrower than in the Dirt Star's gravity. He was looking forward to returning to E-Toll after dropping off his pilot. Donclees cared for his pilot in the same manner that a racehorse owner of Earth would return his steed to the stables, to be groomed and pampered before its next race.

He was in a good mood, as he considered his newly-earned leverage against the Commonwealth, having been subjected to Captain Cudrowe's insulting treatment. It was inexcusable, whatever it was that had so obviously concerned Cudrowe, to have wasted his time in that manner. A trip to a soil producer (not exactly a glamorous task) was made even more degrading by being cast aside by its captain.

*My wasted time and resources were multiplied by Cudrowe's lack of priorities,* Donclees thought.

He responded to Filet's obvious bootlicking thanks. "Filet, we need you rested and well taken care of, if we're to have you fit for the next missions scheduled."

Outside the bridge windows, Quandros was rapidly growing in size as Filet pulled the Ulysses out of DLS, slowing to HLS. Filet's anticipation of a return to his home world after five years, and the bragging to come, swelled his petty heart. They entered the atmosphere and the planet's rotation, and began a slow descent toward its capitol city, Kjett.

Inside the freight hold, Abner was fortunate to find food and fresh water. The hold was connected to the armory by a door with a locking system with which Jenny was well acquainted. She was able to beat the system within a half hour. The seven had eaten their fill, breached the armory, and chosen their weapons within the first two-and-a-half hours of their six hour flight. Ample time remained to master their weapons' functions and break-down, and prepare for what was coming. Each felt a mixture of both excitement and fear.

The Red and Gray Battalions led the way to the landfill's unsealed doors. In transit, they encountered staggering crew members with the telling, white haze growing over their faces. Unprepared for the situation and its unknown danger, they avoided them, pressing on toward the doors after reporting to the captain. The numbers of infected crew grew as they neared the doors.

Obeying Major Vess' command, a facilities technician began setting up his welding equipment. The remainder of the techs set up scaffolding for the tech to reach all the way around the doors. After a few taps on the metal door, he'd struck his arc. Beginning a weld with the ultrasonic, thermally-attenuated system, he completed the twenty-foot-high and eighty-foot-wide doors within the time it would take to walk the scaffolding. They made their way to the other side of the landfill through the side corridors after finishing their work. Upon reaching the doors and similar victims along the way, they set up and began work again.

"Captain, we're finished. The welds look good! We can start a methane burn at your command," Major Myhra reported.

"Let's hold off on anything more with the landfill. We need to get that deck secured as a quarantine," Cudrowe responded.

# The Stanleys

It was Jennifer Stanley's seventh birthday on Tuesday, April 5th, 2044. She was excited. It was 6:00 a.m., and she knew that soon, her parents would wake her with a tickle fight, then make her favorite breakfast (peanut butter and bacon-filled waffles with scrambled eggs). Her stomach reminded her that it was empty as she snuck down the hallway to find her father in his home lab.

Stanford didn't support Professor Timothy Stanley in his theory about the Keyhole Skip Particle's existence in the known universe. Most of the fellow scientists in his work realm had predisposed ideas, all born of thought processes governed by those possessing large sums of money. New ideas needed to fit within the thinking and agenda of the money holders, who usually depended upon specific theories rather than radically different ideas. Professor Stanley wasn't a troublemaker; he only believed his fellow academics had settled for a limited set of truths, and he wanted to know what lie beyond the conventional boundaries of truth in his circle.

His father, William Stanley, the winner of the second Wisconsin State Powerball in 1999, relocated his family west after the terror attacks on September 11, 2001. He moved them to Pacifica, California, a coastal suburb of San Francisco, while his family was still young. William, wanting to keep their financial status private, took a job as a bread truck driver, and his wife Jennifer found employment as a legal secretary. They were able to live comfortably and raise their children, Timothy and Angela, in peace.

Timothy showed promise in mathematics at a young age, and could complete a Rubik's Cube blindfolded in under a minute. During his last year at Pacifica High School, he began to study Quantum Physics in his free time. He graduated a year early, and chose to attend Stanford, followed by MIT. His father considered his education an investment for his future, and one that he was happy to make. Timothy graduated from Stanford with a Phd in Experimental and Observational Astrophysics, and from MIT with a PhD in Cosmology and Experimental Particle Physics. He landed his dream job at the Stanford Linear Accelerator Center (SLAC) afterward. Professor Timothy Stanley planned to add his time spent at SLAC to his résumé, and then apply to CERN in Switzerland within five years.

The professor's theory and fascination concerning the KSP, and the ability to duplicate one within the vicinity of Earth, had cost him his credibility amongst his peers during the prior five years. To continue both pursuits, the academic and a desire for truth, he decided to conduct research from home, and convinced his old roommate, Adam, to help him. Adam became a live-in friend and partner for scientific pursuits. Adam Daxler (who was a genius in his own right) was capable of taking Professor Stanley's theories, equations, and designs into the real world. After six months of collaboration via phone and e-mail, and another five months in the professor and his wife, Kirstin's, basement, they had completed their prototype equipment.

The Machine, as they called it, was similar in function to a 3-D printer, the difference being the medium used and its scale. Building a 3-D printer capable of working on an atomic scale was a challenge for both of them. It was also a bit tricky to have 'borrowed' the equipment and key materials they needed for the Machine to be created. The professor's inheritance, finances that his father had allocated before his death, provided the remaining funds they needed. The final prototype build had begun two years prior, after they 'acquired' cobalt-57 and several forms of antimatter, including antihydrogen and 't Hooftium 5.

While finalizing his theory and completing their machine, Professor Stanley mused that Professor Gerard 't Hooft would have felt justified, as his theory had been proven. His theory posed: "A matter particle in opposite time-direction is an antiparticle, proving that antimatter falls down on earth just like other matter." Professor 't Hooft's trials of justification in front of his peers on this same subject had been fruitless, until now.

At 5:00 p.m., March 31st, 2044, the Machine came to life. They used an electron microscope positioned to view progress, without which the actions of the printer would have been imperceptible to the naked eye. Stitching together the man-made version of a KSP within the vacuum, they began to see it take shape, more beautiful than any jewel known to man, its strange properties visible after the last pass the printer had completed. Drawing in the antimatter about which Professor Gerard 't Hooft had theorized, the particle began to glow and shift before their eyes on the electron microscope's screen. The professor, at first elated and then terrified, shut off the machine. He knew that the sum of his life's work now lie in his basement, and that possibly, it was more powerful than he could've ever imagined.

The man-made KSP had been completed, and it was too late to turn back, now.

# Happy Birthday!

At 6:15 a.m. on Tuesday morning, April 5th, 2044, Jenny made her way into the lab after searching the rest of the house for her parents. She was unable to find them, having had no idea that they were on the beach below the patio, picking up shells for her birthday cake. As she clutched the acorn she had picked up the day before from their trip to El Dorado County, she snuck into her father's lab. Her curiosity piqued and her heartbeat quickened, knowing the room was off-limits. In spite of the rule, she entered the white-walled, sealed cleanroom.

Remembering her father putting on the vacuum suit he wore in the lab, she thought it would be fun to play 'scientist'. She slipped on the much-too-large suit and its helmet with rebreather, and in so doing, fell into the vacuum pump switch. The pumps began running and drawing the pressure of the room down to (10-17 Torr), as she looked at a glass canister on the desk next to the microscope.

Her father had frequently introduced her to wondrous phenomena, and she was intrigued by the glass canister. *I wonder what this could be?* she thought to herself, picking it up for a closer look, and then setting it back in its stand. "Dah used these," she murmured as she turned the electron microscope's knobs. Unable to see anything, she attempted to reposition the canister, and as she did, it fell at her feet and shattered as it hit the floor.

"Now I'm in trouble!" she cried, and observed a faint shimmer of iridescent light for a fleeting second. As she moved her head in different angles, the shimmer would return and then fade, as one would notice when looking into a tiny prism. "Aaaaaahhh," she marveled, mesmerized by the beauty and mystery of the unseen particle—and Jenny reached out, hoping to pick it up.

Abruptly, all motion ceased and all sound stretched and then muted. The cleanroom's white walls contrasted with the various colored equipment within the room, then blurred and melded into the same blinding white light within seconds. The child, Jenny, was suddenly floating in space twenty-billion light-years away from Earth, and a thousand years into its future.

At that exact same moment, the shuttle 'The Savior' simultaneously made contact with the KSP connected to her father's synthetic version. Being a manufactured copy, the time destination was different on Jenny's end. The identical experience was encountered by the children aboard The Savior, however, but with the opposite destination. They truly were 'saved'. The foundation of the house and the basement of the Stanley home (and including the next door neighbor's house) were all at once replaced by a large spacecraft with the title, 'The Savior', on its hull. The lab and its contents were destroyed completely, as were both connected KSP's.

The professor, Mrs. Stanley, and Adam Daxler heard the explosion at the top of the cliff and ran to the house, suspecting a gas explosion and fearing for Jennifer's safety. When they reached the backyard, however, they were astonished to find The Savior with its children inside, peering through the windows. Professor Stanley, still stunned and unaware of the KSP's full potential, couldn't perceive the connection between the two events. He believed his daughter had been killed, and that his life's work had been destroyed by a freak accident. It was altogether too much for him, and he sank to the ground in a paralyzing shock that gripped him for weeks.

First responders arrived at the scene after several people in town had heard the explosion. The nature of the event warranted that the NTSB be involved, and NASA, along with several other agencies associated with national security, were called in not long afterwards. Everyone was baffled. There were no signs of an explosion, no debris of a missing structure was found, and no clues existed to indicate how the ship could've stopped dead at this location. After removing the damaged homes' upper levels and the ship itself, instead of finding damaged lower levels and basements as they expected, they discovered nothing at all. Everything was missing, down to a foot below the nonexistent foundations.

The children were removed from the shuttle and questioned by the authorities, who were unable to make any sense of what they had found. They had no choice but to believe them, since the shuttle was beyond any technology they had ever seen. The children's accounts corroborated with the documentation found on the ship. Following the miraculous event, the Savior children inevitably became celebrities and were placed in foster homes.

It eventually began to make sense to the professor, what had happened to his precious daughter. His knowledge made it even more difficult to deal with his depression, as he suspected that their precious girl may have been killed anywhere, anyplace in the vastness of creation, or that she could possibly still be alive, far from him. He was crushed, knowing that he would never see her again, and would completely miss the experience of watching her grow up.

As time passed, Professor Stanley lost all joy in his life. Try as he did to regain his vitality, his spirit had been utterly crushed. He moved on, becoming a drone of a man, unable to experience anything except his great, devastating loss.

# The Transfer Student

Jennifer was unable to stand within the cleanroom due to the effects of zero gravity. She peered outside its windows, seeing three walls of the basement as she normally would have, but the daylight window's everyday view, of the crashing waves below the cliffs, had been replaced by the most beautiful display of stars she had ever seen. She floated in midair, as the sight of the black space between her and the stars overwhelmed her into a motionless, shocked terror.

Meanwhile, not far away, Captain Ramar Gleek was patrolling the boundaries of the Commonwealth's border when he came across what appeared to be a small asteroid in the distance. "I'm not sure, but it looks like another asteroid in this sector. I'm going to get a closer look, before hitting it with missiles," the captain called in to the controller.

"Keep your distance, Ramar," the controller replied. "Remember some of those things can be radioactive."

"Confirmed, Control. I have sensors up and will proceed with caution."

Ramar approached within a mile of the asteroid and switched off the safeties, thereby arming his missiles. This had always been his favorite part of patrols, as it provided him the opportunity to hone his aiming skills. Any debris or asteroids which came past the Boundary were infrequent occurrences. All at once, however, a funny feeling came over him, and curiosity drew him nearer as he disarmed his weapons.

Coming closer, he noticed what he thought to be an asteroid beginning to crumble. It appeared as if dirt were falling off of some form of square stone and wood structure, definitely man- or alien-made. As he slowly advanced within six-hundred feet, the stone and wood began to float away as well. Only a rectangular white box remained, approximately twelve feet long, twelve feet deep, and eight feet high, floating among the rest of the debris.

When he reached a one-hundred foot distance, he could see, through the windows, a small figure in an oversized suit floating about inside it. He employed the ship's claw arm when he came within proximity of the white box. Pulling it onto the service rack, he turned back slowly toward the Dirt Star. When he arrived at the docks, he manipulated the claw once more, and placed his cargo onto the dock floor. Jenny felt the gravity pull her to the ground, and with a thud, hit her head on the floor of the cleanroom.

Walking down the docks, Major Hicks met Ramar

next to his ship and its payload. "What the hell is this, Gleek?" he demanded loudly of Ramar, who was still extricating himself from his cockpit. "Seems like you do everything but your job! You don't have time to pick up trash from the Boundary all day! This better be something important, or you'll be on night-shift for the next quarter!" Major Hicks' short fuse blew as he turned on his heels and marched back to the offices.

Ramar contemplated the white box that was the cleanroom. "Some white elephant gift?" he wondered, hoping it might be worth the effort. It was unusual for him to pick up debris from the Boundary, but he just couldn't shake the odd feeling he had concerning this strange white box. Stepping off the last rung of the ladder, he approached it. It seemed to be some kind of sealed room, and inside it looked as though it were filled with scientific equipment. In the corner next to one of the plastic windows lay a white adult-sized suit with a smaller form within. Ramar was relieved; he hadn't been seeing things earlier, and his gut check was confirmed.

After making a call, the paramedics arrived with a facilities tech and they proceeded to open the 'gift'. Inside was a small child, no more than five to seven years old and unconscious. The medic first used her mediscan pen to detect any ill health or infectious diseases, and then gave her permission for the suit to be removed. Inside lie a pretty little girl in pajamas, knocked out cold, but in perfect health. They brought her to the hospital and administered tests, and concluded that the little girl was indeed a normal human child, yet wore clothing which had been made in the twenty-first century. When she regained consciousness, she couldn't remember anything except her first name, Jennifer. Clutching the acorn in her pocket, she announced her name to those present as 'Jenny Acorn'.

Jenny was given a special accommodation to avoid the droid upbringing of other Commonwealth children, and instead was adopted by a facilities technician named Foster Dex and his wife Professor Sophia Dex, a physicist. She became the only child in the Commonwealth's history that was homeschooled. Unfortunately, there wasn't a K-12 school due to the droid protocol, so Jenny was educated by her physicist mother and technician father.

Her schooling gave her the gift of the infinite, yet with the grounding of a 'nuts and bolts' practicality. She became the little sister to many aboard the Dirt Star. Her adoptive parents became a comfort to Jenny before and after the memories of her family on Earth had returned to her, and also her recollection about what had tragically occurred in the cleanroom.

Ramar became like an uncle to Jenny from the very beginning. She would go to the docks to watch him leave for his patrols and always attempted to be present when he returned. Every other month, Ramar would invite Foster Dex, Professor Sophia Dex, and Jenny to his quarters, where he would treat them to his one-and-only dinner specialty: meatloaf. Ramar had that one gear, as far as cooking was concerned, but that one gear was all that he required. His meatloaf dinners became a marked event, and the Dex family truly enjoyed his cooking and his company.

As time passed, Ramar witnessed Jenny grow from a child into an adult, and during the last quarter of his career, she watched him mature from a young man into a seasoned pilot.

# Quandros

The Ulysses made its final approach to Quandros and landed at the E-Tollian Embassy in Kjett.

The grounds were surrounded by expertly-landscaped examples of the flora from every region on E-Toll that could grow in Quondrisite soil. Ortric was a plain grain, in contrast to other more colorful and sometimes exotic flora and fauna. Nonetheless, it was the star of landscaping due to the E-Tollians' love of poontrip, the locally-sourced alcoholic beverage of choice on the planet. The landing pad sat in the middle of a field comprised of several varieties of ortric. Their slightly dissimilar colors swayed in the breeze and created a hypnotic display, not unlike the effects of its grain after brewing was completed.

The ship's landing gear touched the pavement surrounded by the breathtaking, ground level view. One could take in the ancient E-Tollian architecture of the embassy building and its grounds, the City of Kjett with its own ancient and modern buildings, theWeljt mountains trailing off to the northeast, and the Quandrosian scenery bordered by the ocean at sunset.

Ambassador Donclees boarded his hovercart, once again being a foot shorter and a foot wider at the bottom now that he rested on Quandrosian soil, and exited the Ulysses. The overnight stays in this particular residence had always been among his favorites destinations.

After the ambassador's entourage of security personnel, secretaries, and personal assistants had exited the ship, Filet assumed he was by himself as he finished shutting down all the systems, and made his way to the freight hold for his bags. As he opened the door, he was suddenly met by a freakishly strong meatloaf individual, and the savory smell of its powerful hand covering his mouth was equal parts mouthwatering and confusing.

"We're taking this ship — you're coming with us!" Abner announced, and spurred on by Loaf's power, added, "This part of a well balanced meal insists! Tie him up!"

The donuts found restraints in the armory, and bound Captain Marcus Filet of the ambassador class ship, the Ulysses. This would not have been an account to add to his normal repertoire of nightly bragging. If only he had had a cup of coffee, he might've enjoyed the donuts more. It was probably the first time in history that a donut had impersonated an officer of the law. Once they had secured him, Filet was put in a corner of the hold to process his bewilderment, as the new crew trekked to the bridge.

The crew powered up the ship as Loaf licked his fingers and then smiled; after all, he was a well-seasoned pilot. He grabbed the helm and pulsed the quantum repellers. The Ulysses shot away from the landing pad through the atmosphere with a sonic boom that blew the front facade off the E-Tollian Embassy, including all its windows. The echo was heard throughout the city, all the way to the canyons of the Weljt mountains, and beyond for hundreds of miles.

A squadron of fighters was sent up as quickly as possible from Quandros Sword Base on the outskirts of Kjett. Fifteen of their fastest fighters added their own echoes in response as they rose above the atmosphere. A small pinpoint of light from the Ulysses was all that was visible, however, as the first pilot lost sight of it. The tracking sensors at the base began to fail as the Ulysses entered DLS.

Just before the fighters returned to the base, the emergency personnel arrived at the embassy. Ambassador Donclees and his staff were transported to the hospital and found to have superficial injuries only, though the ambassador was kept overnight for observation and released the following day.

Ambassador Xytist Donclees' pride had received more injury than any other malady he'dexperienced. This had been a bad day for the E-Tollian, so bad that those nearest him stealthily disabled their translators and made themselves scarce. Their only irritation came in the form of his loud grunts, clicks, shrieks, and sighs as the day drew to an end.

After his short recovery, Ambassador Donclees suspected his captain had made the worst mistake possible of his now short-lived career. Quandros was now in his vengeful sights as well; Filet was, after all, a native.

Captain Marcus Filet of Quandros was now the prime suspect for: 1.) Causing injury to a foreign ambassador and his staff; 2.) Damaging a foreign embassy; and 3.) Grand Theft of one of the fastest and most luxurious ships ever built, worth more than a quarter of the value of the City of Kjett itself.

If convicted, Marcus Filet would be stripped of his title and serve a life sentence for each of his crimes. He was now a wanted man, on both E-Toll and his home world of Quandros.

Taken captive and restrained by what he considered a nightmare, and far away from the destructive drama played on Quandros, Filet remained oblivious of these charges and their consequences.

# The Others

Weeks of toil passed aboard the Dirt Star as Captain Cudrowe and his crew cared for those who had been infected by the Yeasts and Bacterias. They had hoped for the best, but all seemed lost as the victims in quarantine succumbed and became completely taken over by the insidious invaders. Those who were beyond help were placed in another quarantine quadrant in suspended animation, with the hope that a future cure would be found.

On another front within the ship, others aboard the Dirt Star had been under attack from those still under the control of the Yeasts. These new individuals silently 'cured' in their personal quarters until the Collective deemed them feasible tools for its usage. The crew was in a constant state of terror as the newly-converted appeared, intent on spreading themselves to 'cure' their fellow crew members. Captain Cudrowe, unable to keep the information away from the admiral, reported the disaster after two days of failure to control and defuse the situation. The admiral, prime minister, and parliament agreed to contain the problem on the Dirt Star, and provided support in the form of funds, supplies and personnel. The added help made no difference, however; the battle was destined to become a quagmire, a complex fight for which they couldn't develop an effective, successful strategy.

Inside the landfill, a group of eight more uninfected beings traveled to one of the other service rooms and managed to open the seal doors. The new group of beings aboard the Dirt Star were comprised of some the best of the crew's DNA.

Four of the eight beings had come from the second discarded donut box originating from the conference room. Confused by everything that had happened after the first ventilation alarm sounded, they had also absorbed the stench from the ventilation failure's fumes. Each had then been picked up from plates, only to be returned to the second box. Louie, Bob and Rob were unaware of their fates, having been placed in the first box. The second box, too, had been sent from the opposite side of the meeting room which led to the other end of the landfill. This second group of bakery delights then transformed like the first had, and appeared more human than their previous selves.

Three of the four from this group came from the droid parenting dormitory. The three were comprised of a lasagna 'thing' and two mice-people. The fourth was a rat that had been chewing on a hairbrush in his free time; the delicious hairbrush had originated from one of the hair salons on Level 2. He had been munching happily, when the treatments were mistakenly applied.

One of the four, a lasagna, had been served to a child still being parented by the protocol droids. It had been the child's eleventh birthday, but unfortunately, the boy had a tantrum (as many of the children did in isolation), and had thrown his lasagna across the room. The lasagna had subsequently been scraped off the wall, put in a paper bag, and then thrown down the chute.

The mice had been enjoying a discarded, half-eaten peanut butter and jelly sandwich from a child in the next room, the same room from which the tantrum-tossed lasagna had originated. The ten-year-old girl, ten years before, had managed to cut a small hole in the wall between their bedrooms. The boy and girl had become the closest of friends, to the extent that all modifications of personality given to their droids hadn't effectively bonded them to their machines. The children were aware that they were imprisoned, and both had been prone to tantrums. The girl had tantrum-thrown her sandwich, too, and the droids had thrown it down the chute, as well. The peanut butter and jelly sandwich thing that birthed from the ensuing landfill disaster never made it out of the landfill, though the mice that had been snacking on it beforehand (when it was merely a sandwich) did.

The first four beings (of this new group of eight) had interesting backstories, too. Basir, the Persian cinnamon donut, had been handled by Enfrick Fren of Security, who rarely washed his hands. Fren had just licked glaze left over from his last donut from his fingers, and then returned Basir to the plate, where the disgusting stench reached him. Angie and Maude, the twin twists still as beautiful as ever, had been sneezed upon by Dr. Margaret Frost during the meeting, and had been placed in the box before the rest. Claus the Bavarian, lastly, had been bitten by the retired Admiral Torquil Myhra, father of Major Lars Myhra. While on his daily walk, he'd wandered into the conference room after the meeting. The lonely plate of donuts staring him down had been irresistible to the retired Admiral. Claus, rejected and confused, had also been returned to the plate for the janitor to remove.

All eight had accumulated on the same mound below the landfill's starboard exit chute. It didn't take them long to bond together, for safety's sake. Claus took lead of the group as he formulated a plan of escape, utilizing the starboard service bay ahead of them. The eight newborns ran down the mound, avoiding the most aggressive beings as they descended. Memories from unknown origins filled Claus's mind as he entered the code into the door's lock.

Safely inside the service room, they managed to

board a shuttle. Before exiting, they loaded the shuttle with as much food and supplies as they were able, which left little room for themselves. Claus, with his uncanny, newfound knowledge of spaceflight, strapped himself in after he'd secured the rest, powered up the shuttle, and pulled away from the service bay. He drifted away from The Dirt Star without notifying control, as the Dirt Star's entire crew was focused on the newfound Civil War.

They directed their course toward the nearest known KSP, hoping that they might find refuge en route. They would have the best chance of coming in contact with another ship along the way, a journey which would last weeks at their limitedly available speed.

# Leverage

The Ulysses cruised at DLS on a course set to a KSP connected with the Wuxia System. The crew hoped some of its residents would sympathize with their plight, since its inhabitants, though a fierce breed, were also known to be honorable and just.

"We should be in range of the the Wuxia's KSP within a day or so, according to these charts," said Rob, expressing a new-found love for navigation and all things 'mappy'. "We're gonna have to bring him up here to use the KSP controls as soon as we get closer."

"Might be a better idea not to wait—he's gonna be a problem. I can smell it," replied Loaf.

"You have an excellent nose, Loaf! I've dealt with him before...he's a real ass." Abner added with a smile, "Don't breath in too deep!" The three in the bridge chuckled as they contemplated dealing with Filet.

Jenny walked in after having loitered in the hallway, absorbing the complexities of thought and emotion from within the room.

"Want me to spend some time in the hold with him? He's probably hungry. We might get some insight into how he ticks before bringing him up here."

"Might not be a bad idea, but I'd feel better if you took someone with you," answered Abner.

"Flip is a little more intimidating than the donuts," she replied. "You guys should stay here. I'll be back if I get any insight." She walked toward the back of the ship, meeting Flip along the way. "Flip, care to be my bodyguard? I'm gonna bring some food to our prisoner."

"Sure, I can be a fighter. I once broke free from a line after a half hour fight in the river. Back then, I had no idea what was happening. That's where I got this," he said, pointing at the scar on his mouth, which was still present after his transformation.

"Flip, I like you more every day!" said Jenny, after sensing the powerful emotions he felt for his freedom which words couldn't express. They walked back to the kitchen, gathered some food, then headed to the hold. "Just wait in the doorway, Flip. I don't want him to feel like we're trying to intimidate him." Jenny walked in, calling, "Captain Filet, here's some food for you," while handing him a plate. "Are you hungry?"

Filet grabbed the plate from her hands and inhaled the food, as Quandrosites process their food in the lower part of their lungs.

"It's about time! What are you people doing? Do you know stealing this ship is gonna cause a major incident with the Galactic Congress?! This thing's worth over 4000 Furn!" As Filet viciously spat his words, Jenny absorbed more information from him without his knowledge.

She could sense his real concern: his fear that he, personally, was the one they were after. She picked up on a life of past deeds for which Filet had absolutely no remorse. His paramount concern had always been himself, and his energies all concentrated on his ability to manipulate all but the most discerning. This particular tactic was the primary tool he used for acquiring wealth and gaining power over others. The list of lies that he had somehow been able to justify to himself, and to others, was enormously long. Jenny knew that if she lingered, whatever words came from his mouth would be worthless, except to back up her assessments.

Taking the plate, she left the hold, thanking Flip as she walked back to the bridge. Once there, she reported to the rest.

"He's afraid of being blamed for stealing the Ulysses. Says it's worth over 4000 furn."

"Well, we could threaten to send out a distress call backing that up, if he doesn't cooperate," proposed Louie, walking in.

"I feel bad for the guy," said Jenny. "He's a mess! I would hate to be in his world-he's the only one there." Even though Filet was one of the biggest asses she'd ever met, her intuitive understanding about him made her heart break.

# Others Coalesce

The service shuttle was in the shipping lane between the Dirt Star and its nearest KSP, and to keep themselves safe, they remained just inside the boundary set by the Commonwealth.

"Tere's supermax freighter tat haas yust come up on sensorrs affter passeng trough KSP tranzference" stated Basir, "Vee may bee abil to hail dem."

"This isn't going to work, Basir. Those freighters are going to the Commonwealth." Thinking out loud, Claus added, "If we have any chance to get away from the Dirt Star, we'll need to pass the boundary point to be able to hail the ships headed in the opposite direction, or on their way to another KSP. I suspect the Dirt Star won't be shipping or receiving either, after everything that's happening there. A lot of these freighters may be moored within the boundary awaiting berths for weeks or more!" Claus shook his head. "We won't be able to go anywhere, plus we don't know if we're wanted for fleeing the scene, or for taking the shuttle from the Commonwealth. Our faces could've been picked up by CCTV. There could be 'wanted' postings on every monitor that enters the boundaries of the Commonwealth." Drawing on his inner-admiral DNA, Claus's points fell hard on all within earshot.

"I ahgree, tsst...How cood vee bee so stoopeed?" cried Basir, ignoring the fact that only recently, he had merely been a cinnamon donut. "Veel yust haaft to taak oorr chanzes." It was interesting. Nobody knew why Basir spoke with such a strong accent, nor did they even contemplate why he did.

They missed the chance to hail the freighter and decided to use its trajectory instead, changing course to its starboard for two miles, then switching to its aft direction in hopes of passing the boundary. They had no guarantee that there wasn't another KSP in the area. KSP's were unable to be charted, as they could wander from place to place, making it imperative for travelers to have detection sensors if planning to enter deep space.

"My calculations confirm—if we keep our bearing, we should pass the boundary within six hours. You should be able to switch to AI drive. If we hit a KSP, it won't matter if you're at the helm or not," said the unnamed rat.

"Good plan. I'm starving!" exclaimed Claus. "We should all eat."

They all met in the back of the shuttle, and much like their counterparts had done in the appliance box, they introduced themselves (or were given a name) during their second meal together. The fact that the donuts already had names made things easier.

"You were a lasagna, right?" inquired Angie.

"Yep, a rejected one, that is."

"I think you should be called Layerie. You're deep," said Maude.

It was hard to tell because of his ruddy complexion, but he blushed as he replied, "Aw, thanks. I like that."

"And you should be called Maurice," stated Angie decidedly to the rat.

"Why 'Maurice'?"

"It's a suave name. It fits you."

"If you insist," Maurice complied, not concerned in the least about his title. Both he and Basir, bored with the conversation, continued in their prior discussion concerning trajectories and avoiding belligerent starship operators.

"You two seem to be twins, am I right?" asked Angie, knowing the joys and burdens of being a twin.

"Yep! We grew up together before we changed. In fact, we were eating the same sandwich when it happened. I dunno...I feel even closer to you now," the female mouse-person said to her male twin. "Do you know what I mean?"

"I wasn't sure if you were having the same thoughts, but yeah, I do."

"What kind of sandwich were you eating?" asked Angie.

"A peanut butter and jelly," replied the male mouse-person.

"Well, you could be Jelly," said Maude to the female mouse-person.

"And you should be Peanut!" said Angie to the male mouse-person.

"Perfect!" they shouted in unison, realizing that the sandwich had made a huge impact on their lives.

Layerie, Maurice, Peanut, Jelly, Claus, Basir, Angie, and Maude settled in to rest, taking turns monitoring the sensors at the bridge. Being more exhausted than they realized, ten hours elapsed, much longer than they intended.

Maurice awakened Claus. "We're two hours past the boundary. We should be able to course-correct back toward the shipping lane, and if we're lucky, be able to hail a freighter."

"Okay, let's do this!" agreed Claus, eager to find a way toward anywhere, really. "Let's hope this works!" As the shuttle's direction returned once more to the shipping lanes, they set their sights on finding a way out of isolation.

# Disclosure

Aboard the Ulysses, Jenny had an idea.

"Abe, we won't need Filet for long. I can read him...I should be able to sense how to use the KSP tech. I think we'll have to bring him up here so he's focused on it, though."

"Man, that's gotta be a trip to be able to do that," Abner replied. "I don't think I'd want to be in someone like *that's* head. I gotta admit, though—it's saved us more than once, so far."

"Yeah, I'm still not sure what to think about it. There's been so much happening, but this should work, Abe." She spoke with a conviction that added weight to the room.

"Well, we should be within range by tomorrow morning. We can try then. Do you know what this means, Jenny? You'd be the first human to use this technology. It could be a way for us to negotiate with the Commonwealth, a way to go back!"

"The Commonwealth, Abe? Do you really want to be limited to the Commonwealth? They were going to kill us—well, most of us! I'm not sure if I want to go back there. They created the mess we're in, and I don't think we should have to fight to get back into their good graces."

"Yeah, I see your point. I guess I just want to go home."

Jenny, plumbing the depths of his loss, confusion, and longing to be connected with the only place he knew of as home, grew silent. She was taken back in her own memory, first to her adoptive parents, both of whom had taken ill five years prior and passed away. She thought of her Uncle Gleek, knowing it was possible that she might never see him again. There were many people that she loved and would miss from the Dirt Star, but her difficulty was that she knew there was so much more to life than they'd realized, or (unlike her!) even wanted to explore. There was so much more 'out there'. Then again, she considered the Commonwealth's off-boundary law, and once more, her firm desire to leave was renewed. Her thoughts trailed to her family on Earth again, and she felt anew the same pull, loss, and longing for her real home. Abner broke the silence.

"You know what I mean. I can feel you do!"

"I do, Abe, even more now, knowing what you're going through. But there's something I haven't told you about, things about growing up."

"Man, who wouldn't want to forget that? I have a hard time looking at any droid. Even with all the VR sessions we had, I still have nightmares of growing up."

"Abe, I wasn't raised by droids."

"What! How is that possible?" Abner asked, feeling even more isolated than before.

"Abe...I'm from Earth," she responded cautiously.

"You're *what*?!" Abner stood, stunned and blank-eyed, until the truth had registered within him. "With everything that's happened in the last few days, I think this may be the biggest mind-blow of all. Jenny, are you screwing with me, or what?!"

"No, Abe, we haven't been together long and I wanted to tell you, eventually. I was waiting for the right time. Obviously, this wasn't it, but you need to know the truth. I don't want to keep anything from you. I can't imagine being anywhere without you."

"I'm sorry, Jenny...I'm an idiot. Tell me! You're right. I need to know."

Jenny proceeded to recount all the memories she had of her childhood on Earth, including her family there and the accident in her father's lab. She told him how her adoptive parents had explained that she was found near the Boundary by Captain Ramar Gleek, and then brought to the Dirt Star. She added, too, that she could sense Loaf was connected by DNA to Captain Gleek, which was why she was so confident in Loaf's abilities.

"You're amazing! I feel like we're characters in a novel."

"Sounds crazy, I know, but think of it, Abe! We

should be able to go anywhere if this works. I'm done with the Commonwealth. That was existence, not life. I want to see all the places that you've told me about, explore stories you were told at the docks. I want to go to Jook-Sing in the Wuxia, E-toll in the Gomane, even meet the Morfarians in the Antithesis. I can't go back to the Commonwealth, now! Can you?" Abner, with wheels turning in his head, stood still as Jenny sensed everything, and then answered her.

"This is a lot to take in, but now that I think of it...yeah, the Commonwealth is like you said. It's just that thing you grow used to, and when it's gone you want it back, even though you know it wasn't good for you. I dunno. I need to think about all of this. I know it's a fake existence there, but it's all I know. Jenny, you've known that there's more out there your whole life. In the Commonwealth, we were taught to accept the isolation of space and the confines of the boundaries to the Fleet. It was drilled into all of us. We were expected to comply."

"I know. I was told to keep what I knew to myself for the benefit of others. I didn't understand, until I got a little older, how the idea of freedom for some, can be the spark of destruction for others, if they have no way to experience it. The difference now, Abe, is you *are* free. You don't have to go back! Those places you heard about are real, with real people, plants, animals, oceans. Abe! I remember the Pacific Ocean.

It's something you can't describe! You have to see it for yourself."

"As much as I hated the way I grew up, it's all I know," Abner responded. "I guess I'm brainwashed. The door to the prison cell's open, but the cell is still all that I know. Just don't give up on me, okay?"

"Never, Abe! I won't push you, but you have to admit—you've already left the cell, like it or not."

# Supermax!

Two freighters passed, ignoring the shuttle's distress calls. Once a third hour had passed, a Supermax-class freighter with the identifier 'The Ox' became visible on sensors after appearing at the KSP point. This time, their shuttle was given permission to dock. Supermax-class ships were freighters which moved slowly, and were usually three times larger than the average-sized trading vessel. The Ox was a trading vessel from Jook-sing Xíngxīng, (a planet commonly referred to as Jook-sing) which belonged to the Wuxia System. The freighter had picked up its cargo and had been returning to its homeport, when it came upon the shuttle in distress.

To their relief, the group of fresh humanoids found the captain and crew to be very amiable, and spoke English fluently. Over the course of the journey together aboard the Supermax, their hosts explained their custom of always responding to any distress calls in their path.

The captain recounted how their ancestors, the

Mǎ luó, were originally from Earth on China's mainland, but had then immigrated to the western United States of America. They had been drawn there with the promise of a new life, and the opportunity to build railroads and mine gold in California, Oregon, and Washington State during the 19th century. Having been badly treated by their employers and bitter conspirators from China, most had grown to become a people of strong character. Perseverance permeated the culture of those Jook-sing living in the United States. Throughout the 19th to the late 23rd centuries, they had carved out a strong presence in the western United States, as numerous others immigrated from China to join them in the West. Since many were naturally-gifted entrepreneurs, scientists, and engineers, they rose to become pioneers on the forefront of private space exploration.

In the late 23rd century, a large group of ancestors aboard a long-range exploratory starship came into contact with a Supermax trading vessel from the planet Měilì. Their starship was on fire, but at the time, the Jook-sing (which means 'Chinese living abroad') were in suspended animation and had no idea that their ship was ablaze. Similar to the fate of the originators of the Commonwealth, these explorers from Earth had unknowingly contacted a KSP. The source of the fire was never explained, but those on the ancient trading vessel pulled the burning ship into their docks, extinguished the fire, and woke the Jook-sing from stasis. Since their starship was disabled, they joined the traders of the Supermax, and were eventually brought to the planet Měilì.

Over the decades on Měilì, the offspring of the Jook-sing grew in number, and eventually, their culture resumed its love for space exploration. Remaining in the same star system, they found a suitable planet inhabited only by animals, which they named 'Jook-sing Xíngxīng'. In the hundreds of years that followed, the Jook-sing had great influence in their system. They lived on many of the other planets there as well, and even earned the honor of naming the system, the 'Wuxia System'.

Claus and his group listened to the captain. The hearty, middle-aged man of Jook-sing told how he had seen people from many other systems, but never before had he seen anything like those from the shuttle. Luckily, rats and mice were honorable animals in Chinese culture. On the other hand, he and his crew were slightly confused by the donuts and the lasagna-thing. They resembled humans more than the latter, fortunately, and were also welcomed by the Jook-sing traders.

The freighter passed the connecting KSPs, and through the windows, the Wuxia System came into view. They were drawn to the nearby Xióngwěi Supernova.  Its majestically-blended, oblong swaths of gold, purple, orange, and green concentric light presented a hypnotically beautiful backdrop. The captain pointed to the planet Jook-sing as their destination, and as it was still a week's travel away, the captain allowed the newly-welcomed creatures to settle in as temporary crew members.

# Osmosis Sis

Captain Marcus Filet was awoken at 4:00 a.m., Earth Pacific Standard Time, a.k.a. Commonwealth Fleet Standard Time. Abner and Loaf, glad that they must rouse the obnoxious Filet at such an unpleasant hour, brought him to the bridge. Loaf purposefully assumed the captain's chair in the sour captain's presence, and Filet's countenance drooped.

"You will operate the KSP controls to make the jump to the Wuxia," commanded Abner.

"Why would I do such a foolish thing? Quandros is a sworn enemy of the Wuxia. I'd be committing treason against my people."

"You will cooperate or there will be a distress call sent to E-Toll, giving them your exact location," countered Abner.

"The Wuxians are good people. You would be welcome there," Jenny added.

Filet's thoughts raced as Jenny absorbed his entire inner debate. *I would never be able to return to Quandros. How could I live with myself in Wuxia? These idiots have me trapped! This is humiliating. If anyone found out about*

*this, my reputation would be ruined! Well, I guess it's
already ruined. They're right, since nobody would believe
any of these yahoos could pilot this ship. I'm the only one
who would be capable. By the outfits they're wearing,
they've gotta be from the Dirt Star. Still, nobody would
believe it. I'm gonna have to do what they want. I hope
she's right about Wuxia...All I know about them is what
I've been raised to think of them.*

"Okay, you've got me," Filet conceded aloud.
"What are you going to do with me once we land?"

"One step at a time, Captain. If you do this, then
we'll talk," replied Abner.

Jenny observed Filet intently, sensing all he did
and thought. She was fascinated with his
multitasking. He was able to position the ship at the
perfect coordinates within inches of the KSP, then
factor the asymmetrical algorithms corresponding to
it, enter the information and all the projected
eventualities into the AI system, and finally, prepare
the ship's systems for transfer. Jenny realized that the
skills necessary for accomplishing the calculations,
and manipulating the associated controls for the
captain's purpose, contained the intensity of a
focused ballet; no human would be capable of
performing it, except Jenny herself.

When Filet had finished, the AI took control and
the microscopic filament touched the KSP. In a flash,
the Ulysses and its passengers were transferred to the
outskirts of the Wuxia System. All the stories and

documentaries the crew had heard or seen their entire lives, could never have prepared them for the beauty they presently beheld.

Jenny glanced at Abner, and each glowed, connected to each other through the same experience. Abner had imagined this place, as he'd heard tales told to him from the docks. He had shared them with Jenny, and they had long desired to learn their truths for themselves. The sight did not disappoint. The depth of color was magnetic; the system's planets and moons, with their diversity of colors and rings, were spectacularly beautiful. The backdrop of the Xióngwěi Supernova, though, spoke undeniably of the Artisan. Here, indeed, was a place where few could deny its Designer without being considered an utter fool.

"There's Jook-sing Xíngxīng, fourth from the sun!" announced Loaf as he engaged the DLS drive. "We should be there in about seven hours."

"Thank you, Captain." Abner led Filet back to the hold. "We appreciate your cooperation. Louie and Bob are cooking now. As soon as they're done, I'll bring you breakfast."

"One question," interjected Filet.

"Shoot."

"How does a meatloaf fly this ship?"

"Beats me. Must be pretty easy to fly it, I guess," replied Abner, knowing the searing effect his answer would have upon the arrogant captain. Filet returned to the hold, his pride broken, and he slumped down in a corner, hoping to escape into sleep.

Abner comforted himself with thinking there might be hope for Filet, yet. As he remembered Jenny's warnings, however, he decided to keep his hopes to himself, just in case. Captain Marcus Filet was a first rate, master pilot, Abner realized. He hoped Filet's character would change, but he wasn't so foolish as to assume it would.

He spoke with Jenny in the dining room. "Well, how did your KSP class go?"

"Amazing, Abe. What both of us saw was one thing...add to that, what was going on inside his head at the same time? I'm unable to describe it. And, Abe...I can do it now! To think of all the years of struggling to understand certain concepts. All the time spent studying and memorizing—I feel like I'm cheating now, but it's so fun. I'm looking forward to meeting more people, and learning more and more!"

Abner's admiration for Jenny was growing, and as his feelings for her became obviously transparent to the remarkably intuitive Jenny, she blushed.

"Abner!" she cried, and they laughed.

"You know I can't control it."

# Failures and Victories

"We need some answers. We're losing this," Captain Cudrowe mumbled aloud. "More than a quarter of the crew is infected." Their failed attempts to combat the situation had exhausted and discouraged Cudrowe.

"If this keeps up, we're gonna have to look at scuttling," responded Major Myhra. "The ship's contaminated throughout, much of the contents broken down, Captain. I don't see how we can win this."

"I know. It's only been a few weeks and it's just getting worse. I'm glad most of the crew has been pulled out of here in time. After losing so many good people...friends, kids." Cudrowe stopped and stared out the porthole in thought. "Myhra, we need to scuttle, right now! This damn ship's not worth another life. I'm calling the Admiral."

The Yeasts knew its progress would attain its desired result in time, but it had no idea that success would be accomplished so soon. As of now, the Collective had gained knowledge of most of the systems on board. The remaining expertise it needed concerned defense shields and weaponry. The Collective was fortunate enough to have absorbed the DNA of E-Tollians and Wuxians, and could now fully understand KSP tech. The Yeasts chuckled to itself, grasping not only KSP technology, but its theory and engineering as well. The fools would scuttle this ship right into their hands, it reasoned, hands that had previously belonged to them. This would be the final battle; it would need to keep the hands they had taken. Infection had been its conquering tactic up until now. Passivity had sufficed. There would be no mercy exhibited, going forward, and every host was needed. The humans had been wrestling with a difficult cleanup, but the necessary violence for domination would now begin.

The following day arrived, and the captain and his majors met once more. During the twelve hours they had been apart while battling the enemy, the ship's condition had visibly deteriorated, and the number of infected crewman had increased. Majors Myhra and Vess made their way to the conference room to discuss the agenda, exhausted from leading their men at the front throughout the night. Lack of sleep, and the physical wear which ravaged him from leading his own men, rendered Captain Cudrowe gray of complexion.

"We've been cleared with the admiral to scuttle," Cudrowe addressed Majors Myhra and Vess. "This hurts, gentlemen. After all, we've been forced into this fruitless operation. We grew up here, our parents, grandparents. In our race to make things better, we destroyed it all. Couldn't just leave it alone...Progress! Damned idiots, all of us! Seems like technology has corrupted us, more than helped us. What I wouldn't give, to have lived on Earth in the days before Alexander Graham Bell and his cronies. Give me a farm, a wife, a big family, and some friggin' candles over this any day!" Cudrowe shook his head in disappointed frustration, then resignedly commanded his leaders. "Well, let's get all personnel off ship. I want the wounded and cryo-patients off first. We'll need to disable all systems and have a nuke-team pull power supplies. Anything and anyone leaving this ship will need to be decontaminated before setting foot on any pod. Enforcement on this last point is paramount, gentlemen! Use lethal force if necessary." Cudrowe drove home the seriousness of his plan, punching one hand into the flat of the other. "Lethal force! After clean-out, we need tugs at the ready to pull off boundary. The Admiral will decide at that point whether we'll do a methane burn or nuke the whole damn thing."

The removal of personnel began slowly, as pods required decontamination first. Long lines of the remaining crew from every level formed to the escape pods, though most personnel had already been evacuated. The evacuees stood waiting for the decontamination of the pods to be completed, and before they would be allowed on board, they themselves would also need to be decontaminated. Many went back to their rooms, unaware of the necessary immediacy.

The Yeasts struck with lightning speed as its enemy was distracted. The Collective was unable to part with its hosts or any part of the ship. Weapons had been left unguarded, since thus far, the military hadn't considered their enemy anything other than a biological threat. Under direction of The Collective, conventional assault rifles and newer sonic displacement weapons ('SD weapons') were taken without notice.

Hosts began, with the knowledge of highly trained Special Ops warriors, to quietly kill those who were isolated with great speed. It was a highly detailed operation performed without hesitation, as hesitation was a trait exhibited by those with a conscience. The Collective had eliminated any trace of that human tendency, making for a callous and abrupt execution of its objectives. Its mental tools were precisely tuned, no longer hampered by any possible mental inadequacy's lack of drive. Laziness, depression, insecurity, and daydreaming, to name a few flaws, wouldn't register with the Collective. Its inhuman perfection allowed a pure focus of its will.

# Lime Green

One host, whose mind had previously belonged to a manager from the shipping, receiving, and customs department at the docks, stood out from the rest, with his lime green shirt and plaid tie. When in his right mind, he had been an older and lazy man who was eager to retire. He had been born on the Dirt Star, having lived and worked there his entire life. Arush Turgeen had spent most of his vacations aboard the ship, having considered several greenhouse vessel visits to be 'vacations', and having been sent on tours of them to ensure that shipments were accurate.

His benevolent manager, Gerwald Bonageres, who was genuinely concerned for Arush's well being, had mercifully given him the tour assignments. Gerwald had noticed that his supervisor had been becoming lifeless a few years after a brutal divorce from a wife, whom he had idolized. Arush had discovered that his wife, Francis, had been having an affair and confronted her. She admitted to it wholeheartedly, then had subsequently taken everything in the divorce, and most notably, his self-worth. Out of kindness and concern, Gerwald would always send

Arush on any tasks he could find off-ship, hoping
even such small adventures would snap him out of
his blues.

The Yeast's host, Arush Turgeen, was not a lazy
being, however. He was a part of the Collective,
having a hive mind and a powerful will of hate and
revenge. When the time came, Arush, an appendage
of the Yeasts, went to the Armory and outfitted
himself, as a long line of hosts before and after him
did. Arush was one with the Collective—a host
cooperatively sharing the mind of a Special Ops killer,
as well as the mind of a scientist with unknown
numbers of Phds, also the mind of an expert pilot,
and the mind of a doctor who knew how life could be
saved or lost quickly. His past Arush Turgeen
understanding of janitorial, maintenance, and
culinary skills wouldn't be needed, today.

The sonic displacement assault rifle felt good in his
hands.He placed the evil of the Collective into them,
along with the weapon, as he moved down the
hallway. His pale complexion matched his vacant
eyes as the Collective directed his aim toward the
unsuspecting crew members within sight. He
ventured into rooms, quickly killing all men and
women. Fortunately for them, the children had been
sent off-ship a week beforehand, and Arush's victims

were spared the tribulation of enduring their children's murders.

The SD assault rifle he used directed sound waves accelerated by a nuclear power supply. The advantages of the rifles included the lack of need for ammunition, and the ability to direct its charge either into a wide beam or to concentrate it to a pinpoint. Host Arush had chosen a wide pattern diameter, and its blast would spread out from a foot wide to about ten feet away; it could remove a victim's torso or any obstruction which he targeted. It wasn't pretty.

Arush and the other efficient Yeast-hosts assassinated all unsuspecting crew members within a span of five minutes, as they were armed and present on all decks before the attack even began. As the hive mind became satisfied with the stealth of its first moves, the hosts gathered quickly to complete their mission in a combined assault. Side by side, Arush and ex-wife Francis were ironically together again within the Collective, joining an overwhelming number of hosts as they massacred the remaining crew. The poor crew hadn't suspected a thing, having been entirely unprotected, with the exception of the Red and Gray members who only wore the minimally-required sidearm.

Cudrowe and the two majors were completely unprepared for these offensives. The only mercy exhibited toward the victims lie in the speed of their deaths. Communications had been cut just before the attack using a jamming frequency which emitted a false radio silence. The Yeasts, filled with hate and now overflowing with pride, felt every sensation together as one, as it annihilated the helpless crew of the Dirt Star.

"Everyone, fall back! Fall back to the pods *now*! Forget the decontamination protocols—to the pods *now*!" yelled Cudrowe through his useless communicator. Word spread nonetheless, and a remnant arrived at the pod docks to join those already waiting. The survivors boarded in a panic, then Majors Myhra and Vess, followed by Captain Cudrowe. Captain Cletus Cudrowe of the Commonwealth ship, the Dirt Star, gave the command to abandon ship.

His heart sank as he surrendered the home he loved, crushed that their hasty goodbye was so very violent. The pods pulled away from their moorings as bloodthirsty hosts gathered en masse, attempting to block their departure and cutting down all who missed the pods, their faces contorted with Collective brutality. The Dirt Star crew, tragically and heartbreakingly, viewed their loved ones, friends, and comrades for the last time. Gerwald Bonageres looked out the pod window to see his friend and employee Arush Turgeen, with his ex-wife Francis beside him, covered in the characteristic white haze and blood. Gerwald realized that his rehabilitation efforts for Arush had ultimately come to naught, and that he was disturbingly, absurdly united once again with his true love.

The Collective directed its hosts back to the interior of the ship to continue its work of searching for the enemy. Further violence was unnecessary; the survivors would be free to be cleansed by the Yeasts. It was pleased, knowing its intake of necessary knowledge, and the accumulation of host bodies to control the ship in every way, were complete. Its next step would be to give the humans another surprise. However, the Yeasts drastically underestimated the remaining crew's will to survive. The Collective couldn't foresee the persevering crew's fighting determination to outlast and defeat them.

The pods encountered one of the hospital ships that had been prepped for decontamination. They were safe for now physically, though all experienced shock, including Captain Cudrowe and his majors. Processing the nightmare they had undergone and miraculously survived would take time.

# New Seattle

The Ulysses landed at the space port in New Seattle on Jook-sing. Abner and Jenny had chosen the Wuxia System for more than its beauty, for they counted on the inhabitants' inherent hospitality and empathy. Wuxians were known for their appreciation of honor and their lack of concern for outside systems. They earnestly hoped that the Wuxians would be more interested in the crew of the Ulysses than in the ship itself, and they were gambling their odds against complete failure, on both accounts.

The New Seattle space port was not a place where the Ulysses stood out for its grandeur. Though it was one of the most valuable ships in existence, exotic ships of all makes and models filled the port. Exiting the ship, the crew left Filet in the hold as they made their way from the landing pads and toward the city center.

The city itself was a combination of the nostalgia of its namesake, a heavy flavor of ancient Chinese architecture, and many modern buildings that had been perfectly planned into the cityscape. It was built on an inland sea similar to Seattle's Puget Sound. In comparison, though, New Seattle and its surroundings made the original Seattle look like an unpolished version of an eventual master, a prototype. Even the New Space Needle was a tourist destination as the original had been, but the present Needle's top spaceship-shaped structure was actually a true, genuine ship. It would lift from its tripod three times per day, and showcase the best views of the city and the surrounding area for tourist passengers. The nearby islands, half an hour away by ferry, were a remembrance of Puget Sound's San Juan Islands.

Every crew member felt the same overwhelming sensations as the others when they first set foot on the ground, taking in the air, the gravity, the sky, mountains, and sea. It was mind-boggling for all, as none had ever been outside of a ship before, and Jook-sing was only the second planet they had experienced. They had landed on Quandros, yet stayed on board; this time, their feet had actually touched physical land.

Louie, Rob, and Bob spied a donut shop and peered inside, like a parent would through a maternity ward window. It was difficult to spot any resemblances to their original form now, but they still felt a bond with the fresh donuts in the shop. With more petty cash than they would ever be able to use from the ship, each of them carried a pocketful of spending money, and like children, they glanced at the rest for permission as they entered the shop.

"I'm going to get a lemon-filled! I think each of us should get our original forms first, just to see what we were," proposed Louie. "These aren't sentient—see, Wuxian soil!"

"Don't you think it's kinda weird to be in here?" questioned Rob.

"Nah! We're more human now, and I wanna see why humans think we're so delicious!" replied Louie.

"They smell great!" Bob almost shouted.

"One lemon-filled, a glazed old-fashioned and a plain cake." Louie pointed out each to the woman behind the counter, who pulled them from the display case and dropped them into a white paper bag.

"Anything else?" she asked, while looking at Louie. "Coffee or milk for you gentlemen?"

They discerned, due to her large and coy smile, that the serving woman was flirting with Louie. Totally unprepared, he shook his head and stared at the floor as Rob paid for the donuts, and left the shop with a strange sense of awkward flattery.

"Here it goes!" said Louie. They watched in wonder as a former donut ate his past life. "Delicious! To think I used to believe I was just average!"

"Not bad," added Rob.

"Hmm, this is pretty good too," Bob said. Both he and Rob, however, felt underwhelmed at the experience, since they didn't know that a plain cake or an old-fashioned must never be consumed without coffee.

"You need coffee, guys! You're not doing it right!" commented Abner, a professional at consuming donuts.

"Maybe next time," said Rob. The rest agreed, embarrassed.

"We need to get humbows at the market!" said Abner. "I can't count the number of times I heard about them when I worked on the docks."

They traveled to the market, absorbing the atmosphere, sounds, sights, smells, and languages around them like newborns.

# The Wuxian Way

Ancient history of the Jook-sing told of the world that they left, a society that glorified evil in its latter years. It continually filled their minds, saturated it at all times.

Selfishness, arrogance, hatred, and violence were considered virtues, taught and displayed even in its culture's music and films. Using each other for sexual pleasure without care for the other's soul was commonplace. The hierarchy of power, whether in family, business, or politics, had deteriorated among all people. Power had been reduced to a tool for oppression, justified by deceit, and enflamed by the media. There had ceased to be a division between nations in world power, and instead only turmoil within existent power prevailed. The constant pressure of evil permeating the world was the righteous Jook-sing's impetus to leave Earth, as their ancestors had left behind other lands that had oppressed them.

The Wuxian of Jook-sing were full of the genuine Light of Truth. Over the centuries of inhabiting their world, they had cultivated an honor that had affected them physically, giving them a translucent light that shone from their countenances. Though change was constantly occurring in their society, the concept of rebellion was not considered a positive attribute to the Wuxian. To violate a way of life exemplified by honor, justice, love, and peace was distasteful, at the very least. Rebellion was despised and discouraged by all. On the contrary, the goal of most Wuxians was to love and honor each other, regardless of his or her status in life.

The land of Wuxia was heaven itself to its people, and they protected their philosophy of honor and love. All Wuxians were trained warriors, and each was expected to protect the honor of young and old alike, including the weak and the disabled. They knew that the term 'peace' meant destroying anything that threatened the harmony and honor of its fellow man, or the truths upon which their society was built. Enforcing peace with the sword was an honor, yet delivering its power was never glorified; only the Light of Truth was worthy of glory.

The worst crimes committed were rewarded with a 'Certificate of Death'. The criminal authorized their own execution by the actions of their crime. There was no need for a signature by the offender or anyone else for that matter. The offense was all that was necessary to set forth the wheels of justice into motion. Taking another's life, if discovered, meant the loss of your own with immediate effect. The Certificate of Death was delivered prior to the death penalty in trial cases, or it could be delivered postmortem in cases of a witnessing Defender of Honor, or Shǒuhù Zhě. Crimes varied by degree, and those who weren't destroyed when convicted were instead sent to the Place of the Dishonored, a prison colony located on Jook-Sing's second moon, Tolkee. When a suspect's honor was discovered to have left him or her, his greatest penalty was his loss of the Light, a Light that would not have left him had he sought innocence through redemption.

Tolkee was locked in an eclipsed orbit between Jook-sing and the sun, housing it in darkness both day and night. Its view of Jook-sing was that of only a perpetual solar eclipse, its surrounding halo of light showing faintly, and only enough to deliver the memory of light. Tolkee was a dead world of sand and rock, inhabited by dead souls who owned hearts of sand and rock. They knew the Truth, had rejected it, and had chosen their own fates; chaos had been their choice and they were allowed to reap it at will. Their lives consisted of continual stress, fear of others, and an inept pursuit of survival.

The moon minimally sustained life. Its trickle of haloed sunlight allowed mushrooms to grow on rocks in certain areas. Streams provided dank-smelling water. Anything more on Tolkee was contributed by waste ships, which used it as a dumping ground twice a month.

# A Boxed Reunion

The Supermax freighter arrived at New Seattle's port after a week had passed. After being cleared by Jook-sing's customs department, they docked the vessel, and the crew began unloading it.

The dock was similar in design to its ancient counterpart with many exceptions, the most obvious of which was the lack of cranes to offload containers. Each container, instead, levitated under its own power in a ballet of movement, sorting themselves into a holding yard. They would exit their places when cleared, so as not to cause congestion in the airspace. Empty containers would next be filled with export material, then reverse their organized choreography onto their assigned freighters, and finally return to their original, various locations across the universe.

"Thank you so much, Captain," said Claus as he walked toward the gangplank to land. "You've saved our lives and given us so much more!"

"My only hope is that you return the favor to another someday," he replied.

"Thank you, Captain," said Angie and Maude, each giving him a kiss on the cheek as they departed the ship. The others thanked the captain and crew as they left as well, excited for their new lives to begin.

*"To be honor!"* the captain saluted as he waved.

Leaving the docks, they traversed through the port toward the landing pads for commercial and private ships. The ships from around the universe varied in shape and size, many unique and some beautiful in design.

"Vvow, look et thet one!" declared Basir, pointing at the ship docked next to the Ulysses. It was one of a myriad of awe-inspiring, exotic ships that filled the port.

"Gorgeous! Look inside. Posh!" exclaimed Angie, curiously owning knowledge about decorating style and taste.

Coming back from the market, the crew of the Ulysses saw the others admiring the ship moored to their port side. Something about them seemed very familiar to Louie, and Claus' group looked over as the Ulysses' crew drew near.

"Good evening, friends!" welcomed Claus. "Could we have a moment?" The familiarity of his voice resonated with the former donuts.

"Claus...?" asked Louie with some hesitation.

"Louie...is that you?" responded Claus. "How in the world...?"

"Looks like a lot more has been possible in the last

few weeks!" Louie exclaimed.

Rob, Bob, Angie, Maude, Louie, Basir, and Claus greeted each other warmly, boxed reunion style. Their transformations amazed one another and they were pleased with the results. The donuts introduced the others, and in the process, seven donuts, a meatloaf, a fish, a rat, two mice, two humans, and a lasagna-thing became friends.

Louie invited the others to the ship. They boarded, awestruck, questions filling their minds, especially about the beautiful ship they had entered. Everyone spent the next several hours aboard the Ulysses as each shared details about the last few weeks. Laughing, concern, shock, and more laughter filled the ship. That day, everyone had something to add their combined adventures, from Abner wrestling entrails above the rendering department, to Loaf's natural talent as a pilot. Others shared their experiences on the shuttle, too, including their encounters with the Supermax's captain and crew.

"So what to do with this 'Filet'?" Claus mused aloud. "He's surely our greatest problem."

"So far, he's been cooperative," replied Abner. "I can't see him being much of a problem in the Wuxia."

"Maybe not, but just *being* Filet, he'll be a problem in one way or another." Loaf added, "He's a time bomb!"

"I agree he could be a problem, but if there's any hope for the man, this place is it," responded Jenny.

"Accountability!"

"If the stories are true, you're right. Coming face to face with truth can have a strong effect on a person in one way or another." Claus contemplated the depth of his own statement. "For all of us," he added.

"Well I, for one, am *starving*, is my truth for now!" announced Layerie, breaking the weight of the moment. "Let's find something to eat!"

The group, now a large entourage, trekked out of the port again and toward a downtown train. They encountered the city's inhabitants along the way, and noticed the glory of their countenances, their colorful attire, and the elegant weapons at many of their sides. Their light was evident in the peace they displayed, a sense of controlled power infused with kindness. They were nobles, every single one they met was, and meeting them was beautiful and humbling. Many they passed noticed their innocent gawking, and the inhabitants' humility was only inspired, not compromised. A bow here, a smile there—it was odd to be so welcomed in this foreign world, where its peoples' inner beauty equalled the majesty of its landscape.

Jenny compassionately remembered Captain Filet, hoping above everything else that the inspiration of life in this place would improve him. If a place existed that had the power and ability to move a heart, this was it.

Reaching their destination, they found a loud restaurant that served good food and cold beer. The evening continued pleasantly as they ate and drank together. They discussed many issues and problems, some which were agreed upon, and others which they decided to resume at a later date. At the end of the night, they made their way back to the Ulysses, as the ship had ample room to accommodate everyone.

# Roots

After a month had passed, they decided to integrate into society. It was foolish not to do so, as Jook-sing was an easy place with which to fall in love.

Abner found a job on the docks which equalled his prior job in description, but had the added benefit of a fantastic seaside view. Louie returned to the bakery they had visited and obtained a job as a donut fryer, where he felt akin to an adoptive father toward his doughy and fried creations. Rob and Bob joined the New Seattle Parks Department, which boasted the best places to eat lunch. The twins, Maude and Angie, found work in a biotech firm, having the advantage of personal and firsthand DNA transformation knowledge. Maurice obtained a position as a hair stylist, and in a short amount of time, became something of a celebrity. Basir became a security guard with the Port of New Seattle.

Layerie the lasagna-thing, along with Peanut and Jelly the mice-people, had discovered that their mutual bond was due to shared DNA from the two Dirt Star children. They became inseparable, and even decided to attend the community college together. Layerie and Jelly's relationship eventually grew into a hidden romance. Claus joined the Jook-sing Star Fleet Navy, sensing the admiral's presence in his genes. Loaf became a charter pilot to and from the islands. Flip bought a small boat and became a fishing charter captain. Jenny, finally, decided to work in one of the maintenance shops at the port, catering to the private market.

Within the first month, surrounded by life in New Seattle's Wuxian ways, everyone agreed to discuss their shared conundrum, that of the Ulysses. They hadn't planned to steal the ship in the first place; their only goal had been to escape. The most pressing problem was that they were hiding behind Filet in the event of discovery, and actually blackmailing him to comply. All else in their lives seemed perfect, but for that colossal problem. They had two choices: keep the Ulysses and rely on the possibility that nobody would ever find it on Jook-sing, or use the onboard AI to return the Ulysses to Abassador Donclees on E-Toll. They unanimously decided upon the latter, that of returning the ship.

They cleaned it thoroughly, both inside and out. Jenny gave it a tune-up and erased all activities from the logs, including Filet's, for which he was grateful. Filet programmed the AI for the ship's return journey, including the necessary KSP transfers. Everyone had moved into apartments, and as their work for the

Ulysses was completed, the time came for their most recent home to depart. Though they had grown attached to the beautiful machine, it was time to say goodbye. The ship lifted off its pad slowly, banking to port in a long sweep over the sea and islands, gradually gained altitude, and then its familiar sonic roar clapped the atmosphere as it vanished.

When a week living on Jook-sing had passed, they decided to give Filet a chance at an upright and productive life. They were concerned he would flee, but reasoned he would be smart enough not to attempt it. Abner secured Filet a job at the port cleaning ships and shuttling VIPs to and from the light rail station. He had been briefed about Wuxian ways, and was careful not to be conspicuous. The Jook-sing, with their keen discernment of character and their skill with weapons, deterred him from trying to escape.

After a month working as a porter, Filet began to see a different side of life. He had never known what it was to exhibit humility, whether chosen or forced upon him. His new job was revealing to him—what it was to do a good job, yet still be mistreated by those who considered themselves his superior. In reality, Filet was a genius, but it was imperative for him to keep his mouth shut and do his job, regardless of treatment. The mistreatment was never delivered by a Wuxian, but instead inflicted upon him by off-world tourists, businessmen, or politicians. The Wuxian were tolerant of foreign visitors to a degree, and expected their employees to act in kind.

One Monday morning, a notable development occurred for Louie at the bakery. Louie had been in denial about his attraction to Karen. He had just finished the morning run, topping his last batch of crullers with glaze. Karen, not long afterward, started her shift as cashier at 6:00 a.m. Louie resisted his desire to spend time with her, and instead discussed donuts and the universe. Since he kept himself locked within, and froze outwardly whenever she was near, keeping up an appearance of indifference wasn't difficult.

Since Louie had been hired, Karen had also tried to display a reserved demeanor. She had recognized him when he was hired, with his shy responses to her smiles. She couldn't judge where they stood with one another, so she left it alone. Something Karen noticed, though, was how much the donuts improved after his arrival. They were very good before, but Louie had transformed the business into a gold mine for its owners. In less than a month, people from all over the city had been filling the little shop. She had difficulty resisting the donuts, too.

The atmosphere between Louie and Karen was thick with tension. During quiet times of the day, one could hear a donut drop.

"The truth is, I love donuts, but I really took this job because of you!" Louie blurted during a slow time of the morning. He had grown weary of justifying his silence. "If it makes you uncomfortable, I can quit."

"I've been waiting a month for you to say so. You really are the weirdest, nicest guy, you know?!"

"Is that good or...?" Louie asked, unsure of himself and ready to be crushed.

"It's good, Louie," Karen reassured him, smiling widely.

# Bon Voyage

The Dirt Star's thrusters ignited for the first time in anyone's memory. The entire fleet was shocked as it turned to port and away from the armada toward deep space.

The admiral scrambled fighters to keep a reign on the situation, but unfortunately, all attempts at abatement were ineffective. The fighters moved in closely to the soil producer, only to be greeted by its fully-charged defense cannons. With shields engaged, the Dirt Star continued its path away from the fleet, as Commonwealth fighters followed at a safe distance. The fighters turned away and returned to the fleet after their target moved outside of the boundary zone. The fleet watched as the ship passed the boundary, unsure what was happening. They were unaware that, before the assassination had occurred, the Collective had engineered and assembled the necessary equipment for KSP detection and transference. All at once, as the Commonwealth fleet watched, the Dirt Star made contact with the KSP outside the boundary, and promptly vanished.

"Well, I don't know what to think about any of this. I hope to God wherever that ship ends up, that it doesn't cause more harm!" exclaimed the admiral.

The Yeasts delighted in the humans' confusion as the Collective engaged the KSP. The Dirt Star transferred flawlessly to E-Toll within the Gomane System, and they continued moving toward their target. E-Toll's seven moons, each a different color, orbited the massive blue, tan, and green planet. All but two moons possessed their own atmospheres, which allowed for colonies and provided mining, agriculture, and tourism for inhabitants of E-Toll and its visitors.

Ambassador Donclees was alerted to the presence of the Dirt Star within E-Toll's vicinity. He was informed mainly because of his recent visit to the soil producer, and the ambassador was shocked and very curious about its arrival. He ordered his new pilot to pick him up with his new ship, as the hospital had released him a few weeks prior.

Emperor Degsapht of E-Toll gave the order to scramble fighters to protect E-Toll and its moons. The fighters met the Dirt Star, which lurked with its shields engaged and its cannons powered. The fighters interpreted its approach as a threat, and with authorization from the emperor himself, began landing heavy blows against its shields.

The onslaught was merely a training exercise for

the Collective. With its hosts at their stations, the Collective eliminated several fighters with ease. It knew that before long, E-Toll would amass heavy fighters with SD weapons capable of penetrating their shields and destroying the Dirt Star. The Collective directed the hosts to wipe out a few more fighters, and then targeted long volleys toward several of the moons. Fifteen fighters were lost, as well as hundreds of lives on three settlements on two of the moons. The Collective gave the order to power down its cannons, turn to starboard, and find another KSP.

The ambassador's ship arrived near E-Toll out of range of the battle. He stared out the bridge window, dismayed and speechless, at a sight he could never have imagined. Politically, Donclees had been preparing to destroy the crew of the Dirt Star, but the Collective had beat him to his goal, destroying his fleet with the physical equivalent of the wrath he felt toward them. Donclees reeled as he witnessed the Dirt Star destroy fifteen fighters, and then launch salvos at the moons' colonies. Suddenly, all at once, it turned and departed, as if bored with the battle. E-Toll's heavy fighters were scrambled and gathered within range of the Dirt Star as it contacted the KSP. One ship managed to fire two SD blasts that hit their marks as the ship disappeared from view. The ambassador directed his pilot to return to the palace on E-Toll, as the remaining fighters returned.

Aboard the Dirt Star, the Collective moved the

hosts to repair the damaged vessel. Within the vacuum of space, the SD blasts became more potent, and the nuclear-amplified, sonic blasts filled the vacuum of sound and atmosphere as they slammed into the Dirt Star's docks on its port side. The hosts merely sealed off the bulkheads, as the Collective was unconcerned with the areas involved. The Collective wasn't fazed by damage to the Dirt Star; it did not hold value toward things that humans valued. The ship was, after all, a creation of humanity, which the Collective now ironically used to torment it.

Once the KSP transfer was completed, the Dirt Star traveled to another KSP in the Halre System to avoid pursuit by the E-Tollians.

Emperor Degsapht of E-Toll and Ambassador Donclees met, their grunts, clicks, shrieks, and sighs competing with each other into an ever-rising cacophony. They agreed that they needed to contact the Commonwealth about the unprovoked attack.

"What the hell do you mean by sending your crap-maker to us like this?" the emperor's vicious language translated for the prime minister of the Commonwealth. "The Dirt Star has destroyed fifteen of our fighters and killed hundreds of our citizens on two of our moons, not to mention the infrastructure damage it caused! Why?! Why have you betrayed us this way?!"

"Emperor, I am grieved to hear the news of your

losses. I regret to inform you that the Dirt Star was recently highjacked after a large portion of the crew was murdered. We had a biohazard issue that affected many crew members. The result was an insanity-fueled mutiny, and loss of control of the situation," replied the prime minister. "I am so sorry for this, Your Excellency."

"This is unexpected, Prime Minister—but nonetheless, the Commonwealth is responsible," countered the emperor.

"Can we meet, Your Excellency? The sooner, the better."

"We will meet, Prime Minister! Arrange it with my staff. I must get back to my people now!"

# Shifu

As time passed, Jenny gained control of her abilities. It had become tiresome to know so many people's concerns. Her gift was helpful for acquiring skills, but the constant noise of others' accumulated life experiences wore on her. At times when she sensed the value of her supernatural perception, however, she would eavesdrop.

The afternoon was warm on her day off as she sat outside at a market cafe. While she watched a couple pass by to order drinks, she knew that great nobility mixed with skill was in her presence. She decided to keep her 'spy level' low, as she felt that restraining herself was necessary to experience a traditional understanding of another, first. Her approach was nearly Wuxian in thought, honoring strangers with conventional approaches and observations, offering respect to others as fellow beings. To her delight, the older Jook-sing couple sat at an adjacent table nearby, chatting about the warm weather and family.

The lady, appearing to be in her sixties, glanced toward Jenny with a smile. "Good afternoon young lady. Beautiful day, yes?"

"Delicious day, as good as this cup of coffee!" Jenny responded.

"Yes! This day is like a good cup of coffee! Warm, rich, and invigorating!" the older gentleman added.

"Are you visiting the Wuxia long? You seem to be very settled in to me. Oh, pardon me! I am Cheng Píng, and this is my husband, Cheng Chāo."

"My name is Jenny Acorn. So nice to meet the two of you. Can I ask what your names mean?"

"In Chinese, the surname is always first,' Píng replied with a smile. "Cheng means 'sincere, honest, or true'. My name 'Ping', means 'level or peaceful'. Chāo's name means 'to surpass' or 'leap over', but I'm still trying to get him to stop leaping over the dishes in the kitchen!"

"Peaceful! By way of enforcement!" Chāo added, giving Píng a wry smile.

"You two are wonderful! What's the occasion?" Jenny asked, noticing their formal folkwear.

"It was graduation day for our newest class of Shǒuhù Zhě. Chāo and I are Shifu for New Seattle's Defenders of Honor, Róngyù Shǒuhù Zhě in Mandarin. We train our students in honor, ethics, and martial arts to protect our people and values. Today is also our fortieth wedding anniversary. We're going to dinner after our coffee."

"Congratulations. Forty years—that's great! You two seem perfect for each other. I'm sure by now you've got it figured out."

"Thank you, young lady. I think I'll keep him!"

"It's too late now, anyway, and I would be lost without my beautiful one," Chāo added.

"Enough about us. I forgot, I was asking if you're vacationing?" Píng asked again.

"Well, a group of us have come here to see the Wuxia. All of us have fallen in love with your city, and we've gotten jobs, to kinda blend in."

"How long have you been here?" Chāo asked.

"About a month or so. I'm working as a technician at the port."

"Good, honest work," Chāo replied.

"It's so good I met you today. I would love to learn more of your culture and skills. I'm not even sure if it's an acceptable request in your culture to be trained, being a foreigner."

"Character is all that counts with us, although aptitude and a natural sense of agility do help to become Shǒuhù Zhě," Chāo explained.

"Here is our card. The school is just down 1st Street, a few blocks on the right. We would love to have you come and check it out. Bring your friends if you like, Jenny." Píng handed her the card. "It was so good to meet you, dear one," she said, as both she and her husband bowed (and in so doing, paid an enormous honor to her, as Jenny would soon discover). The couple smiled a warm goodbye, leaving behind empty coffee cups, and continued on their way toward a restaurant for an anniversary dinner.

"Thank you, again! And happy anniversary!" Jenny called.

# Shǒuhù Zhě

Jenny walked cheerfully back to the port, excited about the prospect of learning from the Chengs. Inside their after-work pub 'The Crane', half the crew lounged in booths near the windows.

"There you are! We were wondering if you'd been sent to Tolkee!" Abner teased as he sauntered toward her, sporting a t-shirt which bore the logo of his favorite dim sum restaurant. "Glad you're home," he added with a sideways smile.

"Nice, Abe. You guys! I met these great people at the cafe today. They turned out to be teachers at the Honor Defender's School! They invited me, and any of you who want to come to the school to learn. Any of you want to go?"

"You mean, aaah...what are they called? I can't remember... 'So Jofee'?" asked Abner.

"It's Shǒuhù Zhě, Abe... 'So Jofee', sheesh! What a Neanderthal!" replied Jenny with a pompous flick of her hair.

"So, are they like the police around here? I've seen them around town, and they're no joke," Louie said, his mouth full of pretzels. "But they don't look like police. They're like some kinda royal guard or something,"

"Yeah, I think they are what would be the closest thing to law enforcement here. There's nothing bland on this planet, even uniforms. I saw a pair of them the other day. One looked close to seven feet tall, and his partner no more than five-and-a-half feet," said Rob.

"Sounds like a comedy!" replied Karen. She and Louie had become inseparable since the week before at the donut shop.

"I thought it looked funny too, but then this guy shot out of an alleyway with a lady's purse. The lady was yelling and running after him herself! The lopsided pair I told you about whipped around, and gave the lady some kinda signal."

"What'd it look like, Rob?" Bob asked.

"I think it was like this." Rob made a sweep and a downward signal with his hand. "She musta known what it meant, because she stopped and backed away. The guy with her purse stopped dead in his tracks, too—I think he realized he had no escape. He dropped the purse and pulled out a knife!"

"Man! How far away were you?" asked Jelly.

"Close enough, but those two had it under control... everyone in the area backed up. They drew a crowd! Anyway, the tall guy and his buddy slowly pulled their swords, waiting for purse-boy to drop his knife. Nope, he wasn't backing down—then it happened. The big one kinda bent one of his knees as the short guy ran up his leg, and the big one catapulted him off of his knee toward the wall next to purse-boy! The short guy ricocheted off the wall, and before the guy saw him, knocked the knife out of his hand! It was like watching the circus! Purse-boy just stood there stunned, and then held out his hands for cuffs. I thought he might applaud with the rest of the crowd!" Rob had told the story as if he had been witnessing it in that moment. "Those guys looked funny at first, but after seeing them command the situation with style? Well, it was awe-inspiring."

"Wow! I've seen others around town. You're right, they're like nobility—but not like, 'Bow to me!' nobility. They just seem to have a presence that inspires respect. You can tell they're there for you...well, I guess for your honor," said Jenny. "Any of you want to check it out?"

"I'll check it out," replied Loaf, sitting next to Abner. "Might be fun. I'd like to learn to bounce off a wall! Hey Layerie, you've done that—how 'bout it?"

"Yeah, I'll come and help bounce *you* off a wall! I think I could enjoy that!" replied Layerie, grinning.

"I'd like to come!" announced Jelly with a large smile, as Maude, Rob, and Basir nodded in agreement.

# Jūnxiào

The group gathered at the school the next day, and after greeting them, the Chengs ushered them into the classroom.

"Welcome to the Róngyù Shǒuhù Zhě Jūnxiào, the Defenders of Honor Academy," Chāo began. "I am Cheng Chāo. We will start today with the history and reason for our existence within Wuxian society. If this training is complementary to your character and skills, you will be asked to stay. You may stay either way, for your own benefit, but please realize, if you are not selected to be trained to become Shǒuhù Zhě, you are welcome to stay and learn all we have to offer, anyway. This is the Wuxian way of fulfilling the honor of a Shǒuhù Zhě citizen. Because you are off-world, we would like to give all of you the background about life in the Wuxia. Píng, would you like to take over?"

Cheng Píng, glowing with wisdom and grace, walked nobly to the front of the classroom.

"Thank you, dear one. Before the Jook-sing of Earth arrived in the Wuxia System two hundred years ago, only one of the seven planets, Měilì, was occupied by sentient life. Měilìe traders had saved the exploratory ship of our forefathers and allowed them to inhabit our beautiful world. The Měilìe and Jook-Sing make up the majority of the inhabitants to this day, but others have been granted citizenship after fulfilling a necessary need of Wuxia. We are a people of honor; we know dishonor and oppression from our past. When our fathers left Earth in the late 21st century, they knew a world where honor had been discarded. The love of self, and viewing others as a means to an end, no matter how degrading the actions, were standard philosophies. The elders were viewed without honor, and obligations to children had vanished. Ever-increasing depravity within society had become a degenerating pattern. Because of this, Jook-sing was founded upon *honor*. The fathers decided, if one lived his or her life with the intent of friendship to all, dishonor would not be an issue.

"The KSP transfer of the Jook-sing to the Wuxia System relocated them to A.D. 22 in Earth's years. All of creation was soon to be redeemed from its failures. The requirements for spiritual freedom were placed upon creation by the Creator, but were purposefully beyond its abilities to fulfill. Creation's only hope was the Creator himself, who fulfilled those requirements. The Creator absorbed his creation's failures, by actually becoming failure. By allowing himself to be destroyed by his creation, he then renewed his own life, never to die again. He gave this life to all who requested it. All of his creation was affected.

"Here in the Wuxia, those of us who sought honor and life were given the physical representation of our reliance upon the Creator. No one is quite sure how this happens. It may be elements present in this world that react with our spirit. This is the source of our glowing countenance. We keep the Light by giving ourselves willingly to truth and honor, daily. Our forefathers knew Earth's history, and were able to discern why these things happened on Jook-sing. If we fail to stay in a place of honor, our light fades. The Creator never has forced himself upon his own. If we choose our own way, we are free to go, yet we will be in darkness. We will talk more of our ways in the next session. Let's have a fifteen minute break! There is coffee, tea, and donuts in the break room for all of you to enjoy."

The morning classroom sessions were at once fascinating and frightening, as were the afternoon training exercises. The Chengs showed themselves to not only be mentally acute, but their physical abilities were beyond conception, as well. The two began the first session with a display of fighting styles demonstrated by four of the recently-graduated Shǒuhù Zhě. The new defenders were proficient at their arts, but still couldn't match either of the Chengs. There was something other-worldly about both of them; they were equally matched, two halves of the same being, so to speak, and the manner in which they moved was almost dreamlike.

Píng floated with every movement, and whether it was a defensive block, an attack, or avoiding a strike, she was like a ghost. She seemed to move before her opponent—or was it after one would have expected? —and threw all opponents into confusion. She could leap over attackers, knocking them down before they realized what had happened. Chāo's movements, on the other hand, were less balletic than his wife's, resembling lightning. At times, one couldn't see him; all at once a sprint, or a jump and kick, then a flip forward, knocking down anyone in his way, revealed his sudden presence. He exhibited spinning kicks beyond the realm of what was natural, sometimes as many as four revolutions before Chāo's blow would land on its target.

The masters always tempered their blows, though, so as not to destroy their students. Their students displayed different styles, some using swords, others modeling various forms of unarmed combat, and yet others using whatever items were within their reaches, like chairs, books, or even food.

Chāo displayed a fighting sequence one could characterize as half-comedy, half-serious. Even when fighting a sword-wielding opponent, and armed merely with a squash and a box of crackers, he dominated. He delivered the crackers like they were throwing stars to his opponent's eyes, then knocked his opponent in the head with the squash. Everyone would roll with laughter, especially the starry-eyed opponent.

"All of you have the potential to learn and surpass all you have seen here today," Chāo said earnestly. "We know our abilities are gifts, sometimes needing to be pulled from within. You must cultivate your gift like a garden. A gift unused is a dead gift."

Píng added, "A garden is the fruit of the seeds planted. All of you are seeds. A seed looks nothing like the plant it becomes. Just as Chāo and I are different, as from different seeds, each one of you will become a beautiful addition to this garden. That being said, a seed has a difficult beginning. In fact, if you think about it, a seed is as though dead before it is buried. It germinates in the moist soil, and forces its sprout upward and roots downward. It is the dividing point between the seen and unseen aspects of its life. Each of us has our unseen roots and our visible life; only our spirit and the Creator fully know each one."

Chāo stepped back in. "So, to begin your physical training today, you will load bags of seed at the port. Let's meet after lunch at Gate C. We won't hide anything from any of you. If you choose to be Shǒuhù Zhě, our training involves hard work, and humbling yourself to see how your fellow man lives.Our labor also funds your training, and keeps this school tuition-free."

The work was difficult. The ninety-pound sacks of seed were heavy, the heat of the tarmac amplifying the hardship of the experience. The trucks kept coming, dropping their contents onto a conveyor that ran to a hopper, which then filled the bags. The bags felt heavy at the start, but seemed lighter as they continued their work. The last few hours of the day, the bags once again felt nearly immoveable. The group from the Jūnxiào worked alongside men and women who did this same labor every day. The everyday workers ranged in age from their twenties to early-sixties, and were thin, sinewed people, weathered by hard work and the sun. They were free to choose a life of working outside, and the joyful vitality exuding from them was intoxicating. The positive atmosphere provided endurance for the students, as they accomplished their assigned work.

The afternoon dragged until, finally, they had finished. The Chengs, who had been working alongside the students the entire day, called for the day's completion. A few students had left after the first half hour of work.

"Good job to all of you who've made it through the first day!" Píng announced to those remaining. "We will see you Wednesday morning!"

For the next six months, the classes were much the same, starting with a history and culture lesson, then followed by hard work. Each day, the work session was arranged at a new location. Whether at a dock, a ditch, or an assembly line offering lowly tasks, each job had its purpose for building character, strength, or endurance.

Though the Wuxia had an advanced culture, they had learned from Earth's mistakes regarding technology. The Wuxia, unlike those on Earth, chose to restrict the accomplishment all tasks (no matter how lowly) to people only, and decided not to replace workers with any type of technological automation. Menial jobs were filled with people who had chosen them for the benefits they provided. The value of one's work was measured honorably, and this work philosophy allowed a laborer to earn the income of a good life. Work itself was the key; a lazy scientist could be viewed as they should be—lazy—and income would reflect the worker's attitude. Careers associated with vast knowledge were only of great value, if backed with the honor of the individual possessing it.

After the first six months, the Jūnxiào students began a vigorous training program at the school. The Ulysses members who had joined had transformed physically and mentally, and were now being shaped into precision warriors. Jenny had intentionally worked hard to keep her training authentic in nature, without using her powers to ease the experience. The group learned basic and complex moves during the following two-and-a-half years. From time to time, they returned to work at the docks, warehouses, or factories to reinforce the value of humility in their characters.

Graduation day arrived, and each student was amazed that he had lasted to the end. During the ceremony, each new Shǒuhù Zhě was presented with a traditional tunic, belt, and sword of the Shǒuhù Zhě. Each tunic and sword was unique, and mirrored the personality of its new owner. Some were brightly-colored, others multicolored; some had detailed patterns, and others were solid in texture and design. All were similar in cut, however, and bore a design reserved only for Shǒuhù Zhě, a 'non-uniform' uniform.

The brightest and most varied in color and design was created for Jenny, and decorated with Asian patterns of various bright colors and deep earth tones. It was a perfect match for her. Abner's deep blue and red tunic expressed his noble temperament. Each garment was suited perfectly for each crew member of the Ulysses.

The swords granted to each were entirely elegant, from their gold hilts to their blades, all inlaid with intricate designs. Each sword had its own leather scabbard, equal in beauty to their partnered swords, and crafted by an artisan who put his gratitude into every detail. Each gift was provided by the citizens of Wuxia to those who would serve in the traditions and honor of a Shǒuhù Zhě.

The Shǒuhù Zhě of the Ulysses consisted of Abner, Jenny, Loaf, Layerie, Jelly,  Maude, Rob, and Basir. They decided to fulfill the tradition of their offices by committing to two years of service. They spent most of their time becoming acquainted with the people in New Seattle, and in continuing their training at Jūnxiào. Happily, during their service, very little violence or crime existed in the city.

# Stowaway

Filet woke early at 4:00 a.m., washed his face, dressed, made a pot of coffee, and toast with eggs.

The sun rose on Jook-sing at the same time year round, as the planet's axis was parallel with its orbit around the sun. In fact, there were no traditional seasons at all. Its axis angle and its orbit, which formed a perfect circle, prevented variances in the weather. Jook-sing enjoyed a perpetual spring, its temperature measuring in the low-eighties, with light rain in the morning followed by an enjoyable day, every day. Sunrise was at 5:00 a.m., and sunset at 9:00 p.m.

Filet donned his raincoat and walked out the door of the apartment he shared with Abner. He liked to get an early start, so as to return home from work early. His boss made it clear—as long as his work was completed on schedule, Filet could choose his own hours. He still thought it best to start his day before most of his coworkers, as it gave him more time to himself. At this stage in his life, changes were plentiful. There was so much on his mind, that he was glad being a porter was more physical than intellectual in nature; his job freed him to contemplate deeper things.

The one thing that truly amazed Filet was that he actually felt as though he had discovered the value of life—the real value, not the cheap substitute he had accepted until now. There was something about the Wuxia that he would never have encountered, had he not been taken to it against his will (which he had been). Being forced to comply, and humble himself, were the best things that could have happened to Marcus.

His circumstances forced him to see and acknowledge the smaller (and yet more precious) blessings life offered. For one, New Seattle was more than beautiful, and its people matched its scenery. In addition, his relationship with his abductors had changed. It was no longer relegated to that of captor and captive, and instead had grown to become like family, which was yet another aspect of his life that dumbfounded him. Also, he held one of the lowest positions at the Port of New Seattle, yet most days, he was overwhelmed with thankfulness for his job. He lifted his cup of coffee to take another sip, and its aroma filled his senses as he walked toward the port from his apartment. The sunrise lit up the sky in the west, the Xióngwěi Supernova showing faintly in the broad expanse.

Arriving at his station office, he pulled his job

folder and grabbed the needed supplies. He headed to the Shǒuhù Zhě shuttle at the top of the list, the one used for transferring prisoners to Tolkee.

When he opened the passenger hatch, he unpleasantly encountered the smell of stale vomit, and the stench assaulted him immediately. Since the interior was coated with antibacterial teflon, cleaning it out was as simple as attaching a hose to the outer hull connector, and then turning on the interior cleaning system. Water jets and foam washed out the whole area within ten minutes. Filet, watching the system do its job, was thankful that this was his first task of the day, and wished all ships could be cleaned in the same manner.

As the last jets finished their rinses, water ran down the wall, passing a worn seal, and then seeped into the distribution board and relay panel behind the cover. It was likely the thirtieth time it had happened, and caused a lightly-caustic solution of cleaner and water to coat the pin connectors on the distribution board. Undetected by the shuttle pilots and in between services, the problem had yet to cause any concern.

Filet closed the compartment, turned on the dryer, and made his way to the cargo hold. He opened its hatch while pulling in the hose with bucket in hand. The hatch, still on its opening stroke as he entered, came back down immediately after Filet reached the end of the hold. Hastily, he ran toward the door, throwing out his left hand to stop it. In the process, and without hesitation, the hatch cut off both the hose and his hand.

Though stunned, he realized what had happened. He grabbed the light ribbon hose end from the floor and wrapped it around his forearm, forming a tourniquet. Filet lie inside the hold in complete darkness. Unaware that his frantic yells couldn't be heard from the outside, he cried out desperately for help. Filet, weak as he was, slipped into shock, and then into unconsciousness.

This particular shuttle run was Abner's first training mission to the Tolkee prison moon. With anguish in his heart for the prisoners, yet also having the alertness necessary for transferring them, he led the first man out to the shuttle.

Delrash Melnick had been convicted of slowly starving his four concealed children for over ten years. The convict blamed society, his children, and the Creator for his wife's death, and for the consequent pressure of raising four children alone. After his wife's passing, he'd slowly given in to the voices in his head, which constantly reminded him that he deserved better than the hand he had been dealt. The voices gradually changed over the years, becoming increasingly narcissistic and hateful, and Mr. Melnick welcomed their counsel. He eventually shunned the Truth he had once allowed to guide his life. His children became the recipients of his hate and depression, living in the basement and locked away from the outside, and he only gave them rice and water to survive. A video server had been the children's sole source of understanding the outside world.

Finally, one night, one of the oldest children escaped, and the Shǒuhù Zhě were notified. A confrontation escalated as Mr. Melnick greeted the Shǒuhù Zhě with a gun behind his back, and welcomed them inside the house. As they entered, he revealed the weapon and almost killed one Shǒuhù Zhě, and challenged the other. The injured man, a Shǒuhù Zhě Master named Thunderhead, stumbled backwards after a fired bullet narrowly missed his heart. The large, bald Master allowed the impact's inertia to spin him around as he pulled his legs up under him. With a powerful thrust against the wall, he rocketed toward Mr. Melnick and his head plowed through him, knocking him down.

The children, ranging in age from mid to late teens, were released to social services, and then brought into a stable home environment. With ample evidence to justify a conviction, Delrash Melnick's trial came to an end a week later. His confession of all circumstances, and his explicit denial of any wrongdoing, matched his faded countenance in the courtroom. The punishment for Mr. Melnick's crimes was to spend the rest of his days existing on Tolkee. It had been an unusual verdict, as he had attempted to kill a Shǒuhù Zhě during the conflict. The judge determined that Mr. Melnick had only intended to frighten the Shǒuhù Zhě, and not kill him. Regardless, had he been executed instead, his sentence would likely have been more merciful than being exiled to Tolkee.

Abner guided Mr. Melnick into the passenger hold. He said good morning to the guard, locked the prisoner in the restraints, then returned to escort another prisoner into the shuttle. As nine more prisoners with similar stories of their own sat within the hold, Abner and his trainer entered the cockpit and greeted the captain.

# Feeling the Eclipse

The shuttle departed, exiting the atmosphere on its trajectory toward Tolkee. The pilot engaged its ALS drive, and the trip took no more than twenty minutes. As the shuttle entered the thin Tolkeean atmosphere, the effects of the water-damaged distribution board compromised the power to the shuttle's propulsion system. The captain did his best to glide to the surface without thrusters. In the distance, the sensors picked up the drop zone for prisoners and trash. One hundred feet from the ground, the shuttle rapidly approached the surface.

"We're not gonna make it! Better brace for impact!" the pilot yelled as the ship fell like a rock. "Hold on back there!" he yelled through the intercom to the prisoners. The shuttle banked downward as the cockpit slammed to the ground. Tragically, the force of the impact killed both the pilot and Abner's trainer.

Abner woke a half hour later due to sounds of pounding on the passenger hold walls. A cut on his scalp had trickled blood, congealed, and sealed shut his left eye. Looking about him in the perpetual half twilight of Tolkee, he barely discerned the shapes of the pilot and the trainer. The dead pilot was missing half of his face, and he realized the trainer was also dead, as he wasn't breathing, and Abner couldn't locate a pulse. He managed to pry open the cockpit hatch with the trainer's sword and stumbled out, his assault rifle in his hands. He encountered a chaos of surviving prisoners, who were yelling and pounding on the inner walls of the shuttle.

All at once, he detected a familiar voice coming from the back of the ship.

"Help me... someone please help me," it pleaded faintly.

"Marcus, is that you in there?" Abner shouted into the bent opening of the freight hold hatch.

"Abner, that you? Please get me out of here," the voice returned.

Abner ran back to the cockpit for the trainer's sword and returned to the hatch. He pried open the door and found Filet on the floor and blood everywhere, and saw that his hand was missing.

"What happened, Marcus?!"

"Some kinda malfunction with the hatch, I guess. Looks like it may have affected the whole ship, by the way we fell out of the sky. Do you happen to see my hand anywhere around here?"

"No, Marcus. I think you're still in shock. I'll be right back."

Abner ran back to the cockpit and retrieved the

medical kit, injected Filet's wrist with a local anesthetic, and found a cauterizer and a mouthpiece.

"Bite this!" he instructed. "This will hurt like hell." He placed the mouthpiece into Filet's mouth as he positioned the cauterizer near the injury. The cauterizer completed its work, sealing off the stump as Filet writhed in pain.

Filet caught his breath as the local anesthetic took a stronger hold on his pain level.

"Hope you enjoyed that!" he said while feeling the stump at the end of his wrist. "I know I deserved it. After the time I've spent in the Wuxia, things have become clear."

"Marcus, don't go there! Everyone knows you've been changing in a big way since we came to Jook-Sing. Besides, you know of the Redemption—it's not about you, it's how you live after knowing Truth."

"I know...I guess it'll take a while for it to sink in. I still have most of the same thoughts filling my mind."

"We all do, Marcus," Abner said as he wiped blood from Filet's face with gauze. "We just choose not to act on them, knowing the outcome. Failure is a given! It's the reason we need redemption. The difference now is that we choose to fight failure for the Creator's glory, and the honor of self and society." Abner carefully repacked the medical supplies kit, his expression thoughtful. "I remember Píng talking about how we're like seeds. The seed's the dividing point between the unseen root and the plant above ground. I think the difference happens when we choose what soil to be planted in. You're in good soil now. Stay in it, Marc."

"That's a lot to take in, Abe. I've lived for myself for so long, it's easy to feel alone."

Filet looked up as he zipped the kit bag. "I get it Marc, but that's why we rely on truth, and not on feelings. The Creator is able to keep us. We should talk more about this soon, but we've gotta get out of here! If there's anyplace where honor is hated, this is it."

"Do we have a comm?"

"Well the ship's comm is good, but I haven't tried the long-range setting yet."

The darkness of Tolkee was heavy, causing one's mind to be clouded, making it difficult to retain their lives on Jook-sing within memory. The only link Tolkee had to that world was its black silhouette with a faint halo of light in the black sky of the moon. They had been present for only two hours, but Tolkee's oppression was already becoming a ferocious torment. Abner tried using the long range communicator to no avail, as its transmitter was damaged.

"Now what?" Marcus questioned, frustrated, in pain, and wondering how they could last on Tolkee without food and water.

"I'm not sure, but I think we can call out from the comm near the drop point. I remember hearing about a small outbuilding in that area. It's supposed to have a comm inside. I think that's our only choice, if we can't get this thing to work."

"Where's the transmitter?" asked Marcus, hoping his childhood hobby of playing with electronics would help.

"Not sure."

"Well, we'll have to pull the comm and see if there's any network lines connected to it." Filet dismounted the comm, pulling it up and out from its mount, and encouragingly found two network cables behind it. "There's hope!" he announced excitedly.

"Excellent!"

Filet pulled at the wiring, feeling it snake to the right side of the cockpit. He followed the cables downward, knowing they terminated toward the front of the shuttle. Abner carried trainer's sword in his hand as they dropped out of the cockpit. Filet pointed at a section of the ship partially broken open by the impact, and once Abner located a suitable place from which to pry, he ripped open the panel. The compartment was filled with various control modules.

"Can you pull on that cable in the cockpit again?" asked Filet. Abner climbed back in and pulled on the cable, and Filet discovered which cable led to the transmitter. "Got it, Abe!" Filet dismounted the damaged module. "Looks like it may be a lost cause."

"You sure you can't fix it?"

"Well I guess I can try, but...it looks pretty bad." Filet managed to open the damaged cover and found most of the components crushed together, and noticed the telltale scent of burnt electrical insulation, a sign of shorted circuits.

"We're going to have to go with the comm near the drop point," Filet said, tossing the module to the side. "What about them?" He pointed to the prisoner hold.

"I'm not letting ten evil men out of there to make our problems more difficult than they already are. We can let them out after we get help. They'll be safe in there."

"Okay, we better go," Filet agreed, turning away from his repair work and toward his 'get-the-hell-out-of-here' job.

"There's some water and two days worth of rations for two in the side locker of the hold." Abner walked to the back of the shuttle and pulled two backpacks out of the hold's locker. On his way to the prisoner compartment hatch, he yelled, "Hey, you in there! There's food and water in the compartments under your seats. Ration it! We don't know how long it'll take for us to get back!"

In New Seattle, the controller at headquarters realized the shuttle hadn't yet returned, as the one hour round trip was long past. All of his attempts to hail it had failed. They sent a group of five Shǒuhù Zhě in another shuttle for a reconnaissance mission.

When the shuttle arrived at the scene, they discovered the damaged ship with its prisoners still within the prisoner hold. The Shǒuhù Zhě released them and left the area to search for Abner and Filet.

# Metaphor

It was a slow trek for Filet and Abner. In the beginning, they had attempted to go around craters, weaving in between them as they hiked toward their goal. The problem, though, was that it was difficult to maintain a consistent direction while walking the crater valleys.

"I'm pretty sure we're off course, Abner," remarked Filet, although his experience over the first few hours had been distorted by pain killers, and his missing hand was a blinding distraction, as well. Between the two of them, Filet would have had the best sense of direction, but he needed to rely heavily upon Abner for support. "I don't think the light level should be changing, unless we're moving to the dark side of the moon."

"That makes sense," agreed Abner. "I was wondering why it was getting darker. I was dark enough, already. It's hard to see twenty feet away, now."

"I think we should climb one of the craters and see if we can find a landmark," suggested Filet.

"Might as well start with this one. The first crater near the crash site seemed like the biggest one so far. If we can see it, we should be able to get our bearing."

Filet nodded. "Hopefully, we'll be able to see that far."

They trekked up the nearest crater in a switchback pattern to its rim. At the summit, they noticed that the sky was lighter in the east. Unluckily, they had travelled for hours in the wrong direction, so the crash site with its large crater was beyond their view. They settled for the heightened visibility, however, and made for the light in a direct path.

Once again in a switchback pattern, they descended into the crater's interior. In his mind, Abner reflected upon how he had always imagined walking inside the crater of a moon or asteroid. They had fascinated him, when he was younger, as he viewed these impact sites through telescopes. On the Dirt Star, he had only seen asteroids when they passed the Commonwealth. From time to time, the fleet would send out fighters to blow them up before they could come too close to the boundary line, and Abner had always requested time off to view the excitement. This time, though, he was *on* a moon, *inside* a crater, thinking back on his distant thoughts. He couldn't help but be amused.

One thing that he had enjoyed pondering, before, was whether or not evidence of the mass that caused the impact would be present. After a fifteen minute walk through the almost perfectly-flat crater floor, something dimly came into view in its very center, a dark, shiny, geometric shape. From their vantage point, it seemed no larger than a small shuttle or freight container. After another fifteen minutes of walking, as the shape enlarged, they found the form to be about the size of a two-story building. Both stopped to gaze at the amazing sight. It was mottled in color, jet black mixed with a medium gray, with a design looking as if many blocks had randomly been carved into it. The winds of Tolkee had blown its sands and covered the shape over an unknown length of time, giving the landmark a polished, gem-like quality. In this forsaken world, it was truly about the only thing of beauty they had encountered on their journey.

"Beautiful. Makes you wonder how long ago this happened. I can't begin to think of the force of impact this thing made — I mean, look how small it seems next to the size of this crater!" Abner was 'geeking out', enjoying the sight of something about which he could only wonder, when he was younger.

"Never really stopped to think about that kinda thing, but yeah, pretty cool. I just hope there aren't any others ready to hit! I don't think anything on this rock would survive," Filet thought aloud.

"Yeah, let's not think about that. Kinda makes me feel even smaller."

"I guess you're right. Place like this would make

anyone feel small. Let's keep going." Filet's self-confidence was shrinking by the minute.

# Footprints

As they rounded the massive meteorite, they caught sight of footprints trailing off into the distance, originating from the direction of the crater wall toward which they were heading. Filet and Abner stopped in their tracks as they pondered potential dangers they might encounter.

"What ya think?" Filet whispered to Abner, fear evident in his eyes. "I think we're being hunted!"

"Whatever's going on, those tracks look too fresh, considering the winds that've hit today. Keep your eyes open. If we're gonna be attacked, it'll be from the cover of this meteorite. There'd be no surprise in the valley between."

They continued walking and, after another half an hour, began ascending the crater wall once again. To their dismay, nothing revealed itself, and the absence of any new evidence increasingly fueled their fears as they crossed a ten-mile valley between them and the next crater. They arrived at the new crater in the path toward the drop zone, and began climbing. At the summit of the crater, they hiked the last switchback, and hope rekindled within their spirits and brought light to their eyes. There on the horizon, the largest crater was visible, the wreckage of the shuttle barely in view near its base.

"Perfect!" exclaimed Abner. "We need to go that way toward the beacon," he said, pointing north.

"How much longer, Abe? I don't think I can keep going much further. It might be a better vantage point to rest here, if they're still hunting us."

"I was going say the same," Abner agreed. "I think this is the best place to stop for awhile, too." He was exhausted, and couldn't believe Filet hadn't asked to stop earlier than he had. "Here ya go," he said, tossing a bottle of water to and a pack of protein cubes, and a small piece of what looked like bread in the twilight.

"Thanks." Filet tore into the packet and added water, and the catalyst activated, warming the rehydrated cubes. "Am I crazy, or is this delicious?" he asked as he swallowed half of the slice of bread.

Abner opened the seal on the bread pack, when he realized what had been missing. The air on Tolkee was so stale and lifeless, that the aroma of the contents in the packet exploded with life. He removed the thick slice of bread and bit into it. It tasted like eating something fresh, inside a bakery. He wasn't sure if his sense of smell had been altered simply because of its lack of use, or if his own hunger was provoking the experience.

"I don't know! Tastes amazing to me, too." Abner set the bread pack down and devoured the protein cubes. The men felt as though they had just eaten at a five star restaurant.

Abner unpacked the portable heat source and laid it on the ground. He pulled the safety pin from the igniter and bent the tabs toward each other, and the pack slowly started emitting a light smoke before the entire package began glowing red with heat. They huddled closely, feeling a little more at home in the twilight. It had been at least twelve hours since this morning's crash. Abner took the first watch, and Filet lay his head against the pack and began snoring almost immediately. Four hours passed until Filet awoke to give Abner a rest. Using his own pack as a pillow, he too fell into a deep sleep, fueled by exhaustion.

Three hours later, Filet shook Abner from his dream of enjoying a roomful of donuts and coffee. "Someone's down there," Filet whispered, pointing down into the crater. "There—can you see them?"

"I can't see anything down there. You Quandrosites must have better vision than humans. Wait! Yeah, now I can see something, more like just a hazy cluster of movement, though." He continued to stare as his eyesight adjusted.

"Keep looking."

"Okay, looks like four. They're almost to the crater wall. We need to stand our ground. If we run, they'll have the high position," Abner said adamantly as he began repacking their supplies.

"You sure? Well, I guess at least we won't feel hunted anymore," Filet yielded.

"Let's get back out of view. I'll keep my eye on them! You keep the outside of the crater in your sights. There might be more of them down that side waiting for us to run."

"Okay, but I don't have a weapon," Filet reminded him. Abner pulled the trainer's sword from the pack and handed it over.

As he grasped the weapon, *change* was the dominant impression in his mind. Since landing in Jook-sing, Filet's character had begun to blossom, and now his honor had budded. Abner noticed that the man whom he had once considered a waste of space, had transformed into a man who would fight to save his life, even after having been his hostage. The honor of the fallen Shǒuhù Zhě seemed to emanate at the very moment Filet accepted the fallen warrior's weapon. He strapped the sheath to his side and settled in.

There was no activity outside of the crater, that Filet could see. Abner viewed from the opposite position, and witnessed four blurred shapes gaining altitude upon the switchbacks they had traversed earlier. With each completed switchback, the four creatures rose toward the crater's summit, and their disgusting visages became clearer. They were unlike anything known to have been previously human. Each wore clothes fashioned from rags (it was evident that they'd had time to devote to detailing them). They appeared to wear the rags with pride, and though their clothing had been fabricated from refuse, they did not appear as though poorly dressed. The people themselves were a different story, though, and Abner tried keeping his eyes on the situation, and not on them.

All at once they began to run. They passed Abner and Filet about one switchback lower than the top, making one long path to the summit about four hundred yards around the rim. They didn't stop, and instead passed the summit, and descended back down the outside face and away from the direction Abner and Filet had chosen.

"What the hell?" Filet exhaled, relieved and yet confused.

"That was strange," Abner concurred. "I still don't trust them. I don't think they saw us, but I'm sure they knew where we were." Abner settled back down, shaking his head. "Let's wait a while, then get outta here, if you think you're able."

"I'm ready when you are. Sooner we're off this rock, the better!" They watched as the Tolkites faded away into obscurity toward the crash site.

Their exit revived their spirits to keep going. The tedious descending and ascending of crater walls toward the drop zone dragged for hours upon end.

With each rise to the rim of another crater, they were able to maintain their course toward the beacon.

# The Residents

After descending another switchback, they arrived at the outskirts of a settlement. In the distance, shanty huts were visible through the pale twilight. They appeared to be made of whatever had been available from the dump. The inhabitants of this wretched world had developed their own economy, one of its main currencies being the leftovers from Jook-sing. Those who managed to scavenge materials gave a portion of their profits to the more powerful inhabitants.

The dumping grounds' materials had become a source for everything, comprising damaged furniture, cardboard, corrugated steel, cookware—the list was extensive. Items like outdated or disabled electronics could have been cobbled together by some of the inhabitants, had they the will or the necessary electricity to power them. Due to its absence, however, high-tech items were valued only for ornamentation. Building materials were some of the highest valued commodities. The huts of Tolkee were commonly built using corrugated steel for roofs and mud for walls. Four clusters of five huts each were arranged in a circle, with a fire in the center of each cluster.

"Let's get a closer look and see what we're up against," Abner reasoned. "These people seem to be the closest to the drop point, probably the biggest danger here."

"Okay, but I don't want to hang here long," Filet whispered. They headed down the nearest crater face opposite the settlement, and walked around the valley back toward it.

"Keep your eyes sharp...they may have trip wires or something," warned Abner while spying down, the lack of light next to impossible for their vision to penetrate. They had been on Tolkee for several hours now, and their eyes still hadn't adjusted.

Just then, Abner tripped over a thin stick of wood rigged up next to a pile of pots and pans, which fell with a loud crash. The two tried to run back the way they came, but before they could even stop and turn back around in the darkness, a group of fifteen men surrounded them. Four appeared to be the hunters that had been pursuing them all along. Their plan to surprise the two lone men had worked well, and the local inhabitants disarmed them immediately.

The dark shapes whispered to each other as they bound Abner and Marcus and carried them back to the settlement. They returned to the light of their campfire, a blaze fueled by burnt rubber, paper, and other useless things that they had found.

One man, behind them and out of view, spoke. "They look delicious, and if my memory serves me correctly, one's a Shǒuhù Zhě! I haven't seen one for at least twenty years. I could tear one open now, and savor the fine flesh!"

"Yeah!" another responded. "My mouth is watering, sounds tastier than new settlers!"

"We've already eaten one tonight! These'll wait till morrow—annif I catch any of ya samplin' tonight, I'll eat ya alive!" threatened the most evil voice. "Tie 'em up near the fire, I want the meat warm in the morning."

Having been brought close to the light, they could now see their captors more clearly. The group of men were in different phases of transformation from what they once had been. Like deep sea creatures, the lack of light on Tolkee had similarly and severely transformed them. It was easy to guess which residents had lived there the longest, as their eyes had lost most of their color, and had mutated into frosty, white orbs. The residents had also become partially translucent, enabling one to see muscles, tendons, bones, and blood vessels beneath their thin, lifeless skin. The oldest residents possessed an ever-growing evil heart, which matched their shocking appearances. Their physical presences were the antithesis of the Wuxian's glowing countenances.

Abner and Filet were each tied to a post near the

fire, which would have felt nice, but for the knowledge of its purpose. As they were warming, most of the residents left, walking back in the direction of the shuttle's crash site.

"I hate to think of what they're going to do," Filet said, reflecting on what they had mentioned earlier. "Looks like they're going back to the shuttle."

"We've gotta get outta here, Marc!" cried Abner.

For the next hour, they struggled against their bonds, but made little progress. Their toil was interrupted by the sound of the second shuttle's roar overhead as it searched for them in the distance. Regrettably, it passed them, moving toward the drop point. Fifteen minutes dragged by until the residents returned, carrying their catch of five new inmates. They had captured the new prisoners from the shuttle, running them down after the second had left the area. They hog-tied their new catch, including the body of one of the residents who had lost his life in the raid, and dropped them in one pile next to Marcus and Abner.

What next occurred seared itself into both Abner and Marcus' memories forever: the depraved captors slaughtered the prisoners, and then dried their flesh near the fire. The stench which rose from the process was unbelievable, and unable to control themselves, both Marcus and Abner vomited. The sight and smell of the process, combined with their shock, created a trauma which expressed itself in a retching chaos.

"Your'e disturbing my breakfast," protested the leader as he smiled, pointing to Abner and Filet, the torment he was causing filling him with joy. "That's okay...they'll be even more tender eating."

They lost track of time, until the monsters they could see finally finished working, and retired to their huts to sleep. Abner and Filet, exhausted beyond what they thought capable, fell into a deep slumber.

Suddenly, hands clapped over their mouths and they were told to be quiet. The familiar voices of Shǒuhù Zhě filled Abner and Filet's hearts with hope, and they heard blades coming down, shearing their bonds.

All at once, the residents attacked from the shadows. Abner, now hyper-alert, grabbed the leader's arm as he attempted a punch. Fueled with the weight of his body, Abner led the inertia past him toward the fire and released, and the leader fell headlong into the fire. Stumbling to right himself, he instead fell again, and into the burning rubber of a tire. One of the Shǒuhù Zhě, a tall and thin woman, swayed with each attempted blow or kick aimed at her. She managed to lightly tap her aggressor into the fire as well, and both captors slammed into each other in a frantic attempt to remove themselves from the blaze. They fell screaming, one after the other, out of the hot fire and onto the ground. The remaining residents ran, scattering out of sight.

The Shǒuhù Zhě searched the huts and found

Abner's weapons, then led Abner and Filet toward their shuttle near the drop point. They thanked their rescuers over and over again, as shock overtook them due to the trauma they had endured. The team brought them to the shuttle's stairs and helped them board, and as the ship rose above the surface, they viewed the encampments below, in turmoil. Some residents raised torches in defiance, and others fought one another for rank, as their balance of power had now been altered.

Abner and Filet shared agreement in their glances, that this place was where evil belonged. They were only too glad to leave it behind.

# Renewed Vision

The return trip to Jook-sing was filled with anticipation and the restoration of sanity and peace. Abner and Filet delighted in the sun's warmth as they entered into the light again, and it filled each of them with a renewed sense of inner stability and hope. Abner contemplated how odd it had been, that the darkness of Tolkee was able to disorient not only his mind and body, but his spirit as well.

The pilot entered Jook-Sing's atmosphere and managed a low and slow return flight toward New Seattle. Seeing the beauty anew was overwhelming for Abner, and he saw tears streaming down Filet's face as he looked at him. Abner turned away quickly, aware that his own emotions mirrored those of his friend.

Their friends warmly greeted them at the Port of New Seattle. It was a great comfort for them to receive the opposite reaction to their arrival, from what they'd had on Tolkee.

"I was so afraid, Abe. When they couldn't contact you, I couldn't stop thinking the worst," Jenny said, unable to let go of him.

"I'm so glad to be back. I can't talk about it now, but I love you, Jenny."

The crew even hugged Filet. He realized, suddenly, that he needed human compassion and contact more than he'd thought. Many things had changed for him since he had joined them; the kidnapping was just what the old Filet had needed. The changes in him were evident to all of them, and Marcus knew he would never be the same again, that he was a thoroughly changed man. Those that knew him from the past would never have believed it, but that didn't matter to him. The change itself was enough for him.

The group witnessed Marcus develop slowly throughout the next two-and-a-half years. After recovering from the ordeal on Tolkee, he enrolled at the Róngyù Shǒuhù Zhě Jūnxiào. They taught Filet (who was a genius!) that intellect, while an asset when mated with wisdom and honor, was a disability without the latter. Many of his experiences before and during his stay on Tolkee had reinforced this truth Now, the one who had formerly sailed through life and attained goals without effort, finally found the need for tutoring.

The Chengs graciously filled the need for the humbled man, as he made the Wuxian ways his own. The trips to the docks and factories were some of the best methods of character shaping to which he willingly submitted. The experience on Tolkee had cemented in his mind what it was to be a man without honor, without remorse, and without life. Marcus Filet had come to realize that his former life had been leading him down the same destructive path within. He had wisely decided, instead, to take his friend Abner's advice, and stay planted in the good soil of the Wuxia.

Over time, the Chengs continued to serve and be served by Filet. He, like the rest, was taught Jooksing's history and the rich ethics of Wuxian society. He matured in character and skill, his martial arts training balancing equally with the precious value of all life.

In time, he became a close friend to every crew member of the Ulysses. When they had first met, he had been the last person that any of them thought they could ever trust, in any capacity. Now, they were encouraged by his drastic change, and humbly considered their own imperfections. Marcus was a new person, a man of truth and honor, and grateful for the ability to exemplify the values he had received.

His graduation day arrived, and the Ulysses crew applauded their favorite, brand-new Shǒuhù Zhě. Their sincere rejoicing and congratulations became his most treasured achievement to date.

# Graduate School

For the following six months, Jenny began using her intuitive powers while in the presence of the Chengs, but restrained herself from absorbing too much knowledge. As her training continued, she proved her skills—half gleaned through traditional student training, and half through her special abilities, as she 'read' her masters and the other Shǒuhù Zhě of the Jūnxiào. Those of the Ulysses hadn't achieved a level anywhere near hers, but they had become very skilled, in their own right. Jenny had caught the attention of the Chengs before graduation, and she had explained her gift to them. They continued to shape her skills with the hope of passing on all they knew, their mastery of the Shǒuhù Zhě arts, to a younger generation.

The afternoon arrived when Jenny's teachers decided to test her limits. They invited many older Shǒuhù Zhě who didn't know her to the Jūnxiào, and the Chengs instructed them to stay hidden. As planned, Jenny was requested in the training room as the Chengs entered and began a regular routine. At the agreed-upon signal, the elders suddenly crashed through several decorative partitions arranged in the perimeter. They charged and knocked out the Chengs (who played along), and seven seasoned, high-level Shǒuhù Zhě in disguise attacked at once. Jenny, with Píng's wind-like grace, flew above them and stepped onto two of them to gain height. She grew to a whirlwind in Chāo's fashion, throwing kicks between tumbles on the floor or with another opponent. During the skirmish, she 'read' the room, as she was genuinely afraid. Knowing her attackers were focused on their own skill set, she used their concentrations against them with lightning speed. Each fighter lie on the floor when Jenny's fighting storm had passed, all stunned at what they had just experienced and seen.

"Jenny, we must reveal that our training for you today included these Master Shǒuhù Zhě," Chāo explained, presenting the seven masters as they bowed with respect. Chāo introduced each of them in turn.

"This is Thunderhead." A large bald man bowed after striking his head with an open hand.

"Steel Legs." A thin man with large thighs stomped on the floor before bowing.

"Iron Ankle." The master struck a wooden box nearby, which shattered as he bowed.

"Swaying Reed." She swayed in one direction, and returned like a whip to break the boxes on her end of the room; her bow included an exaggerated sway.

"Rolling Hog." He launched himself across the room, then spun horizontally through the air above a display of weapons, eluding every sword, spear, and knife from the rack, and landed with a smile and a wallowing bow.

"Ferocious Hair." His large single braid flew through the air as he jerked his head with a snap, producing a crack like a whip, after which he bowed.

"And finally, Typhoon." A tall, thin lady wore a beautiful, flowing garment which expanded around her as she spun throughout the room. Her garment concealed two swords in each hand, and coming in contact with the remaining boxes, she reduced them to a shredded pile on the ground as she bowed.

All, including the Chengs, stood together and bowed toward Jenny in unison.

"Jenny, we have never before witnessed another with your abilities. Chāo and I have been so amazed by your progress, that we had to test you to confirm our belief, that your gifting is greater than all we have known. You have trained with us for years, now. We will train with you as equals from now on. All of us here today will instruct you in the remainder of our skills during the next six months, as we are blessed to watch you grow even more." Píng bowed again, beaming with the most enjoyable smile Jenny had ever seen her wear.

"I don't know what to say—other than I was truly afraid! But I am honored, beyond anything I could ever hope for today. I would love to train with all of you as much as you think I need." Jenny's eyes welled with tears as the group, with wide grins, drew near to pat her on the back in congratulations.

Jenny continued to train for the following six months. Once she had completed her extended training, the Chengs presented her with a rough gold and silver pendant, fashioned in the shape of a multi-faceted tree beside a stream, and attached to a leather cord.

"This is for you. It symbolizes a tree of many grafted in branches, planted by streams of living water, a receiver of the Light. We would also like to give you the Wuxian Master Shǒuhù Zhě name, 'Receiving Tree'. Jenny, we would like you to consider taking our place as Shifu when we retire," Chāo announced with Píng beside him, as both glowed with happiness. "We know this is a big decision, and we want you to know that we will be satisfied with whatever answer you give."

"Besides, we have many years left before you would need to take over," Píng added.

"You don't know how much this means to me. I will think long and hard on this, Shifu." Jenny bowed with an equally big smile.

# The New Ulysses

The Ulysses crew found various forms of employment in New Seattle. Those who were Shǒuhù Zhě enjoyed some of the highest pay in the city, and were able to work every other day while continuing in their martial arts training.

Peanut, Jelly, and Layerie graduated from NSU with business degrees, and managed a food truck they named 'Peanut Butter and Lasagna'. They created a Thai variation of lasagna, which became their signature dish, and they took turns with other Shǒuhù Zhě patrols before the truck served the lunch rush.

Louie and Karen's success together as a married couple and as business partners flourished, also. They opened a chain of bakeries in the city, named 'Donuts to Humanity', which employed twenty people; Louie continued working twice a week for Shǒuhù Zhě patrols. Loaf's charter tours to the nearby islands and Flip's fishing charter businesses prospered, too. Claus had graduated from The Wuxian Naval Academy and was rising through the ranks as an officer. Maurice's success as a stylist provided him with ample work through a dedicated clientele, and Rob and Bob were content to enjoy their parks department jobs. The Twins, Maude and Angie, rose to the top of their field of biotech firm researchers. Abner and Filet had become close friends following their experiences on Tolkee, and they dedicated themselves, along with Basir, to patrolling full-time as Shǒuhù Zhě. They knew from firsthand experience that a need existed for them.

After returning the Ulysses to E-toll several years before, everyone had joined in a promise to open a joint fund for buying a ship. They found a used KSP-capable ship: a former, upscale, tourist mini-cruiser. It suited them perfectly, and some even moved out of their apartments and into the ship while it was moored at the port. While not as beautiful as the original, they still renamed it the 'Ulysses' to provide a familiar air.

Jenny led the crew to perform all necessary upgrades for its defense and weapons systems. "Shield emitters here, here, and in equal corners at the stern. I'm thinking the SD cannon up top, just aft of the bridge. What do you think, Loaf?" Jenny knew that due to his absorbed DNA, he retained the most experience regarding combat conditions.

"Yeah, that's about right. I would put the laser cannons below on either side. The heat shielding will keep them from burning up the hull if we have to push them," he responded.

"I knew you were going to say that," Jenny responded, which was more true than he could possibly know.

"When are we gonna take it out? I've got the bottle of champagne ready to go!" Louie asked, chewing a donut hole.

"We should be able to finish all the mods in about a week or two. I really don't think it's a good idea to be unprotected if we're going KSP skipping," replied Jenny, while mounting a module to the hull.

"Okay, sounds good." Louie stuffed another donut hole into his mouth. "Donut holes... I wonder if any were changed on the the Dirt Star? I never had a hole taken outta me, but I think it would be fun if you had a detached conjoined twin out there."

"Louie, you're just weird, ya know?" Jenny smiled, actually considering his thoughts. "Thank God there's only one of you!"

"I don't know, it might be good to dunk in some coffee!" Layerie commented.

"Nice. Coming from a Lasagna! You should talk! You lost the best thing about you when you became human!" responded Louie in jest.

"Yeah, what was that?"

"The lasagna!" The crew erupted in 'raspberries' and weak laughter.

"Guess we better put in for some time off, then," Layerie said, still smiling sideways at Louie. "We'll see ya, guys."

"See ya, Layerie!" they said in chorus.

"Alright, we need to get going on this before dark," said Abner. "Where are the harnesses for the emitters?"

"They're in the boxes at the stern," Jenny answered.

Two weeks passed, and with the testing completed, the time arrived to embark with the Ulysses. Champagne bottles shattered as those around cheered their goodwill wishes, and half of the crew boarded; the rest would wait for their vacations to be approved. The crew consisted of Abner, Jenny, Loaf, Louie, Karen, Layerie, Jelly, and Flip. They strapped themselves in while the engines roared to life, and the ship rose upward as those on the ground waved. Loaf took his seat in the captain's chair, Jenny functioned as co-pilot/KSP engineer, and Jelly served as navigator. They used a high-angled thrust to escape Jook-sing's gravity, mainly to test the airframe of the ship.

"Full escape in 10 seconds...There! Looks like she's holding together," said Loaf. "Jelly, where are we going?"

"I was thinking some of you might have a destination. This is the first trip we've taken in years, apart from Meile."

"I would like to go to Earth!" pleaded Jenny. "I really want to see my family again. Life away from them has been good, considering what happened, but I need to see them. I need to know my father is okay, and he needs to know that what happened to me wasn't his fault." An awkward silence fell as all eyes rested upon their friend. Jelly broke the silence.

"Well, I don't think anyone can argue with that. It looks like the KSP to Earth is a quarter of a light-year from the Xióngwěi Supernova. That seems like a destination in itself!"

"I can't think of a better trip—historic!" said Abner, truly excited. His mind began filling with all the possible discoveries they could make, traveling to the home world of the Commonwealth.

The rest of the crew grew more excited as they simply considered approaching the Xióngwěi. There were few things in creation as beautiful as the Supernova.

Loaf engaged the ALS drive, and in the space of three hours, they had arrived within thirty miles of the KSP. The Xióngwěi, in all its glory across the expanse of the heavens, completely encompassed their visibility outside the windows. They were engulfed by it. Its depth, sweeps of color, and light contained an intensity greater than any artwork ever created. The vastness of beauty resulting from a star's explosion, when viewed solely from the point of view of an environmentalist, was extremely wasteful. However, when one considered the expression of beauty, and the energy required to cause such awe in the crew, it wasn't wasteful in the least. Silence reigned, with the exception of the ship's life support systems, artificial gravity generators, and the running of the ice-maker. They paused, entranced, for two hours before moving toward the KSP. There was just too much wonder to absorb, and it wasn't possible to move any faster.

"Well, we can stay here longer on the return trip," Jenny said, feeling as though she was interrupting something sacred.

"Okay, let's get a little closer." Loaf tapped the thrusters toward the KSP zone.

"I've got it, Loaf." Jenny took the controls as they came within a quarter mile of the target. "Here we go."

The ship came within six feet of its target. Jenny began the dance of inputs and control-feathering as she tethered the KSP, and synchronized with the ship's telemetry to Earth. Abner watched as the one he admired the most tweaked the controls with precision, until the time came for the KSP system to govern their journey.

Their sense of time, space, and thought became as one, and light overcame all. The whiteout enveloped everything, and the sound of the ice maker's cubes dropped in overwhelming thuds, as the ship transferred to Earth's solar system. The last cube dropped with a normal sound as they alighted just outside the system's boundary.

# Return to Earth

Pluto was barely visible in the distance, and was merely a large star to the naked eye. While the crew regained their composure after the KSP transfer, the vast loneliness of space surrounded them.

The effects of a KSP transfer upon human anatomy, and those with human DNA, felt as impacting as being beaten with a baseball bat and then hit by a truck, followed by being given a gourmet meal and a massage, and finally awaking on land after having journeyed on a sailboat for a month. The KSP transfer brought one severe pain that was instantly taken away; the traveler was then rewarded with the sensation of a sated appetite and soothed muscles, and lastly the awkward necessity of regaining bodily stability.

Abner wondered if the experience was what death might feel like. He hoped it was indeed like that on the other side, only without the sea legs. The sensations during a transfer happened so quickly that the only way to experience it was in one's memory, except for the unstable feeling afterward (which lasted about fifteen minutes).

"Shall we do some sightseeing, or rifle past all of it to Earth?" asked Loaf, who was still a very young Meatloaf and ignorant of many things. "I've heard the rings of Jupiter are beautiful."

"Well, that's Saturn and Pluto, Loaf, but we've waited this long...we might as well take it all in," answered Abner. "Besides, donuts are a type of ring—I'm sure they'd appreciate Saturn!" The crew reacted in agony to his silly joke.

"Wa, Wa, Waaaaahhh!"

"Boooo!"

"Hissss!"

"Aaaahhh!"

Loaf engaged the ALS drive, and with a quick pulse, they drew parallel to Pluto within an hour. In the distance, it was difficult to discern anything more than a faint, green-gray hue. Closer still lie one of its moons, Nix, which was sapphire blue in color, and appeared to have several volcanos erupting on its surface. They were also able to see the faint, pink shimmer of Pluto's rings, as the weak sunlight passed through them.

"Well, next stop is Saturn, unless you want to go to the other side of the sun to see Neptune and Uranus," said Jelly, adding with a smirk, "The elites left Pluto off the planet list decades ago in this time period, so I think we could drop a planet or two of our own."

"Ha, yeah! I think we can delete a few planets, what the hell?!" Abner sarcastically replied.

"Hopefully nobody lives there. They might feel dissed."

Loaf hit the ALS drive again as the ship accelerated to light speed. Three hours passed until they drew close to the yellow-brown atmosphere of Saturn. The gas giant's surface was a storm of fury, contrasting to its stable, almost tranquil rings. Moving closer to them, they found they consisted of pale, red ice and rock, ranging in size from a meter in diameter to that of dust particles, and moving like balloons as they gently collided and orbited Saturn.

"Looks like me after work," mused Louie.

"Looks like you all day, Louie!" jabbed Layerie, who was actually the laziest of all of them.

"Slight detour toward Jupiter, anyone?" Jelly called. The crew answered all at once.

"Do it!"

"Yep!"

"Okay."

"That's the biggest, right?"

"Yeah!"

Their journey, if one listened to their comments, sounded like it could've been a long weekend of sightseeing from the back of a station wagon.

"OK, here it goes." Loaf nudged the yoke toward Jupiter and tapped the ALS drive. After an hour and a half, they had arrived close enough for a full view of the monster through the windows. The winds, visible on Jupiter, made Saturn's look like gentle breezes in comparison. Its huge planetary eye swirled in front of them, seeming alive with a consciousness, and returning their stares. It felt a bit eerie to them, being stared down by the planet, with its disturbed surface.

After an hour, Jenny couldn't stand it anymore.

"I don't know why, but I kinda feel a little creeped out—can we go?" She wasn't sure whether she was sensing her own emotions, or those of her crew mates, or possibly something from outside the ship and in front of them. Nevertheless, everyone agreed to move on. Jelly provided coordinates for Loaf, and he piloted toward Mars.

The asteroid belt between Jupiter and Mars orbited around the sun, below them. Asteroids ranging in size from dust to that of small moons slowly turned, following a path they had travelled since ancient days. Craters were visible on the surface of the largest asteroids, telltale signs of their ages and mysteries of their very existence. Were they evidence of a long-ago, destroyed world? No one knew. Its ambiguity gave the  asteroid belt an aura similar to that of a cemetery

Once again, The ALS drive roared to life, and they rocketed closer to Mars. In the past, the planet had been a source of fear for Earthlings, but grew to become a second home for many of them. Wealthy eccentrics began making trips to Mars. By the late 21st century, colonization had begun, but most used Mars as a vacation destination only. For humans, its surface could supply a temporary experience, but couldn't adequately provide long-term comfort.

The Ulysses disengaged from ALS using thrusters, and arrived within orbit of Mars. They viewed the red planet below them and its vast, empty surface accentuated by dunes, mountains, and deep valleys. Views like the Valles Marineris made Earth's Grand Canyon seem like a crack on an asphalt road. Mars owned a beauty unlike any other. With the exception of compensating for its weak atmosphere, they could understand why many would want to visit the planet.

"I think we can stay in orbit and get some dinner and sleep," said Abner. "I'm starving!"

"You're always starving, Abe!" jabbed Louie. "I'm glad you dropped me as you did, when the alarms went off!"

"What? That was you?!" Abner was stunned. "You've waited all these years to tell me?"

"Oh, I figured it out about a year ago. Thought it would be funny to shock you with it on some random day! Yeah, actually Rob, Bob, Claus, the Twins, and Basir were in my box, too."

"Louie, you're tripping me out. I think I'm going to have a hard time eating anything again."

"I doubt that, Abe."

"Yeah, you're probably right. Let's eat!"

Dinner was made and devoured, and then each of the crew settled in with a cup of warm tea, and enjoyed the view of Mars' surface through the rec room windows. An hour passed, and one by one, they made their way to their quarters for the night. Jenny and Abner were left alone to finish their tea.

"Did you know?" asked Abner.

"I did, Abe...I just thought they should tell you themselves. I knew they didn't view you like a predator. I think it's a joke between them."

"It's just still weird, even after all this time. I can clearly remember wanting that lemon-filled donut so bad that day. That was until I smelled it, or him. Sheesh, weird!"

The next day, the crew stumbled into the mess hall for breakfast, and Abner caught sight of Louie rounding the corner.

"How can you justify owning a donut shop chain, Louie? Isn't there some great moral rule you're breaking, by selling your offspring or relatives or something?"

"Nah, none of them are sentient. Besides, none were as delicious as me, Abe! I was pretty proud of myself that day, until I was dropped!"

"This is just weird! You're a wack-job Louie. And you, Karen—how can you reconcile this?"

"I had no idea until after I fell in love. I knew he was sweet, but it took some time to know why," she answered, admiring Louie. "He's my zesty boy!"

Her proclamation was met with groans.

"Aaaawww,"

"Boooo!"

"Sheesh!"

They returned to the helm once they had eaten breakfast.

"Last look—too late!" Loaf teased as he engaged the ALS drive without warning, and they rocketed away from Mars. He had taken them off guard, and though they stumbled, they still laughed.

# Earth

Four hours later, Earth grew in their sights from a pinpoint to that of a beautiful blue and green planet. The celestial body was the main attraction in the solar system, a gorgeous gem, from their point of view. The Ulysses came into orbit, and they examined its surface, appreciating its splendor as the planet rotated from morning into night. The lights on its surface shone in an array of studs, giving its night view a star-like quality. Day and night traversed before them. The clouds swirled around the globe, as a small hurricane near Florida's coast came into view.

Jenny's heart pounded, and though Earth's spectacular appearance was beyond what she had imagined, she was eager to see her family. Careful to respect the rest of the crew, she decided to be patient. It had been fifteen years; she could endure another day.

"We can sightsee on our way off planet. Let's get this girl home!" Abner said to Loaf, who was happy to comply.

The reentry was a rough one, due to the effect of

Earth's atmosphere. They felt as heat radiated from the bottom of the ship and warmed the cabin, and they activated the air conditioners.

"Jenny, you remember your address?" called Jelly, her eyes glued to the navigation screen.

"I don't, Jelly. I remember my house was in Pacifica, California, USA. I'll know it when I see it. It's off Cabrillo Highway 1 on the coast."

"That should be enough to go off of," said Jelly, as she typed in the information and forwarded the coordinates. "Here ya go, Loaf!"

"Thanks, Jelly. We're over India right now, so it should be a few minutes before we begin the descent."

The view was striking as the ground raced past below them, their trajectory a low, eastward arch high above India. Nepal flashed past, with Mount Everest only a slight wrinkle below their altitude.

"Okay, we're going to start descending now! Here we go." Loaf guided the Ulysses into a gradual descent.

China appeared below them. As they streamed past, its quintessential design of land combined with manmade structures caught their attention. They quickly glided just north of Shanghai, the busy port city alive with its never-ending work. Ocean freighters filled the Huangpu River delta, and they continued farther inland, deep into the massive city. Loaf matched their descent with a reduction in speed, as the East China Sea, and a flash of South Korea in the distant north, became visible. Japan emerged for a moment as Osaka, one of its 'workhorses', appeared below. Even within the short amount of time that they had seen it, its high-octane, bustling activity had been obvious. For ten minutes afterward, nothing was visible below except the beautiful, blue Pacific Ocean.

Loaf continued to descend, and cut to all thrusters as the Ulysses glided lower in the direction of the sea. Because of the lack of engine noise, flying was a different experience in space than when in the planet's atmosphere. In the vacuum of space, and without the presence of air, the hull of the ship was usually without resistance, rendering it a very quiet flight. In Earth's atmosphere, and with wind resistance against the hull, however, a roar reverberated throughout the entire ship, even with the engines cut. Fortunately, the Ulysses was a re-entry vehicle, created specifically to handle wind drag; many other ships had been built without having being intended for atmospheric entry.

"We're about a minute out, now. I'm gonna return power to the engines." Loaf worked the controls like a thirty-year veteran pilot, and California rose before them, as he maneuvered the Ulysses slightly north. "I'm gonna take us over Sausalito, then head south over San Francisco and Daly City to Pacifica—that way we can get a view as Jenny's memory returns."

"Sounds good, Loaf!"

"Great."

"Yeah, cool!"

Loaf banked hard to the south, and below them, the Sausalito Yacht Harbor emerged for an instant. He continued banking the ship and aligned to the New Golden Gate Bridge, the bridge's modern design nostalgically echoing the former's structure over San Francisco Bay. The city's combined new and ancient skyline encompassed their views from all sides. Fortunately, Earth was unfamiliar with the level of cloaking capability with which the Ulysses was outfitted; they were hidden from all but those who, having heard a roar above them, looked up into the sky. Loaf corrected his flight path to follow Highway 1 south along the coast, and reduced the ship's power to a crawl, as Daly City's traffic passed below at a much slower pace.

"Okay, we should be near Pacifica in a minute," announced Loaf. "I'll move out to sea before we get there, and go into a hover so you can get a better look." Loaf continued tweaking the ship's controls.

"It's so different from above. This might take a while," Jenny said, her excitement growing.

"I think we're gonna need to look for a place to set down. Jelly, got any ideas?" asked Abner, as he scanned the landscape.

"We should be able to set down near Shelter Cove..."

"Wait!" Jenny interrupted. "Did you say Shelter

Cove? That's where it is! It's in Shelter Cove...It
should be right above the beach in Shelter Cove!"

Loaf took the ship closer and just above the beach,
then engaged the anti-gravity system.

"Loaf, can you go further south toward that
point?"

"You got it!"

She pointed. "There! I think it was there. I
remember the brown house with the windsock, and
the blue one with the deck! The two houses in
between don't look right, but that's where it was!"

"Well, let's put it down and ask around," said
Abner. "Maybe a neighbor has some info."

"Okay, sounds good. I think it might be a better
idea if just the two of us go for now. I don't want to
freak them out anymore than what just seeing me
again will do to them."

Loaf landed in a nearby field, and the hatch
opened seemingly out of thin air, as the cloaking
system was still engaged. Jenny and Abner exited
down the stairs and walked toward the street which
Jenny had identified earlier. The hatch closed behind
them, and once again, the ship became invisible.

The sky was clear. The scent of the sea breeze
brought back a flood of memory and emotions to
Jenny, and she struggled to compose herself as the
waves below crashed gently against sand and rocks.
Jenny and Abner turned the last corner toward
Miramar Street, and more memories surfaced in her

mind, of bike rides, of walks with family and friends down to the beach and into town for ice cream, or of walks to friends' houses. Suddenly, they were standing in front of what she had earlier indicated, the spot with the two unfamiliar-looking houses.

"Well, these two are newer than the others in this neighborhood, and this is where my house was before, anyway," said Jenny, fearing she might not find her family.

"There's a transporter in front. Someone may be home."

Jenny pointed. "That's a car, Abner. My dad had a Volkswagen when I was little. This one's not the same, but it *is* a Volkswagen!"

# Reunion

Jenny and Abner rang the bell at the front door, and they listened as footsteps approached. The door opened slightly, and an older version of her father peered out at them. Jenny's heart sank, and she froze, not knowing what to say.

"Yes, can I help you?" he asked.

Professor Timothy Stanley saw two very unique characters, both dressed in beautiful clothing resembling what one might wear for practicing martial arts, and yet different. The fabric was unlike anything he had seen. The outfits matched one another, but each had its own style, as though representing its wearer. The two visitors stood motionless on his doorstep.

An awkward silence ensued, until the professor repeated his greeting. "Can I help you? Are you lost?"

"Dah, it's me, Jenny," she answered, the thought suddenly occurring to her that after fifteen years, a reunion might not go as well as she'd hoped. "I know you probably don't recognize…"

"Jenny?!" he interrupted, "Is this some kinda sick

joke...?" Professor Stanley ceased speaking as he focused on the young woman in front of him. She would have been about this young lady's age after fifteen years, about twenty-two years old. She had a similarly shaped face, and the eyes were...could it be?

For the past fifteen years, he had been devastated by the loss of his daughter. The accident had damaged his marriage, leaving him with only memories of a the best part of his life. The rage inside him began to rise, until he looked back into those eyes. He threw the door open, and clutched her face between his hands, looking deeply into the eyes that he thought he would never see again.

"Jenny! Jenny! It's you! It's you!" he cried, tears flowing down his face as he kissed her forehead. "How?! How, where?"

"Dah, we have a lot to talk about! I'll tell you everything... but first, this is my friend, Abner Oaks. Abner, this is my father, Professor Timothy Stanley."

"No, no! Just Tim! Nice to meet you, Abner."

"Good to meet you, too. Jenny's been so excited to get back here," Abner responded awkwardly.

"Is Mom here?" Jenny interjected, saving Abner from making small talk.

"No, she's at work, but I'll call her! She will be so glad to see you, honey—I can't believe it's you! I see the little girl in there, but I've missed so much of your life! Tell me what happened to you."

The afternoon passed as the three talked, sitting on the deck which overlooked the waves crashing below. Jenny recounted the events that had occurred from the time she entered the lab, and was rescued within the Commonwealth's boundary.

"You were right, Dah! The KSP *is* a real thing! It's being used regularly by many civilizations. We used one to get back here."

"So you've been living within a fleet of starships that haven't left Earth yet? And you've met beings from all over creation, billions of light years away, and thousands of years into the future?" Professor Stanley raised his hand to his forehead; it was all too much for him to absorb. "This goes beyond me, honey. I'm so glad to have you back and to meet your friend, but you'll have to excuse me...I can hardly comprehend this."

"That's okay," Jenny replied understandingly. "This has got to be a lot to take in. Unfortunately, you're probably going to be stretched even more by the rest of what I have to tell you."

"You know, it might be better to wait until Mom gets home before you say anymore. Have you eaten?"

"No, we haven't since breakfast."

"Well, remember 'The Chart House' in Montara? You were pretty little the last time we were there."

"Oh, I remember their mud pie, Dah!" she answered excitedly. "But they closed down a long time ago, didn't they?"

"They just reopened last month, and the food is just as good, if not better! Let's make reservations. We'll leave as soon as we pick Mom up off the floor," the professor said with a chuckle.

Just then, they heard Mrs. Stanley's car arrive, then a door slam, and footsteps running toward the front door. Jenny walked back into the house to greet her mother.

Mrs. Stanley absently dropped her keys and purse, walking toward her. Her husband had explained as much as he could over the phone, but she was still stunned at the sight of Jenny. Her commute home had been in full gridlock, and like nails on a chalkboard, given the situation. She walked toward the young lady, searching for her child.

"Mommy?"

Though it was all Jenny could manage to say, that one word was all Mrs. Stanley needed. Before she had even gotten a close look at her, she had heard the minute inflections of her daughter's voice, different only in its tone. Mother and daughter erupted in tears, and she examined Jenny's face closely.

"Jen-Bug!" Jenny's mother's replied tremblingly. For the next five minutes, they became inseparable. They studied one another's faces, and held the other's hands in their own as they turned them over, observing and remembering the feel of each other.

Abner thoughtfully excused himself to check on the crew as Jenny caught up with her parents.

"Fifteen minutes, Abe!" said Jenny. "You don't want to miss the mud pie! I would travel here—! Wait, I *did* travel lightyears to have a slice!"

"Oh, I'll be right back! You've been talking about that mud pie since you told me about Earth."

The evening passed as the four watched the waves on Montara beach crash against the sandy shore below the restaurant. Jenny described the past fifteen years of her life perfectly, as she was able to sense from them what they needed her to clarify.

She began her story from when she had awakened aboard the Dirt Star, and then described her subsequent adoption. She told them about her growing-up years of being raised by good, loving people, gave an account of her time as an apprentice, and then of becoming a technician with the facilities department. She explained how she met Abner.

There were difficult things to explain, too, especially about the miraculous change that had taken place within her, and the physical effects apparent in her hair. Jenny felt unsure, though, about filling her parents in on her friends, who sat waiting aboard the Ulysses at that very moment. As the discussion progressed, she decided to explain the transformations that had taken place on the Dirt Star, about the myriad of beings she had encountered within the landfill, and how some of them had become her closest friends. She spoke of their life in the Wuxia, the martial arts training with the Chengs, and finally of becoming Shǒuhù Zhě.

"Your life has turned out better than I could have hoped for, honey," Professor Stanley responded, "apart from being there with you through it all." He eyed the slices of mud pie as they were carried to their table. "At least we're together again for mud pie!"

"This is so good, and even better with coffee!" Jenny said with her mouth full, lifting her cup in a toast. "I want to show you what you've been missing, Dah. Mom, you need to come too. The thing about KSP travel? We can spend a year away and get back here tomorrow morning, before you would even need to go to work."

"Well then, let's go!" agreed the professor eagerly. "Let's go tomorrow. I'll call into the office and let them know I'll be out for a few days." The years of doubt and worry were already lifting from his spirit. "I'm ready...Kirstin, what do you think?"

"Sounds even better than the cruise we were planning this summer!"

"Great!" said Jenny. "Let's go home and get some rest, then, and we'll introduce you to the rest of the crew in the morning. Then we'll be off!" Jenny felt a surge of healing course through her body and fill her entire being.

# Clarity

Jenny woke in the morning to the sound of waves crashing and to the scent of sea spray on a beautiful summer's day. She rolled over, reading nine a.m. on the table clock. Jumping out of bed, she dressed, then joined her parents at the kitchen table in front of a large, open window which overlooked the sea.

"I never asked about the house and the neighbor's house. What happened?" asked Jenny.

"We're still not sure, Jen. It all happened at the same time the accident happened," replied Professor Stanley. "We heard the explosion from the beach, and when we got to the top of the hill, a spaceship was lying under both houses, like it had replaced the basements."

"Then it wasn't a dream." Jenny's mind raced back to when she was inside the basement as it floated in space, and to when Captain Ramar Gleek had found her and brought her to the Dirt Star.

"Dream about what, honey?" her father asked.

Jenny recounted how after the accident, she had been in a dreamlike state in the lab within the transferred basement of the house, before the rescue.

"Well, then, you were truly protected for something special, Jen-bug," Mrs. Stanley said. "We seemed to be praying until falling asleep that night. We were devastated and confused about the ship that had replaced you, under the house."

"Tell me about the spaceship. That seems weird," replied Jenny.

"Well, when the accident happened, the lower floors of both houses were kind of... missing. In their place was this spaceship with the name 'The Savior' on its hull."

"The Savior? Jenny! The Savior! That's the name of the escape shuttle that was lost when some kids were playing on it, like, I don't know—a hundred years ago or so in Commonwealth time!" exclaimed Abner.

"That's gotta be it! It was full of kids, too. The authorities declared it was from a different dimension, after finding English literature and some of the data plates on the ship," said Professor Stanley.

"What happened to the kids? Were they okay?"

"They were all just fine. All were adopted. That's been fifteen years ago!" said Mrs. Stanley.

"That's amazing, happening at the same time as our transfer! That's what I mean about how time frames aren't what you would think. That happened so long ago, and the fleet changed protocol for kids under twelve. They've been isolated since that accident."

"What? What do you mean?" asked the professor. "You mean they don't see anyone?"

"Androids, Dah! I thought it was weird too, but it works for some reason, for the most part." Jenny glanced at Abner.

"Nice, Jenny." Abner responded. "Well, I guess if there's no teasing, there's no love. Actually, come to think of it, I guess most of us didn't know any alternative. There are some who do have problems, though."

"How did you handle that, after knowing what the difference was on Earth?" Professor Stanley asked.

"They made an exception for me. The Commonwealth is a good place. Even the isolation of children was intended for their good, after the accident. They know it's not the ideal way to raise them, but while aboard a starship in an area filled with the unknown? It was their best option." Jenny paused, and turning toward Abner, said, "I think we should go now, Abe. We need to introduce them to the crew, and then give them a tour!"

"Okay, where do ya wanna go?"

"I want them to see the Wuxia and meet the Chengs. They need to see where *we* live now." Abner stood.

"All right, let's go! You two ready?"

# Flying Food

Jenny spoke to Loaf through the communicator and asked him to disable the cloaking system, so the experience wouldn't be stranger for her parents than necessary. Loaf met them at the door of the Ulysses, and fortunately, Jenny had forewarned her parents of what they were about to see.

The Stanleys felt as though they were walking into a movie. In the field before them sat the Ulysses, a beautiful ship unlike any they had ever seen, and in its doorway, a being unlike any they had yet seen. Loaf walked down the stairs, addressing them without any concern for his appearance. Loaf had no concept that he was unusual, or beyond imagination; he simply thought of himself as Loaf, and the least changed of the crew.

"Hello!" he greeted the Stanleys. "So good to finally meet the two of you. We've heard so much about you!" Loaf grinned from ear to ear, and his powerfully delicious form bounded down the stairs to welcome them. He thrust out his hand. "It's an honor!"

Professor Stanley, half stunned (though Jenny and

Abner had tried to prepare him), put out his hand without a thought. It indeed felt like the warm handshake one might expect from a live meatloaf.

"Come aboard and meet the rest of the crew."

Loaf led the way up the stairs and inside the Ulysses, where they met Flip waiting at the top. It had been awhile since Jenny and Abner considered the appearance of their friends, but offering introductions gave them a fresh perspective, as they watched the scene unfold.

The professor walked up the short set of stairs to shake the fish-man's outstretched hand. Flip was handsome, tall, muscular, and thin, resembling a human but with one exception: the light-green, iridescent scales which covered his entire body. "Hello! Welcome!" Flip exclaimed. Professor Stanley noticed that his handshake also matched his expectations, as a grasp from a fit, taut man.

They met Karen next, a pretty, Asian lady whom they were told was married to a donut-man. "Hi! Nice to meet you, I'm Karen." Her handshake felt like most female handshakes, a grab halfway to his hand, followed by a light shake.

Louie came into view as Timothy and Kirsten entered the cabin. "Hello, Stanleys! So glad to meet you. We traveled billions of lightyears to do it!" he exclaimed, as only a donut would have. Louie the donut-man appeared to be fully human, as his body had absorbed any donut characteristics during his change. One remnant which remained, however, was a faint lemon scent which emanated from him (though some wondered if it could be cologne). Professor Stanley wouldn't have determined that Louie was the donut-man about whom he'd heard, as the handshake was a normal one, and any difference in its owner was undetectable.

Next in line was Layerie. He, too, had absorbed most of the food portion of himself. "Hi, guys! Welcome aboard the Ulysses!" he said, offering his hand, and the professor grasped it in friendship.

Mice-people are generally shy, as was Jelly, who met the Stanleys last. The professor stood in amazement at the sight of this person of about four-and-a-half feet tall. Her form appeared mostly human, with the exception of her head and tail, and the beautiful, fine hair which covered her. Her head was a well-balanced combination of human and mouse, with large, brown eyes, and small, round ears proportioned as they would be on a mouse. Her hands were also mouse-like. It felt odd to Timothy, as he shook hands with this large, yet kind, rodent.

Mrs. Stanley followed her husband through the gauntlet of new strangers, feeling both amazed and uneasy. She had difficulty absorbing the biological and genetic concepts she had learned about them. She stood looking at their physical bodies, and what they were seeing were realities to which they both must adjust. "Hello," was all she could manage to say, as she was disturbed to her core, yet equally fascinated.

"We have the stateroom for the two of you back here." Jenny led them toward the back of the ship, ushering them to a plush and stately room. "We hope you like it."

"This is great, honey. Thanks," said the professor.

They had been offered the most generous quarters aboard the ship. Showcasing its luxury cruise ship heritage, the room boasted a large bed, a bathroom with a shower, and a reading nook, complete with a library. Its volumes contained Wuxian, E-Tollian, and Meielan works.

"I'm sure you'll find the Wuxian books very interesting," Jenny commented, smiling. "I'll let you get settled. Let us know when you're ready, and we'll take off."

# Return to Wuxia

After everyone had secured themselves, Abner gave Loaf the go-ahead for lift off. Jenny's parents, amazed by their dream-like reality, sat back in their seats, taking in everything as the ship rose into the air without resistance.

The antigravity system engaged, and they ascended above the clouds slowly, careful to avoid air traffic from SFO. The view was spectacular on this bright, summer morning, and the experience was different from than that of an airplane, as the ship slowly ascended. The sight of the subdivision, though obvious before, retreated, and a complete view of Pacifica stretched before them. As they climbed, the ground below became cartoonish; people, vehicles, homes, and buildings slowly shrank and became as though play-toys to the eye. A minute later, they could see San Francisco to the north, and even the lonely Farallon Islands off the coast to the northwest. Eventually, the land below presented itself like a topographical map. They could see several states to the east of California, and as the Ulysses rose higher and higher into the stratosphere, they saw the sunset fall on a portion of the Eastern United States, and night overtake the day.

"Are we ready?" called Loaf, careful to be sensitive to the newcomers.

"Yes!" the Stanleys cried.

"Okay, hold on." Loaf tapped the ALS drive, and the engines roared mightily to life (unlike the absence of sound they would produce in space). It was a good sound, like the feel and noise of a superb sports car. The ship plowed forward, pinning everyone's heads to the back of their headrests, as the ship exited the atmosphere.

"Wow, that's awesome!" the professor attempted to yell above the noise of the engine, but without success. "Ooooohhhh, yeah!"

Mrs. Stanley, terrified in her seat, counted the moments, waiting for it to end. She lie smashed against the seat, white-knuckled, and Jenny encouraged her by mouthing the words, "Almost over." Once the ship had left Earth's atmosphere behind, and escaped its strong gravity, the violent shaking and loud engine noise immediately terminated. The Ulysses, now free of Earth's pull, rocketed toward the moon, and the sound in the cabin lowered to 'pin drop' level.

Jenny turned to Loaf. "Loaf, can you shut down the engines for a bit?"

"Okay." He turned off the thrusters.

"Keep the artificial gravity generators off for a bit,

too."

"You've got it, Master!" said Loaf in his best 'Igor' voice, as he adjusted switches and knobs on the panel in front of him.

"This is the best part about space," said Jenny, and she unbuckled and floated about the cabin. Her parents joined her, and, like playful children, floated weightlessly in wonder. The crew decided it was a good time for space-bowling, and a group of six gathered in a rack formation. Loaf threw Jelly toward them, and she squealed with joy, knocking over four of them. Next, they poured juice into the air, and they drank the liquid blobs as they floated about. They even attempted space ballet and gymnastics, all while enjoying a view of the full moon.

"This is a dream come true, honey!" Professor Stanley declared, as he spun in midair. "Where to next?"

"You'll see! I want you and Mom to be surprised by all of it!"

The return flight to the KSP recounted all that the crew had observed on their path toward Earth, and Professor and Mrs. Stanley witnessed firsthand, that which only unmanned spacecraft had transmitted to its inhabitants on Earth. With Pluto behind them and the KSP ahead, Jenny gave her professor father a basic lesson about the tech involved to harness the element, as they grew close to the particle. His life's work of research set in actual motion, as confirmed by his own daughter, was the most gratifying gift he could have received. Jenny filled in any details about which he was unaware, as Loaf brought the ship closer to the particle. Jenny took over the controls, focussing on the task in front of her. Her parents watched as their offspring's technological dance culminated in a crescendo of time and space manipulation.

"Here we go!" she yelled, as the sound of her voice rose from a natural volume to that of an overwhelming force, echoed by the sights, sounds, and physical manifestations of a KSP transfer upon their bodies.

The transfer coalesced with the sight of the Xióngwěi Supernova, taxing their physical senses. Once again, all were enchanted at its sight; after an hour, the overstimulation of it all had exhausted Jenny's parents. They rested in their quarters, and as the crew decided that an early dinner had been earned, Layerie prepared the meal. They ate together in reverent silence, enjoying the wonder displayed before them through the windows.

They returned to Jook-sing the next day. From their local friends' perspectives, the duration of their entire trip had only been one day. Once the Ulysses touched down on the landing pad at the Port of New Seattle, their friends came running to greet them. The Stanleys had become well-accustomed to the 'unreal realities' before them, by this point, and weren't in the least disturbed as they were introduced to the rest of the crew. They met a half dozen more donut people, which included Claus, Basir, Angie, Maude, Rob, and Bob. They also met the rat-man, Maurice, and another mouse-person, Peanut.

The following day, the Stanleys were introduced to the Chengs, with whom they quickly became friends. Jenny was deeply moved within, as she watched the four together, chatting over their coffee and donuts, the pairs close in ages and temperaments. For her, it felt as though she now had three complete sets of parents.

She noticed her father looking at the donuts a little too long, pausing pensively. As she sensed his thoughts, he saw her staring at him, and they smiled at one another as he picked up a cruller and bathed it in his coffee.

# Loose Ends

After three weeks had passed on Jook-Sing, Jenny's parents informed her that they wanted to remain on the planet.

"We've spoken with the Chengs and have made a plan." Professor Stanley alternated his glance between Kirsten an Jenny. "Honey, this is your home, and we can see why you love it here. The thought of going back to Earth without you is impossible." Jenny beamed as he spoke. "Even if you came with us, I wouldn't want to go back."

"I'm so glad, Dah! What will you do?"

"I'm going to apply at some research facilities, universities, anything. Heck, I'd make a great earth history professor—to me it was yesterday! Mom could do the same, and perform even better than I could! We will need to return to Earth for a while, first. I'll publish my findings in *The Journal*. I'll need to make a withdrawal from my accounts. It'll be interesting to see what the gold-exchange rate is on Jook-sing. If it goes well, we won't need to rely on our incomes."

"Sounds great! When do you want to go back?"

"The sooner the better, honey. That way, we can get back to start a new life."

"Okay. I'll let Abner know. We'd like to get the rest of the crew together for the return trip."

The following day, the second crew met with Abner, Jenny, and her parents at the port. Louie met them on the tarmac and presented them with three boxes of his finest donuts. He made sure to place the less-desirables front and center, as was his custom, reminding them that boring donuts were best served with coffee. The professor, with a big smile, slapped Louie on the back after receiving them.

They returned once again to Earth, savoring the journey this time, instead of cutting it short like before. They took their time and toured the world from above, even making a few stops on their way to Pacifica. Earth's colorful nature amazed them, with its many diverse people, cultures, faces, and personalities. They spent six months traveling Earth and enjoying all it had to offer, including its food. The food! The donut-beings, who had formerly *been* food, seemed to enjoy it the most. Using their hidden translators, they compiled recipes from many countries to bring home to Jook-sing. In the years to come, the recipes became some of their journey's greatest treasures and mementos.

The Stanleys held their precious daughter for a

long while, promising to finish their business within six months and return to the Wuxia. The Ulysses ascended above them slowly, then rocketed away as they walked into the house.

"Am I dreaming, Kirsten?"

"If you are, must be a strong one, TJ!" Mrs. Stanley replied smilingly. "Who knows? After all we've been through, I wouldn't be surprised if even group dreaming was possible!"

Time passed quickly. The Stanleys liquidated their fortune and converted it to gold bullion, and Timothy published his work, which brought him a sense of closure. Ready to move forward with a new life in the Wuxia, Timothy placed their *Last Will and Testament* on the kitchen table for his sister Angela to find. They had left her the house, as well as everything that couldn't fit into the bags they took with them.

The Ulysses roared above them to a stop, descended onto the beach, and the hatch swung open. Jenny ran to them excitedly, and grabbed their bags.

"Ready?" She exclaimed. "I get to keep you from now on!" She walked with them to the ship, feeling the same anticipated thrill she had felt on her seventh birthday, while waiting in her room for peanut butter waffles.

# Future Plans

The Dirt Star appeared in the Wuxia System after transferring from the last planet it had tormented. The Collective had made short introductory visits to several systems, and as many as twenty planets. Its purpose during the prior six months of its journey had been to acquire skills and knowledge, and subsequently strategize. News of its path of terror had traveled to every system. The Collective had learned much while on its travels, and now targeted Tolkee, knowing it held a vast source of wealth.

The Dirt Star, now a drastically different ship from before, drew close to Tolkee. The Collective directed the host at the helm to bring the ship into a low orbit around the moon. Scanning its surface, they found their treasure's source, the most evil and despised group of beings in existence, who had yet to join the Collective. The Yeasts directed the Collective to send out shuttles and fill the Dirt Star with fresh hosts.

The shuttles were sent to the surface, bearing promises of a better life, good food, wealth, and anything else the Collective knew would be a weakness for their spirits. The shuttles, carrying their quarry, docked alongside the Dirt Star. Every Tolkite boarded, reasoning that traveling to anywhere else would be preferable to existing on Tolkee. The new inductees were met by the Collective's most distinguished hosts.

"What the hell is this?" a half-burned monster asked, eyeing a pale man in his late thirties who was formally dressed in a Commonwealth uniform.

The pale, uniformed man looked into the monster's equally dead eyes, responding, "Your new home!" as he offered his hand in partnership. The handshake was all that was necessary to seal the deal, as the Yeasts slowly made their way through the burnt man's hand. They entered his bloodstream, heart, and brain, and saturated every part of him.

The Collective had found what it truly sought, the darkest depth of depravity present in the human condition. It was reborn, whole, for the first time in its years of sentience. The level of evil it contained was welcomed, and it giggled to itself, excited for the succession of handshakes to come. The Yeasts acquired two hundred hosts, their combined wickedness enough to inspire the best. The new hosts, the inhabitants from Tolkee, were now a part of the Collective, and a threat to all but the Collective. As the Yeasts grew within their bodies, they no longer appeared translucent. They became purely white, a purity of another, malevolent point of view.

The Collective gained a new insight into its care of the hosts. As they required feeding to sustain life, the Tolkee inhabitants' knowledge unlocked a way to purify its malicious body, as a whole. The weaker Tolkites themselves became food for the stronger hosts, thereby freeing up vital resources, and providing fresh food for the superior host bodies.

Two of the Dirt Star hosts, once a security guard and a facilities department dispatcher, managed to unknowingly exempt themselves as a food source. Neither realized they had been good friends, formerly. Wildrew Meeks and Enfrick Fren made their way into the reception area for the incoming Tolkites. They were instructed by the Collective to accompany the new recruits to a room, where they could process their withdrawals from independence in comfort. It was by chance that the two friends, though oblivious to their circumstance, had been placed together. The Collective pair led their respective guests to their rooms, one receiving a suite, and the other a standard, single, non-smoking room. It was a carefree walk to their accommodations as the Collective made light conversation with the Tolkites. Meeks and Fren wished their oblivious new guests a goodnight, and then locked them into their rooms for a night of change.

Over the course of the next two weeks, the Tolkites suffered through violent withdrawals, similar to those experienced by heroin addicts. Most lost their minds as they were reborn into the evil Collective. The Yeasts were pleased to pour its full attention and lack of empathy into its new hosts. It enjoyed watching each host lose humanity's greatest gifts, such as honor and self-will.

The Collective, however, provided the necessary items needed for life through older hosts, like Enfrick Fren and Wildrew Meeks. The Dirt Star hosts offered a hospitality crew like no other, preparing tasteless meals rich in nutrients, carbohydrates, and proteins to ensure that the entire host crew remained strong. The older hosts, along with the Tolkites, enjoyed the fruit of their labors as they unknowingly consumed a well-balanced diet of vegetables, fruit, breads, and also the bodies of some of their good friends. The old saying 'you are what you eat' took on a new level of meaning.

As the full, combined knowledge of the incoming inhabitants built up within the Collective, the Yeasts became aware that Tolkee itself could be an excellent base of operations. *Location, location, location,* the Collective chuckled to itself, as every host aboard echoed in laughter. It was the perfect place—a dark, damp environment, with a stagnant water supply. Even the native, growing mushrooms provided evidence that the Yeasts could flourish there. New inhabitants would be brought to them, and, depending upon their strengths, would become either hosts or food sources. The surface of Tolkee had never been under surveillance, apart from the drop zones, so plenty of room existed in which to grow mushrooms undisturbed. Even the deposited trash could become sources for raw materials.

The Collective, filled with sick joy, duplicated its smile upon every dead-faced host aboard the ship.

# Exploration

Jenny's parents were establishing a new life and home on Jook-sing, and had decided not to join them on this particular trip.

No one was certain who had mentioned the chosen planet first, but everyone had found the suggested destination fascinating. Three KSP transfers were required to reach the solar system, as it was several trillion lightyears from the Wuxia. This time, the crew may have underestimated their personal investments. Had there been children aboard, the amount of 'Are we there yet?' questions would have been torturous.

"I know we talked about the time it would take for this trip," said Layerie. "I guess I didn't realize how much a month onboard would be similar to eating liver every day." His complexion was growing more ashen by the minute.

"Well, this last transfer will get us to the system, then it'll be a matter of hours, Layer." Abner felt the same as the rest, but he hid his irritation more easily. He watched others of the crew, as they reached the limits of their frustrations, shifting in their seats or pacing the ship. He hoped that the world they sought would be worth their efforts.

Marcus completed the final calculations for transfer as the rhenium fiber contacted the particle. The crew's spirits couldn't help but revive; anything to break the monotony was welcomed, and a transfer was far from mundane. The transfer occurred just as Jenny, Loaf ,and Louie were finishing lunch. As all sound and vision compressed into echoing thuds and bright light, each noticed that the taste of food amplified significantly. It was as though the food's best aspects became eternally present, in that moment. They found their experiences to be gourmet ones, even though the actual consumed food was subpar, dehydrated, and rationed.

"That was amazing!" exclaimed Louie as the enhanced flavor dissipated.

"Delicious! I can't believe that was just dehydrated grits! It was as though the food was outside of time, back to when it was just picked, only from some kinda heaven garden or somethin'!" cried Loaf, while chewing his now beyond-bland mouthful.

Jenny, attempting to quell her boredom, had been reading them both as the transfer began. She had experienced all three encounters separately, but at the same time, and was nearly speechless. "Grits, tofu, and a peanut butter and jelly sandwich," she said. "I would pay thousands to have that meal at a restaurant again! I'd never have believed it, if we hadn't just gone through that! Think I'm snacking on something on every transfer from here on out!"

As they continued talking, the Ulysses appeared just outside the orbit of the furthest planet from the Maffteak System's sun. Their destination was the second planet from the sun, Dejeal. They chose to explore the world due to its unique characteristics, a place unlike any other, and accessible to outsiders only ten years before.

Loaf powered down the ALS drive and continued the remaining distance to Dejeal with thrusters. There, ahead of them, lie the gleaming sphere. Its outer atmosphere was a thick layer of polished ice, reflecting sunlight toward the next planet in a series of orbits from the system's star. The nearby planet, a grey, red, and blue gas giant, came to life as the reflected light intensified its beautiful image. The Ulysses began its orbital descent of Dejeal, and they arrived outside the path of reflected light, where they could view the surface beyond the ice dome. The dome caused a refractive anomaly from their vantage point, giving Dejeal the illusion of a diminutive size.

The planet had been isolated from the rest of creation due to its atmospheric dome, since Dejeal's ice shield created its unique characteristics. The upper firmament rendered life on Dejeal to be vastly different from any other planet in existence. It allowed for an almost hyperbaric pressure, providing the terrestrial inhabitants many advantages. One such asset included super-oxygenated blood, and both blood cells and plasma were affected. Every intake of breath was like powering a dynamo. Dejealite people could run long distances without becoming winded or tired. Other aspects of life on Dejeal sounded equally fascinating to the crew, too. Already, the toil of long-distance space travel was beginning to pay off.

Residents had never desired to leave their planet, but as the ages passed and each new generation emerged, interest had grown. It was a precarious risk to install a freighter-sized interlock. They constructed the inside of the dome first, then completed the exterior docking port five years later, and Dejeal began exploring its own solar system.

By chance, a Dejealite ship was met by an exploratory ship from the Gomane System, which had been charting the Maffteak System for over fifty years. The E-Tollians were surprised to learn that the explorers originated from Dejeal. Over time, they made an alliance with one another, and E-Tollians became the first visitors to Dejeal. Dejealites, having an aptitude for KSP travel, were welcomed to their world as well, and traded for their technology. The mystery of Dejeal piqued the interest of many, and as a result, became a destination for those who had the patience to travel there.

# Without Reference

The Ulysses was now in sight of the Dejeal Locks Authority. A deep-voiced translation sounded through the intercom, the speaker's tone and speech indicating that he was a being of great power and importance.

"This is Dejeal Lock Authority! Please identify and state your intent."

"This is the Ulysses of Jook-sing. We are a private ship, and our intent is tourism," Abner responded, both intimidated and excited.

"Affirmative, Ulysses. You're cleared for lock position three west. Enjoy your visit." The massive voice, though it appeared welcoming, was nonetheless unnerving.

The Ulysses thrusted forward to its lock position, the bay beyond massive in size, and dwarfing what would be necessary for a Supermax freighter. Five minutes after touchdown, the lock closed overhead, and once sealed, the chamber was slowly brought to Dejeal's atmospheric pressure. The Ulysses had been instructed before the process began that the crew must stay within the lock for twenty-four hours, as their bodies acclimated to the increase in atmosphere.

"So, can we leave? Or do we have to wait on board?" asked Jelly, eager to leave the confines of the ship.

"Yeah, they said we could get out and stretch—we just need to stay in the lock. There's supposed to be like a small town out there," responded Loaf.

"Great! I'm outta here!" proclaimed Jelly. "I can't handle another minute! Anyone wanna come with?" Barely restraining herself from running, Jelly began to power the stairs, her hand on the hatch's exit latch.

"I don't think any of us are staying on board," Loaf said, wanting to push past her and get outside. The rest of the crew agreed, and after grabbing what they needed, lined up behind them.

They trekked out of the ship and into the lock, which was unusually large. The Ulysses was dwarfed by cavernous dimensions, as if parked inside a stadium; their ship happened to be its sole occupant, making the lock's scale appear even more pronounced. They journeyed toward the far end toward what looked like a duty-free mall, which served travelers. As they approached, they saw that the stores were divided into two sections, according to scale. The shops on the right side were of average dimensions, and what a human would expect of a store. The size of the shops on the right side, however, indicated why the dimensions of the lock were so gigantic, and why the voice of the lock authority controller with whom they had spoken had sounded so impressive.

The shops on the right side were constructed to accommodate beings of at least twenty feet or more in height. Presently, the markets were vacant, as the Lock Authority was aware they weren't needed for serving the Ulysses crew. The absence of those who could've filled their spaces made the travelers stop in awe, and an eerie feeling overtook them as they continued walking. They felt like grasshoppers. They gazed up at the unremarkable architecture, and though it was utilitarian in decor, they still felt as though they were treading through a monument, of sorts. Not having the reference of its inhabitants made the experience a chilling one. After walking through the enormous shops and restaurants for about an hour, including the bathrooms, they speechlessly returned to the other side, which was staffed with average-sized Morfarians.

"Welcome! Welcome to Dejeal!" said a very kind-faced woman, as she opened the main entrance doors. They stumbled inside, still aghast after seeing the sideline curiosity of architecture.

"Yes, we see expressions like yours regularly! The Lock Authority attempts to keep our kind separate from those who are recently acquainted with Dejeal." The woman, whose name tag read 'Florance', spoke with a soothing tone and calmed them with her kindness. "I sometimes think that whether Dejealites lived here or not, we would be frightened like a jepseak running from a peesk every time we saw one, because of their size! But, you know, I've never met one I didn't like. Oh, they're big, but their hearts are bigger!"

Jenny's eyes, when locked upon her, verified she was speaking truth. Having seen the rooms next door, she and the rest were relieved to hear the clerk's comforting words.

"So, how big are they? And what do they look like?" Filet asked, reassured by her words.

"Well, they look much the same as *they* do," she replied, pointing at Abner and Jenny, "just bigger! They're breathtaking if you're not ready for the sight of 'em."

"We've heard a lot about this planet, but nothing about them! Do you know why?"

"I think they've tried to keep news of their size quiet, realizing others might be afraid of them! You can imagine how fear of the unknown can play on one's prejudices."

"So, when will we be introduced to them?" asked Abner, his excitement outweighing his fears.

"Well, we can arrange it if you like, anytime. Our living quarters, big and small, are behind the shops. We all get along. Our biggest problem is making sure they see us!"

The crew found a pub across from a fine arts shop,

and they tasted their first bite of the surface's produce. The colors, textures, and flavors of the fruits and vegetables reminded Jenny, Loaf, and Louie of their KSP lunch experience. They shared knowing looks and wide smiles. The pub offered both fruit and green salads, and large glasses of delicious beer. Bread, fresh from the oven, filled the room with a rich, intoxicating scent, and they slathered each monstrous slice with butter and an assortment of cheeses.

One of the crew, looking at a wall clock, suddenly realized that several hours had passed since they exited the Ulysses. Not only had they enjoyed the meal, but they had also started noticing effects from the slow change of pressure within the lock. Relaxedly content, they moved from the pub side to its adjacent lounge, ready to unwind. The room was lopsided, one side built for their proportions, and the other for the Dejealie. The effects of good food, pressure, and heightened oxygen calmed everybody. Florance approached through a small door situated within the large entrance door.

"I'd like to introduce you to a good friend of mine," she said, "if you're ready. She is the daughter of the castack of the Ee-eb clan. The castack is very much like a king, one of the greatest of Dejeal. She is waiting to meet all of you. Can I invite her here?"

It seemed strange to them that a princess of Dejeal would humbly be asking permission of her planet's visitors. A potent impression of honor permeated the room as they considered Florance's request.

"How could any of us not welcome her?" Abner replied, his heart racing with fear and curiosity. Jenny squeezed his hand, and he returned her anxiety and excitement with a squeeze of his own.

# The Drestak

"I present the Drestak Anai." Florance moved to one side of the doorway.

As the thirty-foot high door opened, the movement blew a warm gust of sweet-smelling wind inside. The opposite of what they had expected walked into the room. The drestack's countenance, a mixture of majesty, wisdom, and humility, amplified with her height of twenty feet. At first, due to her proportions, her arrival intimidated the crew; as she gracefully entered the room, though, the elegance which accompanied her surprised them. She was adorned in a long purple dress, of the Eb-eb design. Gold bracelets and necklaces bedecked her, and a thin, golden scroll lie upon her brow. The beauty of her presence was exemplified in her skin, which possessed a perfectly rich, dark, caramel tone.

"Welcome to Dejeal. I am Anai Eb-eb. I was pleased to receive your acceptance to meet." The princess's kind and graceful femininity was contrasted by, yet also enhanced, the power of her voice. They had expected it to be as a man's, due to her size, and were surprised to hear an evenly-toned, female voice, saturated with powerful wisdom. "How can I serve you today?" she asked.

Abner stepped forward, at once feeling awkward and inferior, both in size and caste. "Thank you, um...Your Highness." He blushed and hung his head slightly. The princess grinned at him and broke into free laughter, which eliminated his worries and brought a smile to his face. He straightened his posture. "Princess, thank you for your humility," he said.

She offered her hand in friendship, and her smile reduced the crew's fears, too. She towered over all as she knelt to reach him, which made them grateful that she was a kind being. Abner's hand seemed like a newborn's in hers, and he felt great strength suppressed in her light handshake.

"I am told you are from Jook-sing. A beautiful place, I hear, with a people matching its beauty inside, as well as out. But, I must admit, I was told its human ancestry was of an Earth place called Asia. Only you appear of that land." As she looked into the princess's eyes, Karen remained speechless, but not out of intimidation; the raw power within the room overwhelmed her.

"We are originally from the Commonwealth fleet," Abner began. "We sought refuge in Jook-sing, and fell in love with the land and its people."

"I see. I do not know of this 'Commonwealth'.

Please explain."

Abner and Jenny introduced the Commonwealth fleet and each member of the crew's histories. All observed as the drestack's beautifully massive face altered its expression, as she actively listened. She asked many questions of each member who, once warming to her, began to speak freely. She was amused and concerned, shocked and worried as she listened to their stories. The group eventually turned the questions around to her and to details about Dejeal.

"I am one hundred and ten years old, next week!" she said, beaming with youth, to the shock of everyone in the room. The princess appeared, apart from the palpable wisdom and strong presence she projected, to be very young physically. All would have described her as in her mid-twenties. She understood their reactions and explained.

"Our people live to be over a thousand years old, so yes, I am considered a child by many of my family. In fact, I'm still not done growing! The Creator gave us long lives due to his design of this world." She went on to explain why their planet was so unique, in comparison with other planets. "Dejeal's canopy protects us in many ways. Obviously because of the sun, most planets receive a massive dose of radiation, UV, and gamma rays through their atmospheres. We only obtain the pure, filtered lights, however. The canopy allows the pressure to be sustained for optimum life. We heal quicker than other species, absorb oxygen better, and blow out birthday candles longer! The canopy also explains our size. You have yet to see the surface! You will find all life on Dejeal to be larger, from the plants and trees to insects and animals. It is very similar to how life once was on your planet Earth!"

Abner and Jenny gazed at each other in shock. Jenny, while reading the drestack, knew she was speaking honestly, and she realized that Earth's present condition was that of a damaged planet. Though the distant memories of her home world were loving and appreciative, she now felt as though she were grieving, in light of this new truth.

The princess became sensitive to their realizations, knowing the power that her concepts elicited, and she turned the subject to her life on the surface. She was the youngest of her family of forty-three siblings, and chosen to be the emissary to new visitors. Her father, the castack, had chosen Anai due to her gracious, hospitable personality and her inherent royal presence. She told them of her faith in the Creator, who had balanced everything so well on her planet. She lit up even more, while speaking of her newfound love for a young man of one hundred eighty years old. Once again, the crew was delightedly entertained as they observed her enormous, expressive face. Suddenly, the crew realized that they had been talking for several hours, and had missed dinner.

"It has been my joy to meet all of you. I have been changed by it! I would like to accompany you tomorrow to the surface, if you like. I would love to be your guide."

All agreed excitedly to her overwhelming offer. The princess embraced them, bestowing upon them her final smiles for the night, and said farewell to her new friends. As she rose from her seat, once more the mere movement of her frame disrupted the air within the room, causing a gentle, sweet-smelling breeze to envelop the visitors. The breeze continued to flow as the door closed behind her. One by one, each member exited the room to walk back to the Ulysses.

Though each had been moved by the experience with the drestack, curiously, it was Marcus Filet who had been moved the most of any of them. He had thoroughly transformed, due to the enlightening experiences since his abduction, and had gained great respect for those whom he would've once disregarded or abused. He owned no prejudices associated with race or gender, and Filet honored all with sincerity.

As the crew's acquaintance with Drestack Anai Eb-eb unfolded, it further cemented Filet's new nature. Previously, he'd never had the ability to appreciate honorable, feminine character and power. It surprised him that he had developed a fondness for the drestack, though, and even had a 'puppy love' for her. It was ridiculous, and he knew it, but he couldn't shake how her presence had filled the room with her wisdom, grace, elegance, and power, combined with humility. As he pondered meeting her, he began to realize he had known the same experience before, having subtly expressed itself through many women he had met. His reasoning confirmed it. His past self-absorption had blinded him to the greater joy, of beholding those women as they actually were. His narcissism had reduced them, entirely.

Filet closed the door to his room and got into bed, feeling like a child being tucked in for the first time. His admiration had grown for all of his new friends, but especially for Jenny, Ping, and his precious Anai.

# Facets of Dejeal

The morning began with excited conversation over breakfast. Everyone agreed that the change in air pressure had greatly affected them. They felt more than merely energized, and their moods weren't based upon an artificial exhilaration, like a coffee overdose. They felt a perfectly balanced blend of life and boundless energy. The anticipation grew as they discussed their conversations with the princess the night before, and anticipated what they would experience in a few hours.

"Now I know how a donut hole feels. We were so small next to her!"

"Yeah, you're starting to get it, Louie! There's hope for ya yet!" Layerie threw a piece of cereal at him with a sideways smile. Louie caught it in his mouth and grinned, throwing a handful back, and a group food fight began as everyone joined in the revelry.

Abner pondered that, ironically, he was actually *playing* with food. "Alright, guys!" he said. "We need to clean this up. The lock to the surface will be opening soon! Drestack Anai will be meeting us at the port below."

The lock authority controller sounded over the intercom. *"Ulysses, the lock gates will open soon."*

Filet enabled the Ulysses' hover drives, and the ship raised an inch above the lock gates. They began descending to the surface slowly, passing through layers of atmosphere, their destination in view directly below them. On the horizon lie a vast forest, which surrounded gardens and lakes, and to the east, the seashore bordered an endless turquoise ocean. As they descended, treetops scraped the sky from a height of one thousand feet. When the Ulysses dropped farther, and came within closer proximity of the trees, they could distinguish conifer and deciduous varieties which originated from afar. They entered into a column which had been cleared through the trees, and which led to the landing site below. The clearing itself was approximately ten miles in circumference.

In the distance, to their port side, a Supermax freighter sporting the colors of Jook-sing was ascending toward the open lock above. Below, an array of starships filled the port, including Supermax class freighters, whose size had once been considered gigantic. Other starships of various sizes lie below as well, including small cruisers like that of the Ulysses. Some, obviously of Dejeal design and scale, were moored next to the Supermax ships. The Dejealie ships, triple in size, were not freighters; they were simply cruise ships, similar to the Ulysses, but built to hold no more than fifty Dejealie passengers. The night before, they had experienced the diminutive nature of themselves when meeting the drestack. The view before them, however, revealed an even greater sense of their miniature proportions.

The Ulysses, guided by their slip's homing beacon, lightly touched down on the pavement. The crew marveled at what they saw, gazing out the windows and upwards. Had it not been for the effects of atmospheric pressure upon their bodies, their overpowered senses surely would have caused them to faint.

Abner opened the hatch and lowered the stairs, admiring the colossal engineering displayed in all directions. In the distance, and covering miles within minutes, a figure grew in size, as it ran from the outside of the port and toward them. Her bounding gait shook the ground, as each stride covered a distance of at least twenty-five feet. Still a mile away, she slowed her pace, and Abner calmly recognized her as the princess. She approached the ship with casual, fifteen-foot strides.

"Welcome to Dejeal!" Anai proclaimed in a happily relaxed tone, unaffected by the high speed she had run to meet them. "Are you ready to go?"

They cheered in excitement as they bounded off the stairs and onto the landing pad below. Anai explained that surface transportation was unnecessary, as the effects of Dejeal upon their bodies would allow them to run for hours if they chose, and without becoming exhausted. They tested her reasoning. She led them on an hour-long run from the tarmac and into the woods on ancient paths. Only an hour later, they had covered twenty-five miles. Anai consciously attempted to walk slowly, so as not to outpace them (as the tallest of the crew, Filet only reached the height of her knees).

She announced it was time to eat lunch. They detoured down a different path, entering a lush garden filled with fruit trees, vegetables, and various kinds of melons. The wild garden pulsated with life, as no weeds existed on Dejeal. Anai picked what seemed to be a fruit from the ground, brightly colored and the size of a small watermelon. It looked like a berry in her hand, however. Its bright red hue complemented the delicious scent, which filled the air around them after she took her first bite.

Everyone joined her, partaking of the garden's harvest, as they peppered her with questions: "Can we eat everything here?"..."What is this?"..."This one looks and smells like bread!" Anai encouraged the crew to enjoy themselves, stating that there were no poisonous plants, or any plants or trees that weren't somehow useful on Dejeal. Everyone tasted each other's food, the sizes of which were bigger than what one could consume alone. Each bite, like the sample experienced the day before in the locks, was deliciously tantalizing, and the rich smells of the forest enhanced their flavors.

As Anai called them in the Dejealie language, many varieties of animals and birds began entering into the garden to feed. "This one is my favorite!" she said, bending slightly to nuzzle the neck of a beast. It looked similar to a cow, though with an apparent intelligence dissimilar to earthly bovines. The fifteen-foot high cow gave a powerful, yet affectionate moo as she stroked its neck. "I call her Tina! I believe it's an Earth name. It matches her spunky personality." Tina the cow trotted in place with delight, careful not to trample the crew by mistake. A five-foot tall, chubby, duck-like bird waddled toward Anai as she tempted it with a handful of lettuce. Several more animals drew nearby as Anai called them, and they contained an ease about them, knowing she would cause them no harm. When she had finished, they wandered back to the forest. The duck and the cow were the last to depart, looking back at their master, the drestack, who smiled at them warmly as they wandered off.

"Tonight you will meet the castack and the rest of our clan, if you choose," the princess said, as she offered a gift to Jenny and Abner. "These are for you. They are *chel*, a traditional gift of clothing for our guests." The princess presented robes to the rest. The garments had been created to compliment, but not mirror, their clan's attire. The crew was pleased with their garments, and accepted Anai's invitation. "That is tonight, however!" she said. "We still have much to see before then."

As they traversed hundreds of miles within a day, each was amazed, feeling energized by the journey. They were familiar with the opposite reaction, the resulting exhaustion after a long trip, and collapsing into a chair. On the other hand, the sights, sounds, and smells of Dejeal were without equal, and the entire planet was robustly alive. Death did not reign here. Nearly everywhere one looked, something grew and produced a fruit to eat, or a source of beauty, or a pleasant scent. Most growing things were a rich blend of all three, and their senses feasted upon them.

Anai led them to the sea, and they observed whales draw close to the shore. As the crew walked, Anai explained that their blood was now deeply oxygenated, and that they could hold their breaths longer than they might imagine. Everybody tried; the record holder was Loaf, who reached fifteen minutes before drawing in another breath, and when he did, he felt instantly relieved and not breathless.

At Anai's suggestion, they decided to dive alongside the whales. She directed them to pat a whale's blowhole gently, which signaled the beast to surface. The princess chose a large, multicolored whale. The rest chose dolphins for themselves, which were closer in size to small whales, from their perspective.

"You're right! They're smaller, but they are the

most playful of all. You will need to hold on!" Anai
smiled, knowing what kind of ride they were in for.

She took each dolphin aside and whispered
something, patting each on its head. As she finished,
the entire pod raced around them, flipping and
rolling through the air. They were the 'jet skis' of their
kind, used to playing with the children of Dejeal, and
now excited to play with the visitors. Anai handed
each crew member a saddle, which slipped over the
dolphin's dorsal fin, and allowed for an anchor
between the seat and stirrups. The tack fit
comfortably for both dolphin and rider. The drestack
led the group out to sea, slowly at first, then more
quickly as they raced ahead. She demonstrated that
with light hand pressure just forward of the saddle on
their sides, they could instruct the mammals to dive.
The dolphins and riders took turns at shallow depths
as each rider leaned forward, his breath held. They
eventually grew accustomed to the technique, and the
dolphins and riders became as one, leaping in and out
of the water.

As their confidence increased, Anai led them to
greater depths on a journey to the beauty below.
Creatures, more of them large than small, teemed all
around, and the plants were as abundant below as
they were on the surface. They were glad Anai led
them, as they knew that getting lost could be a simple
fate in the underwater forest.

# To-choobee

After four hours of playing, they returned to the shore. The crew hugged their newfound, aquatic friends in parting, watching as they leapt even higher without their riders, and swam out to sea. The crew departed for nearby huts to change into their chel.

Time had flown quickly, and they were once again famished after the day's joys. Anai led them to the To-choobee, a great hall, not far from the seashore. The sun was setting as they entered.

The entire clan, at least two hundred men, women, and children, stood and greeted them, chanting, "*Chel*-oto, *chel*-oto!, *chel*-oto," in various tones and volumes. Every face of the clan shone brightly with smiles while the chanting continued, and they wore the traditional Eb-eb clothing. Some wore elaborate headdresses, other women and men had shaved heads, and yet others were adorned with intricate braiding in their hair. The crew's *chel* did, in fact, complement the Eb-eb pattern and design.

"They're welcoming all of you to the clan—you are now our cousins!" Anai explained, as the chanting ceremony continued. A group of ten colossal men, each thirty feet tall and very lean and toned, walked forward into the center of the To-choobee. They began to play a variety of instruments which the crew had never seen before, and the men joined one another in an energetic and mysterious tune. Another group of ten men joined them in the center of the hall, and began what could only be described as a combination of dance and gymnastics. The intricate dance included flips and spins, and dancers catapulted from one another's shoulders. Their movements and clothing caused the air to stir into a whirlwind, and the ground to tremble, within the To-choobe. The pure power they displayed was exhilarating. The visitors were deeply humbled, knowing the ceremony was a gift from the Dejealie, and specifically meant for them. All at once, the music and dancing ceased and the dancers froze as the castack emerged from the crowd surrounding the dancers.

He was also a very large man, at least thirty feet tall, with grayed and closely-cut hair. He was obviously Anai's father, as he shared her brilliant smile and air of vast wisdom. He resembled the rest of the clan in clothing and adornment, with the exception of a golden, scrolled band, similar to what Anai wore. He approached the crew and knelt as far as he was able, nearly crouching on his hands and knees.

"Welcome to Dejeal and the Eb-eb! Anai has told

everyone here about all of you, and she is never
wrong in discernment. This celebration is for you,
based upon her opinion of you, and she is *never*
wrong!" His smile broadened, revealing perfectly-
proportioned, beautiful white teeth. "I am Lou, and I
am very pleased to meet all of you!"

Anai introduced her castack father to each visitor
one at a time, finally reaching Louie. "And this is
Louie, father! You have the same name!" They
chuckled as Anai explained that the name 'Lou' in
Dejealie meant, 'rugged outside, gentle inside'. Louie
couldn't help but laugh himself, as he offered his
hand in friendship to the castack, who enveloped him
in a giant hug instead. "Now you are all family!" he
proclaimed to all.

The music began once more, and huge platters of
fresh fruits and vegetables were brought into the To-
choobie, along with many prepared dishes on platters
the size of small swimming pools. Lively conversation
ensued between the crew, the castack, the drestack,
and many others of the clan, some of whom were
members of the royal family, and others common folk.
The feast lasted deep into the night. The crew
discussed how odd it was, considering all that they
had experienced in one day, that they were still full of
energy.

One by one, the members of the Eb-eb began to
excuse themselves to return home, beginning with
those caring for babies and small children (who were

double Filet's height). A Dejealie brought her
newborn near them, so they could hear the infant's
lightly cooing snores as he lay in his basket. He was
three days old, and slightly larger than all of them,
but much more adorable, of course. The crowd
dwindled, and the castack wished the visitors
goodnight, his broad smile beaming as he slowly
sauntered home.

As the group was exiting the To-choobe, Anai
suddenly halted in the darkness. "I just remembered!
Follow me!"

They followed her up a path that led away from
the shoreline and up a hill, and as it was difficult to
follow in the darkness, they kept their eyes on the
princess. Ascending the hill, they found a clearing
among the monstrous trees that had previously
blocked their view of the night sky.

"This is something you can only do here!" she said
excitedly, pointing into to the sky.

As they gazed above them into the firmament, they
discerned what seemed to be anomalies present in the
ice shield. Miraculously, the irregularities were
actually naturally-formed, optical lenses on the ice
shield's surface. "We'll need to wait a bit...watch the
Honchee!" She pointed at one of the five moons
overhead, as it made its way across the dramatic night
sky. Peering into a lens within the firmament, they
noticed that the stars within its circle appeared much
larger than any others in the sky. Without knowing

what they were seeing, they simply assumed they were large stars. After fifteen minutes had passed, however, the moon began to enter the focus of the lens, and its edge grew three hundred times larger than the rest of it. It took at least an hour for Honchee's orbit to pass through the lens, or *gles*. Every second provided astounding, high-resolution detail, as one viewed rocks, craters, and deep fissures on the moon's surface.

Anai explained that each lens in Dejeal's sky was positioned to view all the visible celestial bodies from different vantage points on the planet. There were thousands in the firmament, every one of them differing in magnification power. Dejealies would travel at different times during the year, to view creation through them. After that evening, the crew journeyed to other *gles* sites during their remaining nights on Dejeal, and discovered the glories of the heavens in wonder.

Anai led them to an appropriately-proportioned guest home, and bid them goodnight from outside the door, as she was unable to enter the house herself. Filet stood behind Jenny and Abner and just inside the doorway, unable to pull himself away from his impossible attraction. He had become fond of Anai and her family to a fault, knowing he must soon leave them behind. He reasoned that his infatuation was ridiculous; to even feel the emotions that flooded him, for someone beyond him in so many ways, must be absurd. The group wished her goodnight. Marcus was relieved that his secret love was secure, and that only he knew of it.

The group had enjoyed one of the fullest days of their lives, and they settled in for an equally enjoyable rest. The guest house was beautifully decorated, and full of comfortable beds, each designed to mimic a nest.

Louie made certain everyone remembered that he and the castack shared the same name, found his personal royal bedchamber, and fell asleep. As he slumbered, he dreamed of giant, talking, jelly-filled donuts with big teeth.

# A Farewell to Paradise

They had lived with the Eb-eb for almost two weeks, finding life on Dejeal to be a treat to the senses and heart. The clan members had proven their words to be true, when they had declared that the crew were members of the family. The words weren't merely sentiments as in a greeting card, but were backed by genuine relationships. Their kind, both young and old, had developed a kinship with each of them. Their intimacy was so profound, that their differences in physical size were easy to ignore, for both sides.

The castack had grown fond of Louie and the other donuts. It had taken him time to absorb the truth about their transformation. In the end, he constantly reminded them that he loved food, especially sweets. His relationship with Abner and Jenny was like that of a father, and perceiving that they were meant for each other, he began gently prodding them toward one another. "You two would be miserable apart!" Lou declared, his gargantuan smile complementing his enormous, smiling eyes. "When is the big day?"

"How could we get you into one of our cathedrals on Jook-sing? I don't think we could even get your smile through the door!" Jenny bantered, her smile nearly as wide as his.

"That is why you will have an outdoor wedding, my dear one! Don't think I will be the only large one invited...you must invite us *all*! Don't worry, we'll bring our own food for afterward. I know how little your size eats! Like mice!" Lou belly-laughed, like always, and Jenny and Abner eyed each other in pretend shock, as they laughed with him.

Their last night on Dejeal had come, and the castack and Anai spent all afternoon and evening with the group. The royals themselves prepared a delicious meal for all, commenting that it was easy to make such a small meal. They offered baked roots (similar to potatoes) slathered with butter, and freshly baked bread with hearty, crunchy crusts and tender, steamy centers. Each loaf of bread was the size of Loaf himself. The vegetables and fruits from Dejeal were so abundant, that they had yet to eat the same kind twice. The flavors and varieties of food ranged from familiar to bizarre. Some dishes, when prepared correctly, allowed them to forget meat altogether.

Once the meal and desserts had been eaten, they talked long into the night about any subject that either side broached. They learned that Anai's mother, Lou's 'draystack' or Queen, had fallen ill four years before and passed away. Lou admitted that she was responsible for much of life within the Eb-eb, by producing children, and by infusing the lively spirit of the clan with wisdom and joy. His wife was deeply missed by all who had known her. Lou explained that he had chosen Anai as ambassador to the locks due to her countenance, which she inherited from her mother. Anai's eyes revealed the honor she felt as he spoke.

Their conversations were both solemn and irreverent, and jokes and laughter interwove with prayer to the Creator. The group was nearly in tears as the evening ended, and they said their goodnights, as they knew they would be leaving in the morning. Their last sleep on Dejeal felt just as sweet as the first, as they enjoyed their Eb-eb nest-like pillow beds for one final slumber.

The morning broke early to the sound of the Eb-eb clan singing sweetly outside the guest house as the sun was rising. The Ulysses crew slowly woke to its gentle rouse. They were gathered to the To-choobee once again for one last, elaborate meal. Breakfast was served while young ladies of the Eb-eb joined in a beautifully haunting, heart-wrenching farewell song to their guests. After the meal ended, each member of the clan stood in a long procession of Eb-eb, and they solemnly wished the Ulysses crew goodbye. Some of the children cried openly, not wanting to part from the adults who were only half their size.

The last Eb-eb in the procession were Drestack Anai and Castack Lou, who attempted, without success, to hold back tears for the sake of the Ulysses crew. Lou took Jelly in his hands, gently nuzzling her to his face, as she too began to weep. The procession reversed as the crew said their farewells to Lou and Anai. There was weeping and great joy, as authentic bonds had been created between the friends. Lou and Anai held Marcus closely. His heart was filled with love, pain, joy, and a sense of loss for the people, whose hearts of kindness equaled their bodily hearts, large as they were.

They departed for the Ulysses, waving to the entire Eb-eb clan, as the ship rose above the pavement and headed toward the locks.

"It's such a strange feeling. It's like waking from a dream you're unwilling to believe was only a dream," remarked Filet.

"I can't think of any better dream. I don't think I'll look at anything the same way again," agreed Abner, knowing the weight of emotion Filet was attempting to convey.

"They were easy to fall in love with," added Jenny, speaking sincerely for herself, and also to comfort Filet, knowing his particular pain. "I hope we can see them again someday."

The Ulysses entered the lock and touched down after the lower gate closed.

The crew passed a difficult twenty-four hours afterward, as they waited for their bodies to acclimate to normal pressure. The pressure change was the least of their discomfort, however. It was a relief when the lock authority controller wished them well and cleared them for exit. Their departure was bittersweet, as the Ulysses pulled away from its familiar border. Jenny suggested that they eat during KSP transfers, to make the return to Jook-sing less torturous. They were happiest, though, as they shared personal memories of their experiences on Dejeal, and their cherished friendships with the Eb-eb.

# A Visit to Nomar's

Six months passed, and Abner was given the pick of their destinations. He eagerly decided to visit his friend Nomar Eleeskee, having envisioned the stories Nomar had told him over the years about his farm on E-Toll. He recalled hearing of rivers, lakes, mountains and the Ortric Sea, an uninterrupted field of grain. The vast farmland covered half of the planet's surface, which testified to the E-Tollian's love for the particular crop.

"I'm with Abner, ya know. I don't think about it much anymore, but I was born on E-Toll," Flip revealed much to everyone's surprise, as he was quite an introvert. "I'd like to see the river I was caught in —maybe we can do some fishing!" He had truly progressed from his past, especially after his fishing charter business succeeded on Jook-sing. Flip himself was a curiosity, which helped to reel in customers. His image was visible on his business's promotional materials, but wasn't a shock, until the customers saw him in the flesh. Word spread about the remarkable fish-man, and the strategy worked; customers schooled to Flip not only to see him, but because he actually knew where fish liked to hide.

The crew agreed to visit E-Toll as they filed into the cabin. They had improved in planning the excursions, utilizing KSP transfers to compress the actual time of the trips. Most expeditions only required a few days away from Jook-sing, even if they totaled a year or more in actual time.

Loaf had become the de facto pilot on most missions. Jenny owned the skills of a pilot, but was content to pitch in only when necessary, and for KSP transfers.

Jelly had proven her skill as a navigator, and enjoyed the contrast between the chart and the actual destination, when reached. She had made a game of it in her mind, developing a vision of each destination prior to arrival. She had never yet been disappointed with the realities they encountered, enjoying the similarities and differences between her imaginations and the actual lands.

Layerie acted as cook, since the crew agreed that nobody could compare to the work he accomplished in the galley.

Abner was the one everyone looked to, to lead them. It wasn't necessarily because he was the wisest or most skilled among them, but because he was a born leader, and far from an arrogant one. He was a humble chief that was more willing to serve than command, and was respected by all. Though the crew strived to emulate his character, they were as family to him, and he wasn't alienated in his leadership.

The remainder of the crew filled in where they were needed, knowing that even insignificant tasks were important for expeditions. The process of space travel was never a safe hobby. They loved the experiences they encountered, and accepted all required responsibilities to get them where they were going.

Loaf brought the Ulysses above the stratosphere, and tapped the ALS toward the KSP near The Xióngwěi. Lining up his sights, he relinquished the controls to Jenny, and she made the transfer to the Gomane System. From their distance, the system's sun and three planets appeared as a flashlight surrounded by a few tiny reflectors. A moment after they appeared, as though planned, they suddenly experienced a blinding flash, followed by a violent, shaking push sideways. The U-kooskee Comet appeared in the windows in front of them to the starboard side.

Inexperienced about the star system, Jelly worked in shock as she hurriedly researched the files. "I am so sorry—I had no idea that was there!" she exclaimed, trembling.

"Jelly, it's not your fault! None of us are experts

yet," Abner replied. "We couldn't travel like we are without you. I don't think any of us could take your place."

"I can't stop shaking! If it'd been any closer, we wouldn't be having this conversation." Jelly regained her composure and read aloud from the monitor. "It says here, 'The U-Kooskee Comet: one of the fastest comets in creation, second only to the Kelo Comet of the Delso System. The U-Kooskee Comet traverses the Gomane System every four days. Its trajectory throughout its history of orbiting the sun has always been closest to the planet E-Neldo. The effect of the comet upon E-Neldo has ensured it to be a wasteland.' If that thing can damage a planet, we would have been dust, if it had been any closer! Or if the shields had failed! I'm calculating its distance from us when it passed. Looks like it was less than fifty miles away. That was close!"

"Thank God we weren't any closer," Jenny agreed, trying to calm down, herself. "Jelly, I agree with Abe! You're doing fine."

"Well, I know now that we can't travel like this anymore, without more research beforehand," Jelly replied.

"Yeah, but I think no matter how much research we do, we're still gonna be surprised by what we see out here," said Abner.

Jelly shook her head. "I guess you're right. This has just been a big reality check for me." Their confidence in her provided comfort.

"Loaf, how's the ship holding up?" Abner asked, thinking it best to check the Ulysses' condition before proceeding.

"She's fine, Abner. She's a tough old broad!" Loaf stated in his best New York accent, his humor relieving the tension from their shocking comet encounter. "Shall we continue?"

"Yeah, I think we're good! Let's take it slow at first."

The comet's power was still visibly evident in the forward windows, the vacuum of space silencing its roar. They watched it fly on its path toward E-Neldo, and its size diminished as it sailed away.

"I'm glad that's over," sighed Jelly, slumping into her chair.

Loaf eased into the thrusters, and the Ulysses slowly moved forward. After fifteen minutes, Abner directed them to proceed at full ALS. Loaf tapped the ALS drive as the Ulysses sprang to life, pressing the crew backward into their seats. After reaching full ALS, the forces within the cabin normalized, and they were once again able to leave their seats.

The planet E-Neldo was no longer visible only as a small reflector. Its size had increased in the forward windows, and they decided to get a closer look. The U-Kooskee Comet had just made its pass near the planet, and the Ulysses came into orbit as they viewed its surface from above the exosphere. Below them, they could see recent damage from a windstorm brought on by the comet, having disturbed the planet's thin atmosphere and magnetosphere. A quarter of the celestial body was in chaos below them. As they orbited, they observed that the surface was destroyed; rock and sand were its main characteristics, and mountain-sized rocks had been split from their foundations. The only other feature was a large sea that spread over one third of the planet, and tidal wave damage could be seen on the coastlines for hundreds of miles. It was clearly not a friendly place.

"I think we should get some food and rest before heading to E-Toll tomorrow morning," decided Abner. "Who else could go for some flapjacks?"

Layerie's flapjacks weren't world-famous yet, but they should have been. The crew downed the massive stacks with ease, finished their meal, and retired to their quarters for the night.

# An Eflume

E-Toll, a planet filled with contradictions, appeared in the distance.

Good people resided there, people of the soil, and also those who exploited them. The E-Tollians were a race that resembled slugs in many ways, but were triangular in shape, with unusual faces that didn't resemble slugs at all. Their visages were beautiful, in one sense. In another sense, they were different from what earthlings were accustomed, in that they had an awkward, otherworldly presence about them.

The E-Tollian culture was in flux, as the economy had altered drastically during the last few decades. The change resulted from the discovery of a vast source of the precious metal, rhenium, on one of the moons. E-Toll spread its new wealth among its people, causing equal amounts joy and anguish. The new supply of revenue had usurped the main E-Tollian income of producing poontrip, an alcoholic beverage unlike any other. Ortric, the primary grain used to produce poontrip, was being farmed less in recent days, and in consequence, the planet was suffering. Desertification was spreading as farmers rested on their rhenium dividend checks from the government. Fortunately, poontrip was part of the culture, so the distilleries continued to influence the economy and ecosystem.

Abner was excited to visit the home world of his friend from the docks, Nomar Eleeskee. His address was in his logs, but Abner had never imagined he would be visiting someday.

E-Toll, a green and tan planet during this time of year, grew larger in the front windows of the Ulysses. The tan color arose from a blend of ripened ortric and sand, and the green from the freshwater seas. If they had arrived in spring, green would have been the predominant color of the planet. The underside of the ship's protective layer glowed bright red, as the Ulysses made a shallow descent into E-Toll's atmosphere.

"Looks like everything's still attached—were doing good!" announced Jenny, looking at Abner with a smile which lit the fire in his heart for her, yet again.

"When we get past the E-Huel mountain range, we should begin to see the Ortric Sea. Nomar's village is in the center of it." he said.

"What's the name of the town?" Jelly asked.

"Flumish Glenleit. The address is 9 Darpy, Flumish Glenleit, IP19 3AQ, Klemish Prefecture," Abner read aloud, feeling very excited about seeing his old friend.

"Got it. I'm sending you the coordinates, Loaf."

The Ulysses landed at Nomar's farm in Flumish Glenleit, a beautiful spot of land, with about three hundred acres of ortric ripe for harvest. The crew descended the stairs one at a time to the surface, and Loaf reached the ground first, without compensating for the reduction in gravity. He took his first step and in his excitement, as the strongest of the crew, bounded from the first step to the bottom. His flight path became a twenty-foot arc before he touched down again, where he landed lightly, having laughed the entire way. The rest imitated him as if in a playground. To them, it didn't feel like the zero-G of space, when artificial gravity was shut down; instead, it resembled the feel of a trampoline.

They trekked past the barn. A harvester was being stored inside it, and a large amount of tools, both big and small, lie on benches and were displayed upon its walls. An eflume lie on the ground next to the harvester. Abner was amazed by how much it resembled the way Nomar had described it. On E-Toll, eflumes were the closest in approximation to a dog, physically resembling a bear, but with the mannerisms of a dog. This particular, average-sized eflume was around six feet in length.

Its similarity to a dog-bear ended as it turned its head almost completely around in a lazy, yet intelligent, manner, and then spoke. "May I be of assistance?" The animal's body spun around, repeating the movements of its head in one, graceful motion. Nomar had never mentioned that his eflume could actually speak.

"Um, eh...I'm Abner Oaks, a friend of Nomar. We were wondering if he was home today."

The eflume surveyed the crew, and sensing no danger, responded, "I am —-." Here, the eflume pronounced its name, sounding very E-tollian, with several clicks and a sigh. "My master left here a month ago to deliver a load of ortric to the Dirt Star. I'm so sorry." The unpronounceably-named pet sauntered toward them, as its coat flew into a blur. Its hair resembled thin cords, similar to that of a Komondor sheepdog, and each shaft of hair resembled Jenny's, about one-sixteenth of an inch. Its beautiful, tan mane settled as it reached the group, and it offered its paw to shake.

"Now I remember the master speaking of you! You're the dock clerk, aren't you?"

The eflume's large eyes searched intelligently for honesty, as he returned Abner's gaze. "He always spoke well of you," the eflume stated.

Suddenly Abner realized that the eflume wasn't speaking E-Tollian, but instead a perfectly-spoken English like himself.

"But, you speak English! How, can...what are you?" Abner fumbled in astonishment. "Sorry, yes. I was from the Dirt Star, but that was years ago. He...he hasn't returned?"

"Abner, you must remember, a KSP transfer to a different system is never in the same time continuum. Sir, you could be an hour from when you left the Dirt Star, from their perspective."

"You're right. So, how long has it been since Nomar should have returned?"

"Today will make it one month."

"Do you have an English name? I'm sorry, I don't speak E-Tollian."

"No. In fact, this is the first time I've spoken English, but you're welcome to give me an English name. In fact, I would be honored to have one! I rather like English. It has a smoothness to it which is lacking in E-Tollian."

Everyone was too curiously focused on the eflume to think of a name for it. "Are all eflumes as intelligent as you are?" asked Jenny.

The eflume's eyes met hers as it scanned her, noticing her hair. "Not all, but yes, we are intelligent. We are the best kind of companion for our masters...Your hair is like mine. How is that possible?"

Jenny walked forward, leaning down and stroking the thick mane, and agreed with the eflume. Its hair had the same look, feel, and marshmallow fragrance as her own. Somehow, Nomar must have carried some of this eflume's DNA to the Dirt Star. She wondered if this creature had any other characteristics like hers, and she met the eflume's eyes as it stared into hers. In shock, she stumbled backwards, fell over a stack of boxes, and hit the ground with a thud.

*Jenny, I'm so sorry to disturb you! Please understand I mean no harm. Eflumes tend to be mischievous, in affectionate terms to those they trust. Are you okay?*

"Yeah, I'm fine, just a bit shaken." Upon realizing she had not yet introduced herself to the creature, and that it hadn't physically spoken to her, either, she picked herself up. *So, we indeed have something very particular in common,* she thought. Stunned, she stood as the animal addressed everyone.

"I've been a bit lonely here since my master has been gone, so it's a pleasure to have all of you here. Please make yourselves at home. I'm sure my master would want you to be comfortable. Please, there is plenty of room inside for all of you in the house." With a nearly visible smile on its face, the eflume wagged his short tail and herded them inside the beautifully-furnished, E-Tollian design house.

"If I could, I would prepare a meal for you, but you're welcome to make what you like. There's plenty in the cupboards."

"What do you eat?" asked Jelly, staring at the eflume.

Wagging his tail, the eflume replied, "I enjoy a prepared kibble the master provides. I have my meals in the barn. I would enjoy having a meal with all of you, if you prefer!"

"Sure."

"Yeah!"

"Okay!"

The animal left the house, returned with his bowl of food in his mouth, and set it down. He picked up some kibble, and said while crunching, "Where have you been since you left the Dirt Star?" It looked intently at Jelly, then politely waited for her answer.

"We've been in the Wuxia, on Jook-Sing." Continuing to gaze deeply into her eyes, he stumbled back, himself. He perceived Jelly's origin as a mouse, her change into a humanoid, the trials she had endured, and also her education.

"Ah, the Wuxia! Master has spoken of it and the Xióngwěi Supernova to me many times...it sounds beautiful."

Jenny knew the eflume's thoughts, but decided to keep the others ignorant of what she and the eflume shared for the time being. She knew the two of them understood each other, and that they were in agreement, to keep their knowledge to themselves. Both knew the other to be of noble character.

# Unions

Food was prepared and eaten with fervor, as the crew had been distracted while viewing The Xióngwěi, and hadn't eaten all day. Their fare consisted of roasted ortric topped with freshly sautéed vegetables. Though different than their usual food, it was delicious. Silence reigned, apart from the eflume's racket of crunching as he ate.

"Well, my friends, there are plenty of accommodations for all of you here. I will say goodnight." The satisfied eflume sauntered back to his barn.

"Well, what do you think of him?" Abner asked. "Think it's trustworthy?"

"Abe, I believe that it's part of me," said Jenny.

"What?! What do you mean?"

"It can read us. There was a moment when our eyes locked, and I knew it was taking in everything. It spoke to me without speaking. Did you notice its hair? It's exactly like mine! Nomar must have had something from that animal on him, the last time he was aboard the Dirt Star."

"Well, I guess that would explain a lot."

"As far as I can tell, it seems harmless. Maybe even loyal." Jenny smiled, somewhat relieved that she now understood some of her gift's background. She was almost happy about her association with the eflume, especially this particular one. "Abe?" she said.

"Yeah?"

"I love you. No one else would fit with me," she admitted without hesitation, eyes locked onto his.

"Well then, marry me, Jenny! I feel the same as you do, and I don't have to wonder whether or not you understand me!" His eyes revealed his intensity, as he freely said what he had felt for her, for what seemed an eternity. Thus far, their relationship had been one of mutual respect and friendship, yet masked a hidden passion. Jenny was sensitive to honor it, although she was fully aware of its presence. Surprised at his impulsivity, his heart raced with terror and excitement, as he awaited her reply. He was at her mercy, knowing her answer would provide the wisest decision for them.

"To be honest, I usually keep my mouth shut when I disagree with some of your thoughts!" Jenny reached forward, touching Abner's face as she smiled. The effect upon Abner was similar to that of beholding a drestack's overwhelming, powerful countenance.

"Yeah, I'm sure I'd do the same for you. Must be a burden. I know I don't agree with a lot of my own thoughts, either!" he said, still unsure where she stood.

"Yes!" Jenny blurted, giggling, and focusing upon the eyes that belonged to the one man who loved her, even beyond what her intuitive gift could perceive.

"What?"

"I'll marry you, I'll marry you! I love you too, Abner!"

Abner pulled her close with relief, eyes still locked with hers, their thoughts culminating in emotions that no longer required restraint. Joyfully, Abner lifted Jenny's chin for the first of many passionate kisses.

Everyone overslept, and morning arrived too soon. They gradually stumbled into the kitchen and prepared sausage, eggs, warm, ortric bread with butter, and the choice of hot cups of tea, or a drink similar to coffee called *doe-fee-fee-dur*.

"You all seem well rested!" said the eflume, as he pranced into the kitchen, wagging his stubby tail and rubbing up against each of them with delight. "And your breakfast! It smells delicious!" Jenny knew his affection was sincere, and like most dogs who encouraged leftovers, he retrieved the scraps they threw happily.

"You need a name that we can pronounce," Layerie said, smiling at the eflume.

"Cedric!" yelled Jelly. "You are Cedric!"

"'Cedric'...hmmm, it's Earthling in origin, in Welsh

meaning 'war leader' or 'gift of splendor'. I like it, but now that you know what it means, are you still convinced it fits?" the eflume asked.

"It fits you, Cedric. You are a gift of splendor!" Abner exclaimed. "We'll see if you're a war leader, later."

"I need to ask a favor of all of you," Cedric said somberly, changing the subject. "I must admit I am concerned, not only about my master, but about myself. You see, I am a domesticated eflume, and though I'm sure I could learn to live in the wild, I'm not so sure I would fit in with the wild of my kind. Could you please take me with you? We could leave a note for Nomar, so he would know where I am, but I think he would be glad you did."

"We would love to have you with us, Cedric!" Abner responded brightly.

After having a discussion, everyone agreed upon where their next stop should be. The Dirt Star was at the top of the list, Nomar still hadn't returned, and there was a slight possibility that he was still alive onboard.

"There may be many others alive, too," said Jelly. "There are places to hide on that ship, if you're looking for them." Having once been a mouse, she knew it was true.

"Just remember, this isn't going to be easy," Abner warned. "There's nothing but death there, if the stories are true. That place won't be anything like it was before. The infected ones that are running it are able to do things that other beings are incapable of."

"We would want someone to help us, if we were in their place," asserted Louie.

"Okay, then. With any luck we'll find some survivors," Abner agreed.

"But how do we know where it is? It could be anywhere!" Louie interjected.

"Well, unless it's damaged or they shut it off, it should have its call address generator. All we need is the detect code. Abner, you should have that memorized," said Loaf.

"I couldn't forget it if I tried. Try 7287900-4500," Abner recited, remembering the code filed with every shipping document that had entered and exited the Dirt Star's docks.

Jelly punched in the code, saying, "Well, if that CAG is still on the Dirt Star, it's orbiting Tolkee in the Wuxia!"

"Oh crap! We've got to get back there, now!" Jenny exclaimed, fearing for her parents and her new home.

The crew grew silent. "We're gonna need back-up," Abner said, energized. "Jelly, get on the comm and get ahold of Filet! Tell him to get the rest of the crew's Shǒuhù Zhě and meet us at The Xióngwěi." He turned. "Loaf, as soon as we're strapped in, burn it like it's your last trip!"

# Rush

The crew secured themselves as Loaf readied the ALS drive, and Jenny strapped Cedric in a seat as Abner performed a roll call. Each of the crew answered in the affirmative, and Jenny replied, lastly, "Restrained!".

"Restrained, Loaf!" Abner called. "Hit it!"

Loaf engaged the ALS drive, and the force crushed all aboard into their seats. The ship's ALS drive was programmed to reach light speed at a rate acceptable to human anatomy. The acceleration rate extended to three minutes to avoid injury, but there was no compensation for discomfort, and instantly, its great force pinned each member of the crew against their chairs. Though unlike being exposed to wind pressure (which squished ones face backward in a comical fashion), the power of the ALS drive had a similar effect upon the frames of the ship's passengers, yet without additional wind resistance.

During the ship's first thirty seconds of acceleration, the U-Kooskee Comet flashed past the Ulysses on its port side from less than a hundred miles away. Once again, the uncanny coincidence of another near-impact with the celestial body shocked the entire crew. This time, though, the necessity of returning to the Wuxia had filled everyone with adrenaline. Cedric and his equally-gifted new friend, Jenny, were able to discern the emotions of the crew, and sensed that experiencing the nearby comet's power had actually fueled them in a positive manner. A visceral desire to protect their loved ones and the majesty of the Wuxia engulfed them; the corporate knowledge that pure evil was close to Tolkee had awakened a powerfully defensive instinct within them.

The ship rode the shockwaves of the comet like a car drafting a semi-truck. The acceleration gradually smoothed, increasing by a third without causing discomfort to the crew. Before any of them could react to their resulting dream-like state, the U-Kooskee appeared ahead through the forward left windows. The Ulysses arrived at HLS and was still accelerating. They watched as two tails, a white dust tail and an ion tail, lengthened behind them. Farther ahead, they could discern the massive comet's nucleus, surrounded by its white and green coma, and soon its head became parallel with the bridge of the Ulysses.

The crew watched thrillingly as their ship overtook the hypersonic comet in an empyrean drag race. As they escaped the comet's gravitational influence, a powerful shock of friction dramatically struck them once more. Simultaneously, the ship locked into ALS, and the cabin's insides stabilized, as the U-Kooskee's path traversed into the trajectory of the now-absent Ulysses. The crew were exultant, though blissfully unaware of the destructive collision they had just avoided.

The ship slowed as they approached the KSP, and Jenny took the controls for performing the transfer. Afterward, she relinquished control to Loaf to shut down the drives, and they waited for an hour for their reinforcements to arrive.

As the Xióngwěi glowed brilliantly in the background, the shuttle arrived from Jook-Sing and docked with the Ulysses, and to the crew's relief, the Chengs, Filet, Maude, Rob, and Basir boarded the vessel. The warm greetings of those boarding didn't fully disguise their tension, as they were unsure why they had been drafted to the Ulysses. The old friends, fascinated, noticed the curious form of the eflume as it sat in the back corner.

"First, I need to introduce all of you to my friend Nomar's eflume, Cedric," said Jenny. "If you aren't familiar with eflumes, you will find them to be very intelligent. Cedric helped us discover the location of the existing threat to the Wuxia." Cedric greeted the new members in his own way, and comforted all aboard as only an eflume could. Like most beloved pets, eflumes had a soothing and refreshing effect upon those they deemed worthy of their affections, but eflumes owned the added benefits of intelligence, speech, and wisdom to compliment them.

"I'm so glad we have all of you to depend upon," said Abner. "I asked you to meet us here because we know that the Dirt Star is now orbiting Tolkee." The depth of his seriousness was palpable. "We don't know much about who is commanding that ship— only that wherever it travels, misery follows. Orbiting Tolkee is one thing, but Jook-sing's proximity is another." He made eye contact with each as he spoke. "We're still unsure if there are survivors. We have friends who may still be onboard. I need to know before anything else happens."

A discussion ensued for the next several hours. Supplies were agreed upon, and they decided to keep the shuttle docked at the Ulysses to be used as a tool for the mission. All agreed it would be best to keep the operation as covert as possible. They determined that if Jook-sing were alerted to the threat, the enemy might annihilate the Dirt Star altogether in self-defense, before they could rescue survivors.

As before, the crew strapped themselves into their seats and called out 'restrained', and Abner directed Loaf to engage the ALS drive. Their determination and united drive matched the ALS's power and momentum, as the Ulysses began its overwhelming acceleration.

# Nomar

Nomar Eleeskee: freighter captain, ortric farmer, poontrip brewmaster. If one had asked him, he would've said that his first love was the art of brewing the perfect pint of poontrip ale. He paid the bills with his ortric harvest, augmenting his income with his brewery and freight-hauling business.

Nomar loved his farm. It had been in his family for generations, but he was glad to be away from it for the time being. Nomar's wife of eighty years had recently died three months before. She was a young lady by E-Tollian standards, as an average lifespan extended to about one hundred and eighty years. The love of his life was now gone; leaving the farm had effectively distracted him from his grief.

Nomar finished his first cup of coffee and eyed the plate of lunch coming his way.

"Here ya go, Nomar."

"Thanks, Dorry. Can I get another cup? It's not doe-fee-fee-dur, but it's not bad." His E-Tollian language, complete with its grunts, shrieks, clicks, and sighs, came through her translator in an Australian English accent, which she found appealing.

"Nomar, with a name as long and weird as that, it better be good, and work better than coffee—otherwise, nobody would ask for it in the morning! Most of us can barely say 'coffee' before the first cup!" Dorry smiled, turning back to the kitchen, as her words finished coming through Nomar's translator in a succession of grunts, shrieks, clicks, and sighs.

He finished his lunch. Suddenly, as Nomar sat wondering if his ship had been offloaded or not, sirens blasted, and he witnessed soldiers moving about the docks in frenzied panic. Nomar was leaving for the restroom, hoping the brouhaha would settle by the time he had finished, when Dorry approached him.

"Better take this! You'll thank me later," she said, handing him a respirator.

"What's going on?" he asked in a mildly-irritated tone, which mistranslated to Dorry as a joyful inflection.

"Not sure, but when that alarm goes off? The smell can be terrible."

"Okay, I'll take your word for it," he replied. Nomar donned the mask and slowly walked down the hall toward the restroom, as his hovercart wouldn't fit inside the cafe.

Unfortunately, he went through the wrong door, and entered a long hallway instead. Discovering his mistake, he turned around too late to catch the door, and it locked closed behind him. Hoping to locate another restroom, he searched. All the doors were locked along the hallway, but luckily, he discovered an open restroom near its end. Once he had finished his business, he attempted to exit through the last door, but found that it led to an industrial pantry. He discovered joofstrum, ortric, gestrim, yeast, sugar, and spices inside. Many of the ingredients were stored in two-thousand-pound totes, stacked three totes high and reaching nine feet tall. Enough supplies had been stored there to last several years, for the entire ship.

Nomar, snooping to discover from where the ortric originated, accidentally bumped into a nearby control panel, and a motor activated somewhere in the room. Abruptly, a line of totes moved into position and blocked his way out of the aisle. He attempted to climb out of the self-imposed trap, but unable to overcome the heavy G-force on the ship, he rested against a tote to consider his options, instead.

The day dragged on as he sat, feeling foolish and nosey. The Earthling food to which his body was unaccustomed, but which he always enjoyed almost as much as poontrip, lulled him into a deep sleep. Whether it was due to the food he had eaten, or because he was still weary after completing his haul, two days passed until he finally awoke. He tried escaping again, and finally achieved success, reaching the top of a stack of sugar totes. Given the artificial gravity of the Dirt Star, climbing down involved a high risk for Nomar, but he had no recourse except to try.

An E-Tollian wasn't agile, as its body resembled a four to six-foot tall triangular slug, and had a very low center of gravity. On the ground, stability was its strength, as the gravity secured its mass from above. It didn't have the same anatomy or move like a slug, however. Its undersides rolled, the resulting movement akin to a combination of a snake's belly and a centipede's motion. On E-Toll, the planet's gravity allowed it to move at a quick pace; with the Dirt Star's artificial gravity, and without the use of a hovercart, however, an E-Tollian's movement was laborious. Its arms, too, were suited for its home world, and the Dirt Star's environment rendered it incapable of supporting its bodily frame. For an E-Tollian, mobility was manageable, but not under Nomar's present circumstances. For him, it was a 'fish out of water' scenario.

Nomar grabbed the top of the nearest tote with both hands, and tried swinging to the ground, but directed himself toward an open tote filled with water. He barely missed the ground, and his large body hurled into the tote with a splash as his head clipped its edge. The slight injury sent him into another involuntary rest.

He woke two days later, waterlogged and hungry, and with a terrible headache. Nonetheless, he managed to pull himself out of the tight-fitting tote. Not knowing the time, he decided to return the way he came, and see if the cafe was still open. Once he reached the door to the cafe, however, he discovered that he was still trapped. Though he yelled and pounded on the door for an hour, his efforts were fruitless.

He resignedly made his way back to the pantry, and found a test kitchen attached to the storeroom.

"Well, I won't starve!" he said to himself out loud, and Nomar prepared roasted ortric with gravy and a hamburger. Some blessed soul had even stored a case of poontrip, and he decided he was in heaven. After finishing his meal and downing a few pints, he determinedly searched for a way out, once more.

At the far end of the warehouse, he located a freight door which led to the docks. Once he opened it, though, he heard weapons firing and soldiers running, and then watched as Arush Turgeen walked calmly by. It was Arush's body, but that 'thing' certainly wasn't Arush himself. It was covered in white haze and spattered with blood. The white, bloody man was intensely focused upon whatever he was doing, which was also very unlike Arush. He was so focused, as a matter of fact, that he didn't even see

Nomar. Nomar decided it would be safest to close the door and wait for the chaos to subside.

Nomar spent three more weeks in the pantry, experiencing very little excitement, aside from several KSP transfers. Each transfer was unmistakably detected by Nomar, but he couldn't conceive of how a Commonwealth ship had KSP technology. Though many strange things were happening, Nomar preferred to be bored, and his wish was easily granted while inside his small warehouse. Time passed without making a dent in his food supply. Eventually, he attempted to check on the rest of the ship again.

When he opened the warehouse door, a strong scent of yeast rushed through the gap. Nomar immediately recognized it; three weeks before, the same smell had followed Arush as he walked past, trance-like and covered with a white haze. As Nomar peered outside his makeshift sanctuary, he observed that the same haze was now growing on splattered, dried patches of blood which littered the hallway.

# Intruders!

Just then, three men pushed passed him, fully opening the door and falling into the room.

"Close the door, Hank!" one demanded in a loud whisper. "Thanks!" he said, addressing Nomar. "They almost saw us! I'm Vic, and this is Hank and Gary. Do you have anyone with you?" His translator converted his words into E-Tollian grunts, clicks, shrieks, and sighs as Nomar's shock subsided.

"Glad to see you! No, just me. I was trapped here for a time, and after I saw what was going on, I decided to lock the door and camp out till things settled down. That was at least a couple of weeks ago, and I've lost track of time. Oh, I'm Nomar!"

"Happy to meet you, Nomar. What's in this warehouse?" Vic asked.

"Food. Are you guys hungry?"

"*Yes!*" the three answered in chorus.

"Come this way." Nomar led them to the kitchen.

"We've been surviving on scraps from garbage cans all around the ship," said Vic, his appetite growing.

"Well then, all of you know what's going on out there?" asked Nomar.

"There was some kinda biohazard, and most of the crew was sent away to the rest of the fleet. Whatever it was, it infected a large part of the remaining crew, and now they're like robots. They work together in perfect sync. It's like they're not who they used to be. Four days ago, I saw my boss from the sanitation crew, and he just looked right through me like I wasn't there! Then, all at once he and three others like him turned like they were in some weird dance group, and fired at me, and the other guys I was with! Killed two of us, but us three got away. There's more clean ones hiding out there, not sure how many."

"How are you guys not infected?"

"I really don't know, but I'm sure as hell glad I'm not!"

"Well, you're from sanitation, so you know this ship. You got any ideas how we can take it back?"

"I really don't think we can do anything. Those freaks have changed the whole ship. The controls have been modified, and there's all this equipment they've built from scratch—I'm not sure what it does. So far, looks like you've got the best gig on board."

"Well, we can figure it out later, boys! Let's get some food into you."

Not only was Nomar a brewmaster, but he was a gifted master chef as well, and the kind host treated Vic, Hank, and Gary to a gourmet meal. The hospitality he provided brought comfort to them, a welcome tranquility after the terror they had endured thus far. After their meal, the four discussed plans to locate hidden survivors.

"If all we can do is feed them, it'll be worth the risks!" Vic exclaimed, gratified by Nomar's efforts. It was a profound feeling, having experienced starvation firsthand, and then receiving its remedy. He was eager to find and help as many survivors as possible.

"We can start tomorrow morning, load up some food packs, and see if we can locate them," interjected Gary, sharing his friend's enthusiasm. "Are there any weapons here, Nomar?"

"I don't think so...to be honest, I haven't looked for any, though."

"I think the three of us should split up," said Hank. "It'll be easier and safer that way."

The following morning, Nomar packed rations and water for his three new friends, and cautiously, they left the warehouse to search the ship. Each returned intermittently to renew their supplies, and encourage Nomar with any news of success. Every so often, as circumstances allowed, they returned with survivors. Little by little, the number within the warehouse increased. Some of the survivors began to accompany Vic, Gary, and Hank on their expeditions, and by the end of the week, they had rescued as many survivors as they were able to locate. They fervently hoped that if any others were hiding aboard the Dirt Star, that the Commonwealth could save them before it was too late.

The newcomers were grateful to be rescued, and each relayed their experiences in detail for the group. Nomar enlisted help for cooking and cleaning. All were amazed at the good fortune to have been found by rescuers who possessed their own warehouse of food. The community of friends remained optimistic as time passed, and periodically sent scouts to discover the current whereabouts of the infected ones.

# Above the Dead Moon

It was nearly impossible to see Tolkee ahead through the windows, as it forever existed within a solar eclipse. Locked onto its coordinates, Loaf brought the Ulysses into a low orbit, and steered toward the opposite side of the moon from where the Dirt Star's call address was emanating.

"I can't say I'm enjoying this," Abner remarked, glancing at Filet, and remembering the last time they had visited the dark world. Filet responded with a knowing nod. "We need to somehow board that ship undetected," he continued. "Anyone have any ideas?"

"Well, I can think of two ways." Chāo explained. "The first and most dangerous is to make two trips with the shuttle to the docks. This is probably the quickest way those on the first trip would die. I have a second plan, too."

After several ideas floated among the crew members, everyone agreed that Chāo's second plan was the best of any of their ideas. The best choice was still one of the most dangerous, however.

They decided to eat and rest before executing the morning's plans. Nonetheless, rest was difficult for all as they mulled everything over in their minds, tossing and turning restlessly. Everyone knew the gravity of the situation. Jook-sing was in danger, and they knew that most likely, their combined efforts would provide the best chance of eliminating the threat. The stories about the transformation of their shipmates were genuine, and hell was waiting for them on the Dirt Star. The short amounts of sleep they managed were filled with nightmares; still, their awful imaginings were no match for what they would experience the following day.

Morning came, and the first shuttle trip ensued, with half the crew filling the shuttle to full capacity. It undocked from the Ulysses and headed for the drop point.

Just above Tolkee's atmosphere lie a sparse layer of space-trash that was suspended in orbit. Loaf piloted the shuttle, dropped the first team just out of range of the Dirt Star's short range sensors, then returned for the second team. The first team wore space suits equipped with compressed air thrusters, and they randomly moved closer to the ship, weaving in and out of the debris for cover. They couldn't wait for the second team, due to oxygen expenditure. The trip would take forty-five minutes at their pace, allowing for fifteen minutes of reserve oxygen, in the event that their rebreathers failed. The two teams would all meet onboard. The first team consisted of the Chengs, Abner, Jenny, and Layerie.

One by one, they leapfrogged over one another to the next pile of debris, a damaged satellite here, an abandoned spacecraft there. Tolkee seemed to attract the most garbage out of the entire system, and many theorized that the weakness of its atmosphere prevented the garbage from burning up entirely. Most of the debris was pulled in by Tolkee's gravity, and then remained in orbit above its skies. Once in a while, garbage would enter the atmosphere and crash to the ground, causing further torment to the surface prisoners. The orbiting refuse also disrupted one's vision of the star-laden skies, as it blocked the view from those below. Coincidentally, the trash was a lifesaver to the Ulysses crew on their mission, as the team was stealthily able to move toward their goal with ease.

Jenny and Pìng proceeded from the front, slowly ducking in and out of cover as the team followed behind. The Dirt Star was about a mile away, and slowly enlarging as they approached. Jenny's memories of the ship resurfaced, the place she's known as home throughout most of her life. From her outside vantage point, the sight of it was somehow beautiful. The Dirt Star was not a pretty ship, but as seen through the filter of her memories, Jenny thought it was wonderful.

Seeing it transported Jenny back in time to her youth as a fiery pre-teen, finally meeting others of her age. The majority of them had been full of life, amazed at everything around them. Most had considered Jenny an oddball, but still, they had accepted her, and she had made a few close friends. Since seven years old, she had lived like a normal kid aboard the ship, and had been raised by foster parents who loved her like their own. She remembered the first time she'd seen Abner. She recalled the shyness that had kept her away from him until they were both adults. She was reminded of others that she'd known, young and old, who had been reported missing after the takeover occurred. Jenny hoped that she might aid in helping some of them, if they were still alive.

For some reason, she remembered Enfreck Fren, one of her coworkers from the facilities department. She wasn't sure why she suddenly thought of him; it may have been because she'd always considered it a strange name and fun to say aloud. Enfreck was kind of a 'doofus', but Jenny loved him like a brother. Sadly, he was one of those missing, as was another lovable 'dweeb' from Security, Wildrew Meeks. She wondered why their parents would have chosen those names for their sons.

As her mind continued to wander, she thought it would be torturous, to be required to relinquish a child merely two months after birth to a droid parent. She breathed a sigh of relief, that this practice wouldn't be an issue in her future. *Future.* It was a hopeful concept, given what they were headed for today

# A Homecoming

The ship was now only a quarter mile away from Jenny and Píng. Looking back, they saw the shuttle make its second drop, and Filet, Maude, Rob, Basir, Jelly, and Cedric begin their game of hide and seek among the debris field.

Before the mission had begun, Cedric had come barreling toward Abner and Jenny, carrying a large package in his mouth. Dropping it to the floor as his tail wagged his entire body, he announced, "I will be joining you on this excursion! I'm prepared, I have the best sense of smell of anybody in this crew, and I am an effective combatant!" He bared his ferocious teeth, and then smiled. He raised his massive paws, revealing his retractable claws. "I won't be deterred! Nomar is in fact my master, and best friend."

"What's in the bag, Cedric?" Abner asked.

"Well, it's my space suit. I wouldn't expect you to smuggle me over there in your sock, ya know!" he replied with a wink.

Jenny and Píng waited for the rest, pausing at the last batch of debris before entering the clearing around the ship. Behind them, the rest of the first team approached, with Layerie bringing up the rear.

"I think we should take it slow," Jenny said, "and randomly, one at a time."

"Okay, but I think I should go first," stated Abner. "As long as the codes haven't been changed at the dock doors, we should be good. I'll let everyone know when it's clear. If this goes sideways, I want Loaf to get in here and pull everyone out—don't wait for me. Once we're in, there's no guarantees, guys. All of us have friends in there. Let's get 'em out."

Abner directed his thrusters to slowly launch him toward the ship, and he rolled himself into a ball, tumbling toward the loading docks and mimicking debris. Closer and closer he tumbled as his view rotated forward, the dock intermittently visible on his circus ride. When he had completed his approach, he tapped his thrusters to stop himself and quickly moved into the dock area.

He was happy to discover that the dock's entryway had been damaged by a previous attack. Luckily, the neglected repairs had eliminated any need for the dock's access codes. Abner landed on his feet, switched on his mag-boots, and called to the rest to proceed. He waited with his sword at his side, and his SD assault weapon strapped against his back. One by one, they copied his choreography to the dock, each keeping an eye out for the next to land. They kept a wary eye inward to the ship as well, expecting danger to show at any moment. After ten minutes, the first team completed its arrival onto the dock.

"Everyone do a suit check," Abner directed, looking over his suit, "rebreathers, reserve oxy, check pressure, too. That debris could've vented you without you knowing. I've got duct tape. If we're good, we wait for team two here. Call out when you're clear, okay?"

Everyone called 'clear', except Layerie, who was venting fifteen percent without having noticed until he felt lightheaded. Fortunately, he located the cut in his suit just before he lost consciousness, and Abner sealed the cut as he passed out.

"I was afraid of this!" said Abner, switching Layerie's oxygen reserve on just in time to boost his recovery.

Layerie's eyes brightened, and he sat up next to, what he considered, a bin full of potato chips. "Those look good...I'm kinda hungry!" he said with a peculiar grin.

"He should be okay in a few minutes—he's hallucinating! At least he's hungry," said Abner with a smile.

Team two started their rolling approach with Maude at the front. She made the crossing of five hundred yards a bit too quickly, and had difficulty correcting the roll before hitting the railing off the dock's edge. Abner and Jenny caught her just in time, and placed her on the deck as her mag-boots locked in.

"Thanks, guys! I was afraid they'd see me and I panicked," Maude admitted, aware that her fear could've jeopardized the mission.

"Maude, it's okay. Just being here shows your courage! None of us could've been ready for any of this," said Abner compassionately, as he related to her spoken fears.

After another five minutes, the rest of the second team tumbled toward the dock. The eflume brought up the rear. Jenny and Abner grabbed Cedric and set him down, and his boots locked onto the deck. The teams were relieved at having completed their first hurdle unscathed. Abner signaled the group to follow, and the crew imitated him as he pulled his SD weapon off of his shoulder.

The deck upon which they stood ran the length of the ship, and the docks were inset by about fifty feet from the outer hull. The crew hugged the walls of the outer dock, to carefully survey what lie inside. Approaching the blast holes, Abner examined them. Each was a perfectly-matching breach to the inner portion of the dock, and all twenty feet in diameter, spaced about a hundred feet apart. The group traversed the curve of the hull inward, toward the dock's closest blast hole. The deck and railing abruptly ended at the breach; it was a clean bore into the ship, traveling past the docks, and into the hallway that ran the length of the ship on E-deck. There was no other choice but to use thrusters into the hallway.

"Everyone stay here until I signal," said Abner. He fired his thrusters with a rocket approach, then flew past the docks toward the hallway. He hit his retro thrusters just before his mag boots locked to the deck. As he looked up and down the hallway, which was lit by emergency lamps, he found that it was abandoned.

"Doesn't look like they care much about this part of the ship. No signs of any repairs even started. I think we're okay. Be careful of the sharps on your way over. You should be able to take it slow—there's nobody here."

One at a time, the rest of the group made their ways toward Abner, each catching the next to land, as Abner and Jenny caught Cedric again.

"I think it best to split the group. I'll lead half down toward the stern, and you take the other half to the bow," Chāo said to Abner.

"Sounds good. Surveillance only if possible. We meet back here in two hours," Abner replied.

The group split into two teams again. For the first team, Abner led Jenny, Cedric, Basir, Maude, and Layerie. For the second team, Chāo led Pìng, Filet, Rob, Flip, and Jelly.

Before the teams separated, Abner checked in with the shuttle. "How's it look out there, Loaf?"

"All's quiet! I don't think they suspect anything. I'll let you know if anything changes, Abe. Be careful in there."

"Thanks Loaf. I'm going silent for a while. I'll let you know what's going on in two hours."

"Okay, Abe. Talk to ya soon."

# Separation

The teams separated, heading in opposite directions down the hallway. As each team passed the seal doors in their respective paths, they found that all seals were missing. There was no presence of breathable air on this level, either, which explained the lack of repairs to the dock.

The hallway was lit dimly with green emergency lights. Abner passed through, followed by Cedric, Jenny, Basir, Maude, and Layerie. They made their way toward the bow of the ship, carefully checking all connecting hallways and doors along the way. On the doors connecting to the main hall, they found most of the seals were intact. They were unable to see any activity from the port windows, until they reached the bow observation deck. They encountered a mass of people, and from what they could tell, they were infected (form what they gathered from those closest to the port windows). They looked like a group of swaying dolls in storage, as all of them faced forward with dead eyes, as one unit. It was a disturbing sight. They were hollow, lifeless, like tools that had been set aside. Remembering the stories from the Commonwealth, and that they were connected to one another, Abner was careful to maintain a covert stance for the team. Signaling for quiet, he motioned each to view the situation.

"We need to find a place to operate from. This looks like a holding area for them—we need to find out how many more of these storage areas they have. The records show there are about two hundred and ten missing from the logs. There were about a hundred in there. It would be great, if most were contained this way."

"Hey, I've got an idea!" said Jenny. "I brought a Porta-Weld pen. We can seal off this door, and maybe we'll have a chance against the rest."

"Great idea, but I still think we need to find a place to fall back on first, in case it goes sideways," Abner replied.

The group, agreeing, retraced their steps down the hallway, looking for a suitable place to use as a base. Abner thought about the last time he had seen Nomar, and turned to walk toward the diner, the rest following him.

"I know there's air to breathe here, guys. Basir, can you check to make sure it's not contaminated?"

Basir used a scanner to take an air sample. "Az fair az e ken see hered, et lukes guut Aebnir," reported Basir with a smile.

"Okay, but make sure to keep your suits and

gloves on. This place *is* contaminated. Don't touch your hands to your mouths! And Cedric, don't lick anything!" said Abner, grinning.

Ahead of them lie the door to the 'Trucker', the diner closest to the docks. A few years before, it had been the place where Abner had eaten most of his lunches during the week. For him, it felt strange to see it again, now empty and dusty. Absent were the good scents and familiar sounds of the kitchen, now replaced with a smell of decay and silence. The glass case next to the register displayed moldy donuts, cinnamon rolls, and pies. After passing the pile of donuts and cinnamon rolls, Basir stopped and looked at Maude. They shared a solemn moment of silence for the death of their relatives, after which they proceeded through the restaurant.

The place was abandoned. Burnt food sat on the grill and rested in the fryers. The emergency system had shut down the power to the kitchen, so it hadn't been destroyed by fire. One could tell people had left in a hurry. Personal items had been left in the booths, too.

Abner investigated, searching for clues. He found Nomar's favorite seat, one made especially for E-Tollians. There, on the table, lie the moldy remains of Nomar's usual a Monte Cristo sandwich, fries, and a salad. More clues were evident: Nomar's keys and keychain, which bore the crest of the Eleeskee Brewery. Abner handled them, and noticed that the edging around its leather consisted of a single strand of eflume hair. Nomar's favorite newspaper lie on the table, too. Translated into E-tollian, it was made especially for the diner (newspapers were a novelty, and fit perfectly with the diner's retro-trucker theme).

The remainder of the eatery was decorated with an overabundance of tchotchkes associated with trucks, truckers, and ancient diners. Truck grills and doors hung on its walls, twelve-volt fans were bolted to the tables, and even CB radios had been installed for customers to hail waitresses. It had been a popular place, mainly because the food was amazing; but it was a fun place, too.

"This was his! Let's check the back rooms," said Abner. Walking down the hall in the back of the diner, Abner paused and unlocked the door before proceeding further. They checked all hallway doors, discovering a bathroom and a few supply closets. The last door they approached was locked. In case they might need it, Abner had borrowed a crowbar earlier from one of the closets, and he made quick work of opening the door. They entered and found a warehouse full of totes.

For some unknown reason, Abner knew his friend was inside this room. His excitement mounted as he pushed the door open the rest of the way and allowed the others to enter.

# Grunts, Clicks, Shrieks, and Sighs of Joy!

"Is there anyone back there?" Abner called.

Hearing his voice, Nomar wondered if he could be hallucinating after ingesting a fourth bottle of poontrip. He raised himself halfway out of his chair. "Yes...I'm back here," he responded uneasily. "Who's asking?" Nomar raised himself from his chair.

Abner motioned to the others to stay low, then ran forward with the rest of the group trailing behind him. "Nomar! It's me, Abner!" he called. "Are you okay back here?"

"Abner Oaks! Well, I'll be damned!" Nomar exclaimed. "What the hell are you doing here? Don't you know this is a dangerous place?" Nomar's answer translated into an un-Yorkshire-ized form of E-Tollian, full of grunts, clicks, shrieks, and sighs. Abner discovered Nomar walking toward them, healthy in both spirit and body. Cedric came running, overtaking Abner to meet his master, his joyful cry sounding like a mixture of a dog's bark and an owl's screech.

Nomar, excitedly confused, vocalized several clicks

and a sigh.

"What are you doing here, boy?" Nomar exclaimed, as Cedric continued barking and wagging his whole body, rubbing his side against Nomar. The E-Tollian stared at Abner in astonishment, his mind whirling. Here in front of him stood his friend, a mere shipping and receiving clerk; he was here to the rescue, and bringing his favorite pet, no less. Nomar was dumbfounded.

"We went to visit you at your farm," Abner happily explained. "Once we realized you hadn't returned, we decided to see if you were still here. Hope you don't mind that we brought your eflume. He was determined to come with us," said Abner, flashing a gigantic smile.

"I'm glad you're here, Abe! I need to introduce you to the rest." Nomar motioned toward his recent alliance. "This is Vic, Hank, and Gary," he said, as each waved in succession.

"Nomar, I'm Jenny. Are there any other survivors on board?"

"Is this the one you were talking so much about, Abe? She's a beauty!" He nodded affably. "Good to meet you, young lady. Yes, there are survivors! These gentlemen have been searching throughout the ship since we've been here."

Vic stepped forward. "As far as we can tell, there are about twenty or so survivors hidden away in various places all around the ship. The three of us make the rounds to bring food to certain drops every day. We've brought about twenty more survivors back here. They're in the back of the warehouse."

"How long has it been going on like this?" asked Abner.

"I've lost track, but I think about six months," answered Nomar.

"Yeah, that's about right," Vic agreed.

"Okay, we need to sit down and discuss logistics," Abner said. "I'm not sure if you're aware, but we're orbiting Jook-sing's moon. It's been years since I've seen you, Nomar! The KSP skips have distorted time for all of us. We've been living in the Wuxia on Jook-sing since we left the Dirt Star. We're here to stop these invaders, and rescue the rest."

The other team entered the warehouse and met Nomar and his friends, and together, they strategized about what they would do next. Vic shared his observations of the hosts and how they functioned as a whole. They began to realize that they were dealing with an unseen force, which moved its pawns for its own pleasure. This malevolent force was working through the hosts; most of the hosts were unknowingly being manipulated, but some had full knowledge and understanding of what was happening.

Hank told them about a man he had seen within a team of four hosts a few days before. Hank observed that though the man was conscious of what was happening, he was obviously opposed to what his own body was doing to an unfortunate survivor that they had discovered in hiding.

"They found Harold in the machine shop's bathroom," described Hank, "and I had just dropped a pack of food for him. I watched through a vent from inside a locker, as the man picked up a knife and stabbed the victim in the chest. That was bad enough for me to witness. Harold was a friend, but the guy who stabbed him...I dunno, it was weird. I could tell from the neck up, the guy was freaked out. You could see it in his eyes—he didn't want to do any of it! He would try to turn away from seeing, what his own hands were doing. It was crazy. He was crying while Harold died with his blood on his hands. The rest of his body calmly turned the knife in Harold's heart." Hank, still shaken, was clearly willing to try anything to help, including dying in the attempt. "I'm in, just tell me what to do. I can't watch as we're picked off by whatever is controlling them."

Gary spoke of the hosts' daily movements, and how their numbers were few for patrolling the ship. "Most of them are kinda stored, like in the room you guys found earlier," he explained. "There's two other rooms like that. One's down the hallway at the stern, and the other up one deck, midships. Most of them are there—they're rotated in and out to keep 'em fresh, but there's never any more than I'd say, about twelve throughout the entire ship, at one time.

They're in three groups of four on their patrols."

"So, sounds to me like we can't see a leader? These hosts are controlled by an unseen mind?" Chāo asked.

"That's true mostly, but when the ship came here last, I started to see new faces. Disgusting faces," replied Vic. "It seems like one in particular might be a leader, or *the* leader now, I'm not sure. Looks like a monster, half burned. I watched him a couple of weeks ago from a ventilation grate. He didn't look like a zombie—just, well, evil."

Abner's eye caught Filet's with confirmation. "I know who you're talking about!" Abner responded in shock. "Marcus and I were his prisoners on Tolkee. He was the leader of a group of cannibals down there. I gave him those burns! If he's a part of this now, well, we don't have the luxury of failure. He's pure evil."

A somberness fell inside the room, as they contemplated what they were up against. They had arrived with a certain expectation, only to find that the reality was much worse than they had anticipated. Abner and Filet had only shared a small amount of information with the group, but it was enough for them to realize that the force's malevolence contained a certain purity. As the conversation continued, all arrived at the same conclusion, and were willing to sacrifice their lives to end the threat.

Nomar and Layerie provided a feast for all, bringing comfort and encouragement to their stomachs and hearts. That night, a resigned peace rested upon them as they slept in the warm warehouse. They lay upon piles of clean clothes which Vic and the boys had found to distribute to the survivors.

While the rest slept, Abner and Chāo remained awake together, fine-tuning the morning's strategy.

# Revelations

In the morning, a shuttle from New Seattle carrying new inmates began descending into a low orbit over Tolkee. The pilot and co-pilot weaved the shuttle in and out among the debris.

"Looks like there's more trash out here than usual, doesn't it?" commented the pilot. "You can barely see the surface." He was unaware that the Dirt Star had been collecting debris across the galaxy, depositing it in the atmosphere above Tolkee, to further camouflage their nefarious dealings on the moon. "We're gonna need to alert sanitation to get up here and vaporize some of this." Just as they began their descent to the surface drop-zone, they saw it.

"Look at that!" the co-pilot cried.

"What?"

"To starboard on the horizon. Looks like a starship, a big one."

"Yeah, damn right! What the hell's it doing out here? Could be in trouble. Let's check it out after the drop." said the pilot.

They completed their drop of prisoners at the

drop-zone, then returned the shuttle to its previous low-orbit coordinates. The pilot alerted the base. "Command, this is shuttle 252 orbiting Tolkee after drop. We've spotted a starship in orbit over Tolkee, and are moving closer to provide assistance."

"Confirmed, shuttle 252. Proceed with caution and advise."

"Affirmative, Command." The pilot applied thrusters as he steered toward it, navigating the debris field. A mile from the Dirt Star, the sensors sounded a hostile alarm, indicating they were within range of the large starship. "Shit! That's the Dirt Star!" the pilot muttered under his breath.

In the command office, his fearful voice sounded through the speaker. "Command! Command! Visual on the Dirt Star. Repeat, Visual on the Dirt Star in orbit over Tolkee. We're turning—" All at once, the speaker's sound turned to static, as the Dirt Star's SD cannons vaporized the shuttle. After the SD weapon had found its mark, nuclear-accelerated sound waves instantly turned the shuttle into microscopic space dust. In dramatic fashion, a cloud of debris replaced the targeted vessel and its occupants.

In response, the Jook-sing Space Force sent out its first squadron of fighters to meet the threat. Piloted by expert Shǒuhù Zhě, each ship broke away from formation to engage and distract the enemy.

The Collective spoke calmly through the Monster as every host repeated the commands vocally. "Battle stations," he reported, revealing a twisted smile on the left side of his face. Its right half was burnt into a permanent grimace of pain, and the right eyeball was missing, replaced by a deep gouge in its socket.

Inside the pantry warehouse, Abner's crew could hear the noise of battle. The shields were taking the brunt of the SD blasts from the fighters, and when coupled with the noise of the Dirt Star's return fire, their ears rang. They were relieved that the Collective was now distracted by battle. Chāo reminded everyone of the danger in which they might find themselves, if the Shǒuhù Zhě were successful in destroying the Dirt Star. Abner sent out members of their crew in teams of four, as he joined Vic, Gary, and Hank to gather survivors. Nomar stayed behind in the warehouse to care for any that might arrive.

The battle outside carried on for hours, but the Collective was no match for the Shǒuhù Zhě pilots in their fighters. However, nobody could deny that the Collective was a brilliant force of evil, a strategist like no other. The Monster's scowl revealed frustrated thought as the battle raged. For hours, the Collective had been unable to prevail against the combined effort of the Shǒuhù Zhě fighters, as their wisdom and skills avoided the Dirt Star's cannons. The fighters directed fire upon the aft shield generators, and before the Yeasts knew what was happening, they had become defenseless. A Shǒuhù Zhě pilot shot a final, direct hit toward the aft shield generator. When three more fighters attacked from the sides, taking out the main engines, the Collective was rendered unable to respond, or give the command to retreat.

The Yeasts furiously changed tactics. With a shrill, hate-filled contempt, the Monster ordered the hosts to abandon the cannons and prepare for hand-to-hand combat.

An hour and a half before, Abner, Vic, Gary, and Hank made their way easily through the ship, as the hosts were occupied. They spread word to all survivors to meet in the galley warehouse. Abner, having confirmed Vic's report that all survivors had been accounted for, told Vic, Gary, and Hank to stay behind with the survivors for their protection. Once his mission was accomplished, he returned to Jenny, Rob, Flip, and Cedric on the other side of the warehouse.

Each team supported the survivors as they made their way back to Nomar's hideout, stealthily ducking in and out of hallways and doors. Their objectives stated firstly, to avoid detection, and then secondly, to avoid killing all but the Tolkee hosts. Thirdly, if a protective maneuver was unavoidable, they were to kill swiftly, unseen by the Collective.

As their plan unfolded, the teams succeeded, and they managed to smuggle everyone into the warehouse. Out of necessity, they had cut down five

Tolkee hosts, and then quickly hid their bodies away from sight. In the end, all survivors were sequestered securely within the warehouse, and a noticeable silence rested upon the Dirt Star.

"Now what? It sounds like the fighting out there has stopped, and I can't hear the shield generators anymore," said Nomar.

"I would guess Jook-sing has disabled the ship. They're probably preparing to board now. You, Vic, Gary, and Hank need to stay here and guard everyone," directed Abner. He smiled at Chāo. "We need to do some surgery," he said.

The teams regrouped and set out to do what they could, to contain the threat of the Yeasts. As the last Shǒuhù Zhě walked out the door, Vic and Hank locked it, and used a pallet jack to move two totes of ortric in front of it, creating a barricade.

# Poontrip

Nomar Eleeskee the E-Tollian had been raised according to the customs of his culture. The planet's rich history and civilization were founded upon traders, farmers, explorers, and most importantly, brewers.

Nomar's father had taught him the craft of brewing poontrip at an appropriate age of accountability to consume the venerable symbol of E-Toll. Poontrip brewing was an art form. The ortric wort was combined with water, sugar, yeast and gestrim, and then placed into a vat to ferment. Fermentation, the process of yeast consuming the sugars within the batch, would conclude with the yeast converting the sugars to alcohol and carbon dioxide. The process's conclusion resulted in the death of the yeast microorganism, which produced ale. Once it was filtered, the ale was poured into aromatic resin casks to age.

To be taken seriously as a brewmaster, the beverage must be shared at a 'meet' on the brewery grounds, where the village would sample the vat at the expense of the brewmaster's apprentice. If the desired characteristics were found, the apprentice would be declared 'brewmaster', and given the title on the spot. In E-Tollian culture, it was a title akin to lord or esquire. The newly-titled brewmaster would be compensated for the batch, and then awarded according to its value. The endowment could be as small as a pint of poontrip from a brewmaster of higher caliber, or as large as great riches. Thousands of acres of ortric farmland, complete with outbuildings and homes, were awarded to those who exhibited a rare gift. This custom ensured that the highest quality of the beverage would fill stores to suit the E-Tollian palate.

Nomar had been declared brewmaster at the age of twenty-eight, having apprenticed under his father, the current brewmaster title-holder of the Eleeskee family. His father was near retirement from their small farm/ brewery in the center of the Ortric Sea in Flumish Glenleit, and he was hopeful of his son's skills.

The day of the meet arrived, and to the joy of both, Nomar was declared brewmaster, and awarded two thousand acres of ortric farmland which adjoined the current property. In addition to land, the village gifted him with a new harvester and brewing equipment. Though the award of these gifts overwhelmed Nomar, his favorite gift was one he received from a young lady he had known in his youth, the present of

an eflume cub from her dame's last litter. A few
months later, she also gave him her heart and hand in
marriage.

Nomar held his title well, and the demand grew
for his ale. He hired workers during harvesting, but
was able to accomplish most of the work by himself
the rest of the year. There was much to do, between
planting, harvesting, and brewing, and also casking.
He would then ship the product globally. Eventually,
the brewery's fame expanded and brought off-planet
requests. For many years, he sent his shipments using
a carrier. As time passed, he educated himself as a
pilot, and then purchased his own small ship to
deliver his prized poontrip.

Ten years later, he began making trips to the
Commonwealth. He was fascinated by its people and
customs; humans were unlike any beings he had ever
seen before, and they were just a portion of those
aboard the Commonwealth vessels. The
Commonwealth was a place where all species known
in existence converged. Visitors of many forms
existed there—some beautiful, and others so strange,
like the humans, that they were difficult to
comprehend. Language differences did not hinder
communications between the various kinds, as they
had the assistance of translator modules. Nomar's
language, complete with its grunts, clicks, shrieks,
and sighs, were understood by all, provided that their
receivers were tuned properly.

It was here, in the Commonwealth, that he had met his friend Abner, an apprentice on the docks. As time passed, Abner became a good friend, and Nomar considered him like a son.

At that time, Nomar had begun carrying freight from many other planets, and his wife, Undra, would accompany him during many of his explorations. They enjoyed learning of the cultures, histories, and personalities of those they encountered. His poontrip became less than half of the loads he carried. Nomar had the best of every part of life as an E-Tollian, but apart from Undra, his foremost joy was his brewing of poontrip.

# Facing Evil

When they had exited the pantry warehouse, a Shǒuhù Zhě master led each of the three Shǒuhù Zhě teams: Chāo led Layerie, Cedric, and Basir; Píng led Jelly, Maude and Flip; Jenny led Abner, Filet and Rob. The teams split into different directions, their primary objective being to stop the Tolkite hosts, specifically. The other hosts were innocent victims themselves, unwillingly controlled by the Collective. The teams would do their best to merely incapacitate them when necessary, and inflicting bodily harm upon the non-Tolkee hosts was to be avoided at all costs.

Jenny's team ducked into the same conveyor room where, years before, she had accidentally fallen into the landfill chute. They narrowly missed being sighted by a group of hosts as they trekked en masse to the armory. Memories flooded back to Jenny, and she pondered the changes in the Dirt Star's atmosphere since her time working aboard. They cautiously returned to the hallway as a group of ten Tolkite hosts approached from around the corner, about twenty feet away.

Immediately, the Collective knew of their presence. Jenny didn't hesitate as the hosts did, however. She ran full speed toward them, holding fast to the knowledge of what this sinister plague had done to the world she held dear. At Olympic speed, her sprint turned to a flip, terminating in a flying side-kick which crashed into two hosts' heads. Her efforts wiped out four hosts in total, the sheer force of her kick killing them instantly. Abner, Filet and Rob stayed close behind her, swords drawn, and cut the remaining hosts down before they could react. The Yeasts were furious, and the Collective directed its most-favored hosts to the battle. When they arrived, they found nothing but the dead, as the Shǒuhù Zhě team had vanished. Jenny's team continued searching carefully throughout the ship to locate the highest concentration of Tolkites.

Chāo's team, finding the upper deck host hold empty, traveled to its armory. Once they arrived, they discovered a long line of hosts waiting placidly for their weapons, as twenty armed Tolkite hosts stood at the rear, guarding them. Chāo cried aloud, sword raised high, as he and the team charged. Cedric overtook the rest, teeth bared, as he sailed over Chāo, running at the Tolkites with claws outstretched. The awesome sight stunned the rest of the team, who paused to watch as Cedric obliterated ten guards with blinding speed. They snapped back into fighting mode, as soon as they saw the remainder of the guard respond to Cedric. Chāo, Basir, and Layerie cut them down in a beautifully choreographed attack, and the team disappeared down an adjacent hallway, leaving behind the remaining, stunned Dirt Star hosts.

Meanwhile, Pìng's team was making its way to the bridge, hoping to discover as many Tolkites as possible. In the emergency stairway leading to the bridge, they could hear a group descending from the landing above them, and they swiftly exited the stairway until they had passed. Reentering the stairway, Pìng gave a loud, threatening yell that echoed throughout the column of the stairway. The Tolkites were unable to tell from which direction the threat had come, and seizing the opportunity, Pìng sailed above them, sword singing through the air. Her sword had been created with special vents cut into the blade, which allowed for a song of doom to sing for any foe she faced. It contacted the necks of two Tolkites, relieving them of their heads, as she landed upon the heads of two others, rendering them unconscious. Her dance of death proceeded to cut down any remaining Tolkites who faced her.

Jelly and Maude, fueled by Pìng's bravery and skill, surprised themselves and joined in the attack. Swords drawn, they entered the fray before Flip could join them. By the time they finished, they found twenty-five dead Tolkites lying at their feet. They paused and wiped their blades. Knowing that the Collective was expecting them to be in the stairway, they altered their plans.

Jelly, Maude, Flip, and Pìng departed through the nearest exit, and a group of fifteen Tolkites surprised them as the evil hosts came walking from thirty yards down the hallway. Two thunderous SD blasts narrowly missed Pìng and Maude, as they managed to cut across the hallway toward the opposite doorway. SD weapons in hands, all four Shǒuhù Zhě responded with their own SD blasts in rapid progression, a move only experts would dare attempt. (SD or sonic displacement weapons were unpredictable, when fired with the incorrect frequency. Weapons training made it imperative to fire more than one weapon at a time in perfect harmony.) Their timing was beautiful, allowing for the four blasts to combine into a musical sound of fury, disintegrating all but four Tolkite guards.

As the sound of destruction surrounded and bewildered them, the remaining hosts staggered, unsure what to do next. With an enraged yell, Pìng led the way as the Shǒuhù Zhě ran toward the four guards. The hosts reached for their SD weapons too late, and the four warriors swiftly ended their lives.

There would be no Certificates of Death issued for them that day.

# The Brewmaster

The Shǒuhù Zhě teams left the survivors in the warehouse to wait for their return, from what seemed to be a suicide mission. Nomar attempted to lift everyone's spirits as the minutes stretched into hours.

"Anyone hungry?" came Nomar's translated invitation. Most had already sampled his creations, and knew that he was an excellent cook. "Come, let me know what you think!"

They gathered at a large table spread with sliced bread, soups, and pasta, and piles of desserts and snacks, as well. Nomar, unsure how the day would unfold, decided if it were to be their last, they should enjoy it.

"Do you have anything to drink, my friend?" a survivor smilingly requested, who was more interested in something to slake his thirst than in food.

"I knew I was forgetting something. Wait here, my man!" Nomar went to one of the many pantries in the warehouse and found what he was looking for. He rolled out a large keg of poontrip, and with the help of two men, hoisted it up onto the table. "Hope you like this one! I brewed it myself four years ago. Should be extra special today!"

As Nomar stabbed a tap into the face of the keg, an idea suddenly struck him, and he paused. Barely containing his excitement, he turned to Vic. "That's it!" came Nomar's translated cry. "I've got an idea that might just work! Do you know where that chute goes?" he asked, pointing to a door near the corner of the floor.

"It runs to a sort of retaining pond in the landfill. It's for graywater," answered Vic. "I've had to clean it a few times. It's a kinda pan, built into the floor. Thing's huge, like a swimming pool. The whole thing was cleaned after the last batch. Should be empty."

"I can't begin to tell you how good hearing that makes me feel, Vic!" said Nomar. "This is what we're gonna do." Nomar took Vic aside to explain his plan, then called everybody present to gather around.

"I need all who are capable, to assist me with a large project. I think we may be able to help win this battle!" Nomar beamed, knowing their chances were good, if they followed through with his idea. "We're going to brew some beer! Trust me, you'll understand later. There's shovels in that room. Grab one and follow me!"

Most of the group, glad to be included in a useful task, rose to join him. Finding several empty totes in the returns area of the warehouse, they moved them near the industrial milling machines. Nomar directed one mill to be filled with ortric, and the other with gestrum grain. Over the next four hours, he and his workers created the largest batch of mash the brewmaster had ever attempted. They emptied the grain totes into the machines, milled the ortric and gestrim, then filled the empty totes with the lightly milled grain, brown sugar syrup, and water. They heated the warehouse vats, and once the wort was completed, Nomar ordered that each batch be sent down the chute to the pan in the landfill.

Finally, they had completed their work. The pan, resembling a large swimming pool, was filled to a depth of five-and-a-half feet with the main ingredients necessary for creating ale, with the exception of yeast. If Nomar's hopes were realized, obtaining yeast wouldn't be an issue.

The Collective became restless, as it sensed the strong pull of the sugars present within the landfill. The sugar's attraction challenged the Collective mind and will of the Yeasts, as its seductive scent began to permeate the lower decks. Inner conflict grew within the Yeasts, and the Collective was distracted as its hosts carried on, their compliance waning. Its focus was clouded, and the hosts' abilities to work in unison began to deteriorate. Slowly at first, they peeled away from their assignments. The Yeasts grew furious, screaming commands through the Collective.

Each host echoed the screams, while smelling the sugars that were becoming irresistible. Over the next several hours, their numbers reduced, as deserters sought for the enticing source which lured them.

Jenny noticed a change in the host's determination to fight. "Abner, do you see what I see?" she asked.

"Yeah, it's like they're not interested anymore, even though they're yelling commands opposite of what they're doing. This would be funny, if it wasn't real."

"I'm worried about Nomar and the rest. We should check in with them."

"Good idea—it's been a few hours." He reached for a nearby communicator. "Nomar, do you copy?"

After a few minutes, Nomar replied, "Abner, you okay?"

"Fine, just checking in with you. Everyone there okay?"

"Everyone's great here. We're more worried about what's going on out there."

"Well, we can't figure it out...it's like the hosts are AWOL. Most are just walking away!"

"That's *great*! It's working! Just keep your focus on the Tolkites. We don't want them in there, too."

"In where? What are you talking about?"

"We're brewing some ale, Abner! Yeast can't resist a good batch, and this'll be the biggest yet! If you can, try to draw them toward the landfill!"

"Nomar, you're a freakin' genius! You think it'll

work?"

"Sounds like it already is, from what you're describing, Abe!"

"We'll keep the pressure on for a good brew, buddy!"

The Shǒuhù Zhě, led by Chāo, Píng, and Jenny, worked hard to track down as many Tolkites as possible. The hosts manning the SD cannons were some of the first to abandon their posts, as they were on the same deck as the landfill. To prepare for hand-to-hand combat, Shǒuhù Zhě pilots from the battle outside the ship began filling the docks with fighters, and Chāo organized the reinforcements which arrived. He issued the instruction to focus on the Tolkites, and move the rest of the hosts to the landfill.

# Dedication

The Tolkites of the Collective were not as easily swayed, as their passionate impulses were already born of evil. The Dirt Star host numbers continued to dwindle, as more and more Shǒuhù Zhě from Jooksing entered the docks. Their numbers replaced the missing hosts. The Tolkites grew increasingly vicious; their connection with the Collective intensified, though the Dirt Star hosts were disconnecting from it. Guerrilla tactics became the Collective's modus operandi, as it looked for opportunities to kill as many Shǒuhù Zhě as possible before its own hosts were apprehended or killed.

The Monster, the half-burned leader of Tolkee, was unwilling to relinquish the joy he had found in serving the Collective. His personal, original thoughts had never left him, and the Yeasts manipulated his catatonic, weaker ones. The Monster acted in the capacity of an advisor and co-conspirator. His value was never limited solely as counsel to the Collective, as it enjoyed viewing the cruelty he perpetrated, through his own eyes.

Shǒuhù Zhě met many of the Tolkites near the

entry point to the landfill. When they challenged them to surrender, most Tolkites refused, insatiably drawn by their lust for murder. They were no match for the Shǒuhù Zhě, who promptly ended their lives of torment.

The Monster subsequently changed his strategy; if this was to be the end, he reasoned, he would make it a joyful one. He was a cannibal, and the hosts had been been a source of food for the Tolkites. The Monster cunningly began to maim or kill as many hosts as possible as they abandoned their posts, determined to gorge himself with the 'not-so-fast' food.

He met his first Shǒuhù Zhě near the stairway to the docks. He was one of the fighter pilots, inexperienced with armed combat apart from the training room. The Monster greeted him from above as he was chewing on his last victim's finger. He pulled it out of his mouth and pointed it at the young man, saying, "I'm sure you'll taste good, too! I've been saving my appetite for fresh meat!" Bearing a long knife in his hands, he leaped off the landing to meet him, eyes filled with empty depravity. "I'll even let you have some!" he taunted.

The young Shǒuhù Zhě worked hard to fend off his enemy, landing many sword blows against his unflinching torso. They accomplished nothing, however, except to increase the Monster's smiles and aggression. In the end, the young man lost his life quickly, unable to block a slash to his neck. The Monster added the hand that wore a wedding ring to his lunch bag, and moved on as though he were in a cafeteria line, loading a tray with food.

Píng and her team stumbled upon the Monster as he was exiting the stairwell. They paused in shock, surveying what looked more like a mutilated beast than a man. Before he could react, Píng gave a piercing cry and jumped high against the opposite wall from the Monster. She pushed off with an unseen power toward him, sword singing through the air. Her outstretched foot made contact with his upper thigh as her sword came down, sheering off his right forearm. The Monster wailed in pain as he swung the stump toward her, knocking her out cold, then turned to fend off the attacks from her comrades.

With his left hand, the Monster pulled a large knife from his belt, and lunged toward Flip. The knife narrowly missed his face as Flip ducked out of the way with a backflip. Jelly, in turn, ran up and over the Monster's back, landing a back kick to his face and causing him to lose his balance. His shocked expression revealed more than he cared, as Jelly spun around with a back-slashing slice to the Monster's waist. Flip turned as Jelly's moves landed at a lightning-fast pace, and once again came at the enemy, landing several blows to his head and disorienting him further.

All at once, as though in a trance, the animal

rebounded. He chose to inflict the easiest damage he could, and ran his blade through Píng's heart while she lay unconscious. Afterward, the Monster ran out of the hallway and back into the stairwell, as the rest stopped cold with shock.

# Health Spa?

The sweet scent of the freshly-poured wort emanating from the landfill's pan filled the hosts with an insatiable lust, and they frantically shoved one another to find it. They were more motivated than ever before, as the rebel Yeasts within them tore at their minds.

The hosts filled the stairways and fell over each other, flooding the hallways and straining through doors to reach their obsession. The Yeasts within them had abandoned the Collective, and had become separate colonies unto themselves, driving each host they possessed like a jockey on a racehorse. Drool streamed from the blank-eyed beasts as the minds of their captors dominated them. From all corners of the ship, hosts were now deserting the Collective. The hallways overflowed with hosts climbing over each other, creating moving piles of bodies which reached the ceiling. Humanity was absent, and the order belonging to the Collective was absent; only a concentrated narcissism pressing on toward its goal within the landfill remained.

They streamed through the landfill's doors, crossing mountains of rotting compost, to the portion of the cavern dedicated to graywater containment— the pan. They hiked the hills and valleys like distracted tourists unaware of their surroundings. Once seeing the source of their fixation, the mob's pace increased, as did its stumbling and pushing. Approximately two hundred men and women, either within the landfill or en route to it, comprised a struggle nearing its end.

The graywater pan, no longer filled with its designed substance, attracted the hosts more strongly than a clean pool on a summer's day would attract a vacationing child. Graywater had been used in the landfill to balance the moisture content of the composed soils, and also to balance the air's humidity within the rooms. Most of the hosts had never been inside those walls, and wouldn't have known the difference between the wort and graywater. The desperate hosts began falling into the pool, belly flopping, diving, and pushing into the wort in rapid succession.

It was a frantic baptism, as the Yeast-driven hosts entered the liquid. The Yeasts were blinded by their lust, and without realizing it, their passionate ambition was orchestrating their own deaths. Once their bodies slipped under the thick brown liquid, they became docile to its control. The yeasts surged through their frames, much like they themselves had surged through the ship and into the pan. The host's white haze, that had covered them inside and out, dissipated, and their eyes began to clear. The Yeasts streamed out of their bloodstreams and excreted through their skin.

After thirty minutes or less, many regained consciousness, standing in the wort in a state of confused relief. Little by little, the pan became like a huge pool party consisting of calm people. They were once again The Dirt Star crew with a past, present, and future.

One man at the center of the pan, after regaining consciousness, became cognizant of his own thoughts. He felt as though he were emerging from a dream, as memories flooded back to him, yet was still unsure what was happening to him, and to those all around him. The memories unveiled themselves, as sights and sounds perceived in his own mind, yet knowingly controlled by an unseen force. Memories surfaced of weapons in his hands, and of murder committed without remorse. He recalled vast amounts of time he had spent, simply standing in a large room with others like him, wearing blank expressions just like he had worn. The memories now plagued him, as he knew that his past compliance to this force had been due to an unchallenged slavery.

Arush Turgeen's thoughts receded from the present into the past, back to when he had first sensed the infection, of being unable to stop the madness, of highjacked thought, and ultimately of his complete compliance. He felt the cold memory of his manipulated thought, yet was also aware he was now free of bondage. The rapid detoxification produced two results—an unfettered awareness, and also regret.

At that moment, Arush was outside of time, and fully grasped who he was, in the present. He, like all of humanity before and after him, was physically caught in time; yet, emotionally or spiritually, he was a composite. He carried within him his earliest memories, as though still present within childhood. Just as concretely, the present held him as he stood within the warm brown liquid. He was also in the future, in his thoughts. Whether or not the actual circumstances he pondered occurred, was irrelevant. A legitimate truth was that he existed in the future, in the same moment as he existed in the present, and existed in the past. Pondering this fact, he realized that everyone he had ever known was in the same condition, living a composite of experiences outside of time. His emotions erupted and he sobbed, partly with joy for his freedom, yet also with pain from the recent past, and what his body had obeyed through his tormentor.

He knew its title, the Collective. He knew its being, the Yeasts. Somehow, he began to perceive the reason he was standing in the pan.

The dichotomous Yeasts abandoned their hosts to the wort. Finally within their grasp, an insatiable panic ensued on a microscopic level, and the sentient Yeasts began consuming the sugars present in the wort. Once each yeast microorganism had been satisfied, it emitted its own carbon dioxide and alcohol. As they voraciously devoured the sugars present in the ortric, gestrim, and added refined sugars, they still continued feeding, and the alcohol levels within the pan slowly increased. The surface became active, not only with recently-arriving hosts, but also with the carbon dioxide and basking yeasts, which produced islands of brown bubbles and foam at the top of the liquid wort. The Yeasts multiplied, exponentially adding to the batch.

The remaining hosts streamed into the pan as their tormentors vacated them. The wort, now saturated with the dissident Yeasts, became less crowded as the revived crew members exited the pan. The sentient nature of the yeast escalated fermentation, and the alcohol level within the pan grew to sixteen percent within two hours. The Yeasts, though sentient, were intoxicated with their lust for the sugars, and they ignored the rising level of alcohol.

All at once, the deceived Yeasts became aware of their dire situation, but couldn't save themselves. Their hosts had left them, and they died, one by one, in the trillions of trillions within the fermented brew. The landfill—the very same place that had unknowingly birthed them—had now cruelly eliminated their existence.

Once again present in their own minds, Wildrew Meeks and Enfrick Fren stood together in the middle of a pool of ale.

"Dude, where are we? Think we can drink it?" Enfrick asked excitedly, and fortunately unscathed by any memory as a host. "I feel like I'm at Willy Wonka's new factory, man!"

"En, you're a freak! You're standing in it!"

"Yeah, but it smells great, man!" Enfrick called to Nomar, "Can I drink this, dude?"

Nomar's grunts, clicks, shrieks, and sighs translated, "Not yet, my friend, but welcome back! Welcome Back!" Nomar welled up with emotion as he witnessed the crew returning from their bondage, and he leapt with joy for each individual transformation (and jumping was no small feat for an E-Tollian).

After the Dirt Star crew departed from the landfill, Nomar and his crew went to work. They filled as many aromatic resin casks as could be found within the warehouse.

Vic became concerned and raised a red flag. "Nomar, I'm not so sure that this stuff is worth saving. The whole crew's been swimming in it!"

"I would agree, if you tried to drink it now—but the trick is in the casks! The resin they're made from will kill any known bacteria. We use it on E-Toll as a remedy for many ailments, as well. The resin also adds to the alcohol content, once it ages. In a few weeks, it'll be about fifteen percent."

Nomar named the resultant poontrip ale 'Poetic Justice'. It became one of the most sought-after ales that any brewmaster had ever produced, making Nomar Eleeskee brewery on E-toll the most famous of all poontrip producers.

# Tender Loving Care

The wounded animal, the Monster, cried out in agony as his injuries throbbed. The Collective knew it must stop the bleeding before proceeding. *The belt. That would work*, thought the Collective. Taking off his belt, the Monster wrapped it around his forearm and pulled the end tightly, inflicting such excruciating pain that he nearly blacked out. *I'll need to stop the bleeding*, the Collective said to itself, knowing the beast was one of its last surviving hosts. It was deeply concerned, and poured all of its energy into preserving the life of its friend and colleague. Once the loss of blood was contained, the Monster resumed his attempt at escape.

Several stumbling runs down the stairs caused him further injuries as he left the staircase exit, and entered a lower-level hallway. The Monster found the maintenance department a few doors down. Just inside the room, the storage locker contained what the Collective was after, a torch. Pulling it out and lighting the blue flame, the Collective didn't pause to fortify the Monster's courage, but immediately turned the flame upon the bleeding stump. His pain rose to a blinding level, and the Collective compensated its awareness for the Monster's failings as he passed out. The Collective, now in complete control of its host, finished the work the beast had begun, and burned the stump to cauterize the wound completely. Once it had dealt with the stump, it turned its attention to the lesser, yet no less life-threatening, wounds. The torso had been hacked badly in several areas, and it now received the same treatment as the other wound.

The stench of burning flesh filled the room as the Collective carried on with its labors, and as it did so, it called out to summon the remaining Tolkites. Aside from the Monster, twelve hosts remained. They were the elite hosts, and were the Yeasts' ultimate hope for survival. The Collective called to the Monster's saviors. They would protect him. They would even die for him, at least while under the Collective's control.


Brian Jung's life on Jook-sing had progressively deteriorated after losing his abusive mother to the addictions that ran her life.

Jook-Sing was a difficult place to exist in a state of addiction, but she had managed to provide for her needs, paying for sources by a means which diminished her honor. Years earlier, before an overdose precipitated his own death, Brian's father had introduced her to her tormentors. The course of time dragged for ten-year-old Brian as, daily, he had watched his mother make her forlorn agreements with death. Coldness reigned for the family of two. Every day, upon waking from the latest escape, she would begin the routinized torture for herself and the child she had never wanted. The hours of persecution they endured between her fixes was agonizing.

Brian, after receiving beatings to motivate him, would wander the streets of New Seattle's slum neighborhood. The Habitat District was the inevitable destination in the city for those who refused to take responsibility for themselves, and the borough was also home to a small population of non-conformists. The area was known to produce criminals, yet Jooksing was a place of freedom—freedom to walk in its ways, and freedom not to, as long as that freedom didn't encroach upon the lives of others.

Had it not been for Brian's special abilities, his mother would have had trouble continuing in her self-destruction. He was a natural when it came to stealth, agility, and theft. He became their main provider, often eating some of what he'd stolen before going home. She traded everything he stole for drugs, and ate very little, as her tormented body desired its fix.

Her wasting, enslaved habit led to her early death one morning, while Brian was out on his usual rounds. He'd begun his day eating a quick breakfast (whatever he could steal unnoticed), then had lain for a few hours on the park's grassy lawn, under a great oak tree. After his rest, he'd journeyed downtown to where he was an unknown face; his anonymity made the job of moving in and out of the crowd easier, as he added several wallets to his stash. Every night, he would come home to the familiar smell of mold, which grew wildly in the dank basement apartment. This night was different, though. He saw his mother in the same chair, as always, but somehow, he knew she was dead. He could sense that her presence was missing. He was free.

It cut him to the heart, knowing that the hope of her change would never be realized. Brian fell at her feet, reaching out for the hand that had usually touched him only when it was clenched into a fist. He held it, weeping all night for himself and for what he could have had, had his parents not been fueled with selfishness. Since she had allowed her disease to overshadow all of living, it eventually took her life completely. Brian left behind his hopes that day. He left behind the place that held his memories, that held everything in him associated with a dream of love, kindness, and honor. The side effect of his parent's addictions, their unintended cruelty and neglect, would define his character from that day forward.

He eventually became the product of his thoughts as he focussed on 'self', like his parents, and was unwilling to turn away from his deathly path to embrace an honest life. As time passed, he grew, stealthily passing through his teen years without drawing the law's attention toward himself. He worked hard to stay in the shadows, existing through thievery. He took advantage of others to satisfy his greed for more, influencing people through fear. He either maimed those who crossed him, or his wrath ensured they were never heard from again.

In his adult years, Brian ruled the Habitat underground through threats of torture and murder, and became known as 'the Monster', his title describing nothing less than the truth. His pleasure in others' pain made it easy for him to manipulate the weakhearted. His mind was as brilliant as it was twisted, and covering his tracks wasn't difficult for him. Eventually captured for reasons other than his greatest evils, the Monster was sent to Tolkee to spend the rest of his living days.

Brian Jung — the Monster — would become the figurehead of the Collective. Ironically, his ancient ancestor, Carl Jung, had developed the theory of 'The Collective Unconscious'.

The Collective finished with its patient as the team of surviving Tolkites arrived. Instructed by the Yeasts, they lifted and brought him to the last escape pod on board, which had been inoperable during the first siege. The hosts had repaired the problems with the pod, and had retained it for use as a final option, if necessary. As the Tolkites brought Brian, the now-unconscious Monster, to the pod, the remaining hosts piled inside with him. They closed the hatch and ejected toward Tolkee, the debris field providing perfect camouflage, as it once had for the Shǒuhù Zhě.

# The Thin Line Between

Píng lay on the floor, unresponsive to Jelly's cries.

"Quick! Get a Cryo-bag! There's one down the hall, on the right!" Desperately, Maude pointed to the medical cabinet halfway down the hallway. "Grab the med kit too!"

Flip ran to the cabinet, retrieved the needed supplies, then returned to Maude's side. "She's lost a lot of blood...can she be saved?" he asked fearfully, dreading her response.

"I'm not sure—help me get her into this." Maude removed the Cryo-bag from its container and started pulling it over Píng's feet. Together, they quickly tugged it over Píng's petite frame, as Jelly read the instructions aloud.

"*Place subject inside bag, remove inner Cryo-pod. Firmly grasp Cryo-pod in both hands and rotate halves oppositely with one firm action. Return Cryo-pod to holder within bag. Seal top of bag over subject's head...*She's gotta be in completely, Flip. Pull the bag over all the way!"

"Won't she suffocate?!" Maude interrupted, her question heavy with concern.

"I've seen it done before—don't worry, just do it!" Jelly collected herself as she continued reading. "*Cryo-pod reaction will occur within ten seconds.* Okay, grab that and turn the halves. Okay, good! Now put it back in that pouch...Good. Now we have to seal the top." Maude and Flip tucked Píng's hair inside and sealed the opening shut. A few seconds later, the pod within started discharging a white fog, filling the bag. They watched as Píng's body began to freeze.

"What do we do now?" Flip asked, as Jelly continued reading.

"Okay, it says, *subject will be preserved for future surgery within five minutes and will be stable for transport at that time.*" As she finished reading, a large group of Tolkites quickly passed twenty feet away, at a 'T' in the hallway. Jelly, Maude, and Flip looked at each other, eyes wide in panic, unsure what to do.

"I'll stay! Go!" cried Maude, as the others turned, ran furiously down the hall, and turned right. "Abner! Abner! Do you read me?" she called into the communicator.

"This is Abner — go ahead Maude."

"Abner, Píng is down..." Maude's voice quivered as she held back tears. "We have her in a Cryo-bag. We were attacked by this—thing! It got away, but Píng's hurt pretty bad, Abe! I'm here with her on the D level main hall. Jelly and Flip just ran after more Tolkites."

"Hold tight, Maddy! We're not far! We'll be there in

a minute."

Once Abner relayed the information to Chāo, both teams discarded their search for Tolkites and raced toward Píng and Maude. They arrived at the scene three minutes later, finding blood everywhere. Píng lie inside the Cryo-bag with Maude by her side, sobbing. Chāo fell to his knees, leaning over her as the weight of the circumstances settled upon him.

"We can't stay here," Abner said evenly, hesitant to intervene. "Layerie, Rob, help me carry her to the docks. Chāo, it's up to you if you're coming with us or staying here to fight."

"I'm staying," he answered resolutely. "Take care of her. She may be in more danger if we don't stop this evil. Píng is a warrior...she would have it no other way." Chāo fought back tears as Abner and Rob bent down to retrieve the small form, whose power and influence was now shrouded in her perilous condition.

Píng's frozen body felt like a plank of wood, as they picked it up. They quickly transported her toward the docks, where Loaf was waiting in the shuttle, and carefully loaded her onto the sickbay's restraint table.

"Loaf, take her back to New Seattle. I've already called the trauma team at Freedom—they're expecting you at the landing pad. We're going back for those bastards!"

Loaf shut the hatch, as Abner, Rob and Layerie ran

back toward the hallway from which they had come, the intercom calling aloud."Abe, we can't find any of them," came Chāo's voice. "I think we're gonna need to split up the teams into twos and search the whole ship again."

"I have a better idea. Everyone, meet me at the docks."

Ten minutes passed until everyone gathered at the docks. Standing together, their rage was palpable. Abner broke the tense silence.

"Every hostage on this ship has been treated and cured. They're on shuttles back to Jook-Sing for recovery. Everyone in the warehouse has been evacuated. New Seattle's Shǒuhù Zhě are finished. It's just us and the remaining Tolkites we need to worry about. I say we get back to the ship and nuke this pile! Chāo it's you're call."

"I must meet my wife's attacker face to face, Abner. I'm sorry, but I must know he has been met with justice," Chāo solemnly replied.

"I understand, Chāo. I can't imagine what you're going through, but I think it best if you take the lead from here."

"Abner, your lead is clear...I can follow like the rest, just lead us to them. I'll take care of the rest."

"Okay Chāo, if you insist," Abner conceded. "As you suggested already, let's break into twos. Jenny and Flip, Maude with me, you with Jelly, Marcus with Basir, Cedric with Layerie. Each pair spread out starting on the lowest deck. Let's work our way to the top."

They exited the docks in pairs, and jogged to the staircases which led to the bottom deck. Their search for Tolkites lasted for three hours, and though they didn't locate any, they happily discovered five more survivors. They had been hiding in supply closets and storage bins, had peered through cracks in the doorways, and to much relief, had seen the Shǒuhù Zhě. The crew, though proud of rescuing survivors who would've perished without them, was frustrated at their inability to locate any remaining Tolkites. Their dead were strewn across every deck, and they stood out among the other dead hosts. Tolkee's lack of sunlight had caused mutations, and the Tolkites were battle-worn, grotesque, and scarred, due to constant civil war. The teams finally gave up the search. They knew that, though the Tolkites were easy to differentiate from the rest, none were as mutated or mutilated as the Monster, and he wasn't there.

They made their way back to the last Shǒuhù Zhě shuttle. Once they had boarded and secured themselves, the pilot hit the thrusters, and proceeded quickly on a direct path toward the Ulysses.

Chāo called in their intention for the Dirt Star to New Seattle for authorization, and once approved, all shuttles and fighters moved away from the blast zone. Chāo gave the order. Two DF-35 Heavy Fighters armed and then released two missiles apiece. The four missiles rocketed toward the Dirt Star, each trailed by a blue flame which stretched for two hundred miles in length.

For a moment, silence ensued amongst those who had, at one time, called the Dirt Star 'home'. Memories flooded their minds. Ultimately, everyone agreed that the most recent memories of the ship, couldn't integrate with the good memories from the past. Destroying it was a mercy killing. In a sense, it brought relief, witnessing this incarnation of home annihilated, and its elimination made way for better memories.

The missiles each made impact half-seconds apart in succession, as the black expanse of space instantly turned blue-white with each impact. When the silent explosions terminated, nothing remained except a void, as the blast wave hit the shields of the Ulysses.

# Trauma

Loaf landed the shuttle onto Freedom General's emergency pad as the trauma team rushed to meet them. Loaf joined the team as far as they allowed him, until he was asked to sit in the waiting room. It overlooked a wide view of the harbor, adorned with islands and rimmed with mountains. In shock, he slumped into a chair, knowing his mentor and friend's chances were slim at best.

The team quickly removed the Cryo-bag, venting the white fog within. The surgeon worked quickly, using a laser scalpel to cut through the frozen chest. Removing the still-frozen heart, the team put Píng into a cryo-chamber while he worked on the heart. They thawed and scanned it, finding that the Monster's knife had pierced the left ventricle and nicked the aortic valve. In due course, the surgeon repaired the valve, and stitched its damaged muscle closed. They refroze the heart in its own, specially-sized cryo-chamber, as the team brought Píng out again to repair the damage to her torso and lung.

After his surgery was completed, the doctor joined the group in the waiting room. "Everything went well in surgery, Master Cheng. All we can do now is wait. It'll take about three days for her body to come back to temp. We've seen success many times here, so there's hope."

"Thank you, doc," was the only response Chāo could muster.

"You're welcome to stay here, but we have a room down the hall that you're welcome to use."

"Yes, I will take the room. Once again, thank you."

The group led Chāo to his room. Jenny and Abner stayed by his side and far into the night until eventually, he fell asleep out of exhaustion. Jenny and Abner returned to the waiting room, where they also collapsed from the day's heavy labors.

Morning arrived, and Jenny woke on the floor next to Abner. Wiping drool from her face, she headed in to freshen up, as well as she could in a public restroom. Still finding Abner snoring on the floor when she returned, she lovingly went on a search for coffee.

The roasted, comforting scent slowly roused Abner, and he blinked as his eyes adjusted to the light streaming through the windows. "I can't believe I slept that well on the floor! Any news?" he questioned while rubbing his eyelids.

"Nothing yet, Abe," Jenny answered. "I don't think

much will change until the third day, anyway. I just want to be here for Chāo."

"Yeah, me too. How's the coffee?"

She handed him a full paper cup. "Well, it's coffee! I've had worse—it's definitely not do-fee-fee-dur!

"Speaking of that, I wonder how Nomar's doing. I want to hear about the brew. Can you believe it? Who'da thought beer was that good for your health?" Abner quipped with a sideways smile.

"You dork! Yeah, that's funny, but it makes sense how it worked out," she replied.

Abner called Nomar on his communicator, who explained everything to them regarding the brew, and the recovery of the hosts. "Good news is," Nomar said, "not all was wasted. We managed to cask about fifty kegs!" Nomar's E-Tollian, along with its grunts, clicks, shrieks, and sighs, translated his exultant news.

On the third morning, Chāo called Jenny and her parents, asking them to come to the hospital. Jenny, Abner, Jelly, Loaf, and the Stanleys joined Chāo and Píng in her room, where she lie in bed, beaming with joy through a cut and bruised face.

"You came! I'm so glad you came, dear ones!" Píng cried, as lively as she'd ever been. "Look! I'm still kickin'!" The seventy-year-old warrior smiled, her face shining brightly with victory. "My Chāo's gonna need to do more dishes for a while, but I think I'm gonna be up, takin' down baddies any day now!"

Each drew near to her bedside, and she received hugs and tears from all.

Last of all, Jenny approached, sobbing, "I thought we had lost you! I'm so glad you're well, Píng!"

"It'll take a lot more than that to hold me down again. Jenny, I hear it got away, huh?"

"As far as we can tell, that's what happened. We couldn't find the body and there was an escape pod missing, so..."

"Well, looks like we'll have to do some hunting, sweetie! Just wait a few days for me to get some strength back."

"Days? I don't think so! I'm gonna be doing dishes for a while!" Chāo interjected.

"We'll see if you can hold me back, old man!" Píng teased, feigning a sneer.

# The Returning Shifu

The days turned into weeks as Píng regained her strength and healed from her injuries. She was healing faster than most other patients had, who had arrived with the same type of trauma she had incurred. She, with Chāo at her side, spent merely two days in the hospital after having awakened. It was as though, both physically and mentally, she simply shrugged off the damage the Monster had inflicted. After two months, she eagerly began training again at the school with Jenny and the rest of the Shǒuhù Zhě.

Píng's first day back at the school began with a celebration in her honor, and those attending cheered as Píng entered through the front doors. It was a large party, filling the entire school's three levels, and spilling out into the streets. The celebration honored Píng and the rest of the Shǒuhù Zhě's work to free the captives of the Dirt Star. News of the joyful event drew people from many systems who had been touched by its terror.

Nomar floated past on his hovercart, towing a trailer of poontrip kegs behind him. Approaching a microphone, he addressed those present. "I read an account of an ancient American named Benjamin Franklin who once said, 'Behold the rain which descends from heaven upon our vineyards, and which incorporates itself with the grapes to be changed into wine; a constant proof that God loves us, and loves to see us happy.' All I can say is, here's more evidence of his love—the ale that cured the crew! It's on me, folks!" As the glasses were topped with poontrip, Nomar raised his. "A toast to Píng, and the rest of those who saved us from that nightmare! We thank you folks, and praise God for giving you the courage to fight to free us!"

The crowds cheered inside and outside of the school, and even down the streets as the party began. Abner and Jenny took the opportunity to announce their engagement, receiving replies of, "Took you long enough!" from many in the crowd. With enormous smiles, Castack Lou and Drestack Anai each raised their kegs to toast the happy couple. Though many in attendance ran away in fear, Abner and Jenny rushed over to greet them.

Toward the end of the night, a figure dressed in a shocking combination of unmatched colors approached Abner and Jenny. "Abner," he said, "I want to thank you. Thank you for all that you and your teams did. You can't know how grateful I am, and how I've regretted the way I treated you as my apprentice. You've truly grown to become a man of honor. I hope you can forgive me for those days on the docks." Arush Turgeen's face glowed with equal parts thankfulness and embarrassment.

Abner threw his arms around his former supervisor. "Arush!" he cried joyfully, "I'm so glad you're well! I have nothing but happy memories of the docks, Arush. I knew you were going through a lot. All is new, my friend! So good to see you well again!"

Many others had assembled for the celebration, too. Captain Cudrowe ribbed them all good-naturedly about blowing up his ship. Majors Vess and Myhra joined in, happy to see the outcome of the Shǒuhù Zhě's efforts, and they requested the introduction of Shǒuhù Zhě training for their forces. Cedric waddled next to them, sitting down to listen and absorb what he could from the military guests. Last of all, to the shock of the Ulysses crew, Ambassador Donclees approached them. Filet attempted to position himself behind Cedric, who intuited everything, and began chuckling to himself.

"Nomar Eleeskee!" the ambassador began. "What an honor to meet the most famous E-Tollian brewmaster in the known universes!" He raised his glass of ale. "This is the best poontrip I've ever tasted!" He continued, turning to the rest of the group. "So good to see that the rest of you have restored your honor. The Ulysses was returned! Though I suspected you had stolen it for a time, Captain Filet, that's in the past. Truth be told, Mr. Filet, I haven't had a pilot with your skills, since you left. I would love to have you back!"

Filet, stunned, wondered if Donclees had drunk too much poontrip. He emerged from behind Cedric, who was laughing aloud, as the others were taken off guard.

"Seriously!" Ambassador Donclees assured him, "All's forgiven—if anything should be, that is! I'd be a fool to be against the heroes of the Dirt Star Conflict, anyway! After finding out about the extent of what happened in the beginning, to those infected? Well, all I can say is I started to understand over time. Oh, and I've kept my eye on you over the years, Marcus! I have to say, I was surprised by what I was told. You, of all people, a Shǒuhù Zhě? I couldn't believe it! Well done, man!" Ambassador Donclees took advantage of the stunned silence of the group (with the exception of Cedric's chuckling), saying goodbye to all with a smile. He turned his hover cart around, as his translated E-Tollian—with it's grunts, clicks, shrieks, and sighs—faded into the crowd.

Above the skies of Jook-Sing, Tolkee continued in its silent orbit within darkness. Its atmosphere still shrouded the surface with collected debris from across the expanse of space. Several of the moon's once-abandoned huts now housed a brooding power which required revenge. The Yeasts, enraged by the defeat, began sending spores from the Tolkite Hosts to the huts and beyond. The spores floated outside the encampment, touching everything, even the native mushrooms of the prison moon. The Collective remembered its knowledge of genetic engineering, and each sinister Tolkite host smiled.

In the following weeks, shuttles began arriving at the drop zone, carrying new inmates for imprisonment. The Yeasts were filled with glee, and the Collective's contentment grew with each handshake.

# Index of Characters
(in order of appearance)

**Abner Oaks:** intern of the customs, shipping, and receiving department of the Dirt Star.

**Louie the Lemon-Filled:** a sentient, lemon-filled donut born aboard the Dirt Star.

**Claus the Bavarian:** Louie's box-mate.

**Basir the Persian:** a delicious cinnamon donut with an accent nobody could explain, as he was born in the same donut shop as his other box-mates.

**The Twins, Angie and Maude:** box-mate cousins of Basir by relation of cinnamon. Known for their good looks and superior intellect.

**Arush Turgeen:** supervisor of Abner Oaks in the customs, shipping, and receiving department of the Dirt Star.

**Gerwald Bonageres:** manager of the customs, shipping, and receiving department of the Dirt Star.

**Bob the Plain Cake:** Louie's box-mate.

**Rob the Glazed Old-Fashioned:** Louie's box-mate.

**Nomar Eleeskee:** an E-Tollian brewmaster, freighter captain, and ortric farmer. Friend of Abner Oaks from the system closest to the Commonwealth, the Gomane.

**Undra Eleeskee:** beloved late wife of Nomar Eleeskee.

**Jenny Acorn:** a Dirt Star facilities technician. Girlfriend of Abner Oaks.

**Flip:** a fish-man.

**Loaf:** a meatloaf-man.

**Ambassador Xytist Donclees:** ambassador of the planet E-Toll. An official granted the use of the ambassador class ship, the Ulysses, one of the most valuable ships in existence.

**Captain Cletus Cudrowe:** captain of the Dirt Star.

**Captain Marcus Filet:** a Quandrosite, and an employee of Ambassador Donclees. The official captain of the Ulysses.

**Enfreck Fren:** the Dirt Star's facilities department dispatcher.

**Wildrew Meeks:** a Dirt Star security guard.

**Delt:** a Dirt Star facilities technician.

**Officer Daley:** a co-worker security guard of Wildrew Meeks.

**Captain Ramar Gleek:** a fighter squadron captain of the Dirt Star's Division 2 Security Force of the Commonwealth Defense Force.

**Major Hicks:** Captain Gleeks' commanding officer.

**Professor Jamus Lantooto:** genetic scientist of the Dirt Star.

**Hank Thomas:** the Dirt Star's head of security.

**Jimmy Roberts:** a Dirt Star facilities department engineer.

**The Yeasts/The Collective:** the engineered yeasts present within the landfill used in the production of soil. They were changed by the failed genetic treatments within the landfill. Needing hosts, they possessed the bodies of anyone with whom they came in contact.

**Janice:** Captain Cudrowe's secretary.

**The 41st Red and the 30th Gray:** two Commonwealth security battalions present aboard the Dirt Star.

**Major Lars Myhra:** leader of the Commonwealth 30th Gray Battalion.

**Major Vess:** leader of the Commonwealth 41st Red Battalion.

**The Seals:** an abused cousin of the Yeasts. A product derived from fungus, modified to become fungus based polymers, or FBPs.

**Kurts:** a highly decorated soldier of the 30th Gray Battalion.

**The Bacteria:** a lesser-motivated force than that of the Yeasts.

**Jennifer Stanley:** aka Jenny Acorn.

**Professor Timothy Stanley:** Ph.D. of Experimental and Observational Astrophysics, Cosmology, and Experimental Particle Physics; father of Jennifer Stanley.

**William Stanley:** father of Professor Timothy Stanley and grandfather of Jennifer Stanley.

**Jennifer Stanley Sr.:** mother of Dr. Timothy Stanley; grandmother of Jennifer Stanley.

**Angela Stanley:** daughter of William and Jennifer Sr.; sister of Timothy.

**Adam Daxler:** genius friend of Dr. Timothy Stanley and engineer of 'the Machine'.

**Kirsten Stanley:** wife of Dr. Timothy Stanley; mother of Jennifer Stanley.

**Professor Gerard 't Hooft :** (Non-fiction reference taken from wikipedia):
**Gerardus (Gerard) 't Hooft** (Dutch: [ˈɣeːrɑrt ət ˈɦoːft]; born July 5, 1946) is a Dutch theoretical physicist and professor at Utrecht University, the Netherlands. He shared the 1999 Nobel Prize in Physics with his thesis

advisor Martinus J. G. Veltman "for elucidating the quantum structure of electroweak interactions". His work concentrates on gauge theory, black holes, quantum gravity and fundamental aspects of quantum mechanics. His contributions to physics include a proof that gauge theories are renormalizable, dimensional regularization and the holographic principle.

**Foster Dex:** facilities technician of the Dirt Star. Adoptive father of Jenny Acorn; Husband of Sophia (below).

**Physicist Professor Sophia Dex:** adoptive mother of Jenny Acorn; wife of Foster Dex.

**Dr. Margaret Frost:** sneezed on Angie and Maude before their change.

**Retired Admiral Torquil Myhra:** father of Major Lars Myhra. Took a bite out of Claus before his change.

**Layerie:** a rejected lasagna-thing.

**Maurice:** a rat-man.

**Peanut and Jelly:** sibling mouse-people.

**Píng Cheng:** senior co-shifu with her husband Chen of New Seattle's Junxio for the Róngyù Shǒuhù Zhě.

**Chāo Cheng:** Ping's other half and fellow seasoned war veteran Róngyù Shǒuhù Zhě.

**Brian "The Monster" Jung**: Leader of the elite group of Tolkite mercenaries allied to The Collective.

**Florance:** greeter within the Dejeal Lock Authority.

**The Drestak Anai Eb-eb**: a princess of the planet Dejeal.

**The Castack Lou Eb-eb**: the King of Dejeal.

## About the Author

Erik R. Eide was born in a Chicago suburb. The family moved to a small coastal community south of San Fransisco while he was still in grade school. After a decade in California, the Puget Sound region of Washington State became home for over thirty years. He enjoys writing subject matter leaning toward relationship and philosophy, with as much off-kilter humor injected as possible. He lives in the San Antonio area with his wife and three children.

# Find Erik R. Eide-

**Web:**
http://www.eideologically.com

**Facebook:**
@eideological

**Instagram:**
@erik_r._eide

**Twitter:**
@Eideological

**email:**
erik@eideological.com

Made in the USA
Monee, IL
27 December 2020

55677561R00260